TRU LIFE PUBL

A LOVELY MURDER

Down South

AUTHOR OF BLOOD MONEY

PAUL JOHNSON

Also by Paul Johnson

Blood Money Crime Incorporated

A Lovely Murder

Down South

Paul Johnson

***

TRU·LIFE·PUBLISHING
Brooklyn · New York
11202

To every woman who has been hurt by a man and wanted to do something about it.
And to all the hustlers that leaked in the streets or have the system shackle their feet, I hope we find an easier road to riches.

Pe

A Lovely Murder Down South © 2006. *All rights reserved. No part of this bo may be reproduced in any form or by any means including electronic, mechani or photocopying or stored in a retrieval system without permission in writing fr the publisher except by a reviewer who may quote brief passages to be included a review.*

ISBN: 0-9774575-0-8

Cover Concept Design & Layout:
ocjgraphix.com
Typesetting & Interior design:
Industrial Fonts & Graphix

Manufactured & Printed in Canada
06 07 08 09 10 BCT 10 9 8 7 6 5 4 3 2 1

Acknowledgements

Special thanks to all the women in my corner, especially: Karen, Jennese, Sherice, Elaine, Laurel, Rhonda, Shian, Sue, Cheryl, Victoria and Renee Johnson.

Shouts to a few that keep it real:

Javone, Kareem, Kyran, Nyshawn, Ebin, Joe, Bishop, Ernie, Mel, "E" Pete, Dre, Chino, Jazz, Pound, Ray, Dog, Hut, Lunatic, Dawu, Hassan, "P.I", Breed, Troy, Hugh, Rome, Little A, James, Ruck, King, Walter, Bone, Neil, Tunc, Paulie, Lucho, Mike and a lot of men behind bars for being a man about theirs.

To those I missed fault the memory, it can't always keep up with the heart.

Part one

Every woman is beautiful in her own right,
but sometimes…sometimes things go horribly wrong
and Beauty can become a beast.

1

I Hate 'em

Lovely Sinclair's fourteen-year-old body couldn't handle the pain.

"Get off me Rick! Stop! Please! You're hurting me!" cried Lovely.

"Shut up and hold still," grunted her stepfather. "You know your fast ass want it. You better stop kicking your legs all crazy for I slap the shit out of you."

Lovely could feel her panties tear and knew the opportunity she had to convince her stepfather not to rape her was quickly slipping away. "Get off me Rick! If you don't I'm gonna tell my mother you raped me," Lovely threatened.

"Shut up bitch." Rick growled, "She not gonna believe you, and you will get her and you an ass-whipping."

Lovely knew he wasn't lying; her mother was madly in love with her husband and ignored anything that interfered with that, and Rick was fond of beating her mother's ass. Lovely didn't want to be the 'cause of another vicious beating and the heavy make-up to cover the bruises was becoming a permanent part of her mother's face. Lovely tried to force her body to relax and endure the violation being forced upon her—hell it wasn't the first time Rick or one of her mother's men had forced themselves on her. She tried not to holler out, because she suspected that Rick enjoyed that. She hated Rick, she hated all men and she hated her mother. Lovely couldn't understand how a woman so pretty could repeatedly chose such ugly men to share her life with, and she hated her for it.

THE NEXT DAY Lovely stood naked in front of the mirror inspecting herself. Rick and her mother had left for work and for a little while she felt at ease in her own home. A large bruise across the top of her chest from Rick's forearm holding her down was still visible. Her young but full breast had purple bite marks. Her privates were still aching. She turned around and looked at her outrageously too big for a fourteen-year-old African ass, and saw the scratches from Rick digging his fingernails into her. Lovely hated the way she looked; she hated her long, straight black hair, the hazel eyes, cocoa-butter complexion, full lips and high cheekbones. She also hated her large ass, big thighs, five-feet-eight inch height and womanly hips, all of which she blamed on her Black side—everything that made her attractive.

Lovely's mother was also mixed: she had long straight hair, light brown eyes, and a thin nose. But she also had full lips, nice size ass, and hips, a fondness for soul food, soul music and soul brothers. Men in Georgia went ape-shit over Delores, and now they were going ape-shit over her daughter.

Lovely's sexual abuse started as early as eleven-years-old when her mother's then boyfriend Randy started touching her. When she was twelve-and-a-half years old, a mean son-of-a-bitch named Jeff who was dating her mom raped Lovely one night while her mom was out working at the bar. Jeff had a well known reputation around the hood for shooting and stabbing people, so when he told Lovely she better not say anything or he would kill her and her mother, she believed him and kept her mouth shut. Even though she knew they were very bad men, she blamed herself.

"Why does this keep happening to me? I don't even like boys. I don't ever wear revealing clothes, I do all my schoolwork, I pray at night and I never flirt or be too friendly. Why won't they leave me alone? I just want to be left alone," she cried to herself. So she blamed her looks for the unwanted attention, since it wasn't happening to her girlfriends. So she stared in the mirror and wished for blemishes, acne, a flat chest and a flat ass so men would leave her alone.

Knock, knock, knock, someone was knocking on the door, so Lovely quickly got dressed and went to let her best friend Joy Murphy in.

"Hi Joy, you look so cute. Is that a new outfit?" Joy came in doing a full circle so Lovely could survey the outfit.

"Girl ain't it fierce? I boosted it last week. I'm telling you, you should come with me."

"No, no not me. I'm scared to get caught and my mother wouldn't have any money to bail me out. I'm not gonna be stuck in jail."

"Girl they send you to juvy not jail, and you won't get caught. You're just a scaredy-cat."

Joy was fifteen and lived down the block. She was street smart and envied. Joy was thin, tall, dark, had short hair and an aggressive personality—no boys or men ever messed with Joy. Lovely wished she could be Joy instead so men would leave her alone.

They both went to Therell High, so they caught the bus together, Lovely was in the ninth grade, and Joy was in the tenth. Boys frequently approached Lovely in the hallways, the classrooms, her locker, but she wasn't interested in any of them. She especially hated when they would touch her arm or shoulder when talking to her, that gave her the creeps. She was so glad summer break was almost there.

Joy wasn't stupid, she knew some weird stuff was going on in Lovely's house, but Lovely refused to tell her anything. She saw the way her stepfather looked at Lovely all lustful like. Joy had come to recognize that look in many men's eyes even though they never looked at her like that. Sometimes she wished she was beautiful, and exotic with a developed body like Lovely, but she had grown comfortable with her looks. She knew her dark complexion, flat ass, and short hair made her undesirable to the boys, but so what—she didn't give a fuck about them either. She especially hated the young hustlers; she knew they were the 'cause of her brother's death. Her brother, Calvin Murphy had been the best basketball player at Therell High—probably the whole state—and the neighborhood thugs had been jealous of that.

They knew he was on his way to an NBA career and couldn't stand to see someone do well without them. They was always with the bullshit: "Calvin let's go get a forty. Calvin let's go smoke a blunt. Calvin come hang out with us—we having a hooky party." *Why couldn't they just leave him the hell alone*? They knew he didn't drink didn't smoke and was a good kid who went to school everyday and got excellent grades. Joy and Calvin's mother was a good person at heart, but she was an alcoholic so brother and sister had become best friends and guardians to each other. Even though Calvin was two years older than Joy, they hung out together a lot and spent crazy hours together on the basketball court. He taught her a very good jump shot and strong game in the paint. Calvin was the older but because of his sweet disposition she felt protective towards him. Calvin was being reported in the Atlanta newspapers as the next straight to pros basketball star, but that all ended last year and so did Joy's interest in the game.

JOY REMEMBERED DECEMBER with pain. It was pleasantly warm even by Georgia standards. The crime rate was down, jobs were plentiful, and everyone seemed happy. Even their home was uncharacteristically well off at the time; their mother wasn't drinking as much, had a good job at Otis Elevators in downtown Atlanta, and was talking about different Christmas gifts for Joy and Calvin. Basketball season had started and Calvin was heating up the scoreboards. He was averaging twenty-seven points and thirteen rebounds a game and the Therell High School panthers were undefeated. Calvin was the starting strong forward and his best friend was the starting point guard—Avery "Quick" Williams. Their friendship was based mostly on basketball; they lived too far apart to hang out much outside of school. Avery lived in Kimberly Court apartments and Calvin lived in Stanton Homes, but they usually stayed after school in the gym until five o'clock everyday working on their game.

At the time both Stanton Homes and most of Stanton Road had become a drug emporium and Kimberly Court was even worse. Calvin stayed as far as he could from drugs and any other illicit activity, but the same couldn't be said for Quick Williams. The hustlers all over Atlanta knew Quick's package moving skills were even quicker than his crossover. Quick had one problem though: he was an ugly motherfucker—he looked like road kill had been regenerated. And you know- the uglier you are- the hornier you are, and under his eye- offensive conditions he had to trick and trick hard. So he was fucking hustlers' packages up left and right, but he could move two or three thousand a night and in the coke game greed supercedes caution so he never had shortage of dealers looking for him to move their work.

One night, it was after seven o'clock and Calvin hadn't come in yet. Joy had an uneasy feeling, but didn't voice it. Around 8:30 her mother sent her to look for her brother.

On her way to the courts she passed the hustlers controlling their twenty feet of real estate, the more successful ones had many pieces of city pavements. They sat on their cars surrounded by fascinated boys and girls, men and women and smiled their gold toothed smiles that matched their gaudy jewelry. For the poor whose lives were a boring survival spiced with the occasional come-up, unexpected return to pregnancy, brutal death, someone big arrested or someone important returned to freedom, ordinary letdowns damn near went unnoticed they were so commonplace. But in the South, poverty was shared, so one didn't feel alone; here everyone was family. Joy saw one of her classmates standing on the corner.

"Hi Joy. Damn everyday you look more and more like a dude."

"Fuck you Pete. Everyday you look more and more like your wrinkled grandmother."

They both broke out laughing because Ms. Jerri was wrinkled as hell, but still sashayed around Stanton Road like she was sexy.

"Pete have you seen my brother?"

"Nope, you want me to walk with you? He's probably at the courts."

"Nah, I'm okay thanks," and Joys continued on.

She walked past some working girls dressed in their business attire: tight mini-skirts and undersized shirts that accentuated their large breasts and displayed their midriffs. One was definitely gonna get paid because she was built like country girls are: ass thick and tight like she had been squatting with refrigerators on her back, legs like she raced horses and a face innocent enough to sell the Keebler Elves some Girl Scout cookies. Her girlfriend was gonna have to settle for chump change, she got in the game too late. Her face had the wear and tear of too many years in poverty, her stomach had the stretch marks and kangaroo paunch of a mother with humongous kids, and she wasn't even smart enough to cover it up. A car pulled over and tried to proposition them, but their pockets were probably filled with lint 'cause the girls laughed at them. Joy hoped they were not trying to make Stanton Road a hoe track, most girls worked near The West End Mall or downtown Atlanta.

"Shit," she said to herself after discovering he wasn't at the courts, so she headed back home hoping he was there already.

"Hi Joy, how's Calvin doing?" asked Ms. Mary, one of Stanton Road's oldest residents.

"I'm looking for him now Ms. Mary, have you seen him?"

"No I haven't, but I'm sure he will be home soon—he's such a good boy, probably at the library or something. Tell him I'm going to try and come see one of his games this year, and whenever y'all want some goodies come see me, y'all credit is good."

"Okay. Ms. Mary have a good night and I'll tell Calvin what you said." Ms. Mary had the biggest candy store in her house and only a privileged few received credit, but she gave little kids a lot of free stuff.

When Joy got home Calvin still hadn't arrived and her mother really started worrying when Joy showed up without him. They waited up for him most the night; Joy constantly looked out the window and her mother chained smoked her Kools cigarettes. They both fell asleep in the living room. It was 6:50 when a loud knock woke them up. It was a policeman who wanted Joy's mom to take a ride with him. He said two boys had been found dead and one had this address on him.

"Oh my God! Oh my God no! Please no! Not my son," Joy's mother cried.

The officer tried to calm her down. "Ms. Murphy please check first. Do you need someone else to come with you?"

"No, I'm going to be able to handle it," her mother said as she gathered her strength, got her purse and left with the officer, after telling Joy to continue to wait by the phone. Joy knew. She just knew her sweet brother was dead and that somebody had killed him for nothing, they just didn't want to see him make it out of the ghetto, they hated that he kept to himself, they thought he was acting better than them, but he wasn't, he just had a softer heart and couldn't relate to their rough ways. Joy went in her room, locked the door, lay on her bed and cried. She lay there and cried all day and in those tears a hatred was born.

The Police had no idea who had killed Calvin Murphy or Avery "Quick" Williams. A woman on her way to Greenbriar Mall to catch a bus spotted their bodies along the road. Stone Hogan Connector was a quiet road at night and witnesses would be hard to find. The up-and-coming drug dealer G-Man knew that when he chose the spot.

"YO STAN I DON'T KNOW why that bitch ass nigga tried to play games with my dough, I ain't hardly 'bout to let no nigga beat me for three thousand dollars," G-Man loved to sound gangster.

"Yeah, but why you have to kill that guy Calvin? Damn he was our best basketball player–now Therell ain't gonna be able to win the championship."

Nigga I don't give a fuck about no basketball player, homeboy shouldn't have been with Quick, plus he probably had something to do with it."

"Plus G, now it's gonna be police trying hard as fuck to find their killer, the boy Calvin was all in the papers and shit." Stan didn't like the move at all but G called the shots.

"Ah man, stop crying, you act like you did something – me and Ron the one that took care of them." G-Man started describing the scene.

"Yo! You should of seen 'em, they was coming from the school bouncing a basketball back and forth to each other like they was Michael Jordan and Scottie Pippen. We had the tinted

Caravan and crept up on them. Dumb motherfuckers didn't even hear us. We pulled beside them- pointed those guns at 'em and made them get in." It was like G-Man was reliving the scene as he described it.

"Fellows what's this all about?" Calvin asked.

"Your homie knows what this is all about, ain't that right Quick?" replied Ron.

"G-Man I swear to God all I need is a few days and I'll have your money," Quick pleaded.

"Nah bitch ass nigga, you shouldn't been avoiding me in the first place. I needs my money now," G-Man was dead serious.

"Take me around my way and I can get the majority of it for you, Quick figured around his way he could escape.

"Listen fellows I don't have anything to do with your money." Calvin interjected.

"Yeah G-Man he didn't have anything to do with this," Quick added.

"Quick it's been three weeks. What happened to the two and a half ounces I fronted you? Where's my three thousand?"

Quick decided to tell him the truth, "I was at a hooky party in Kings Ridge getting with this girl and someone went in my pockets."

Ron drove them to a house they had on Honeysuckle Lane. As soon as the garage door closed G-Man made them get out the van.

"Ron tie their hands behind their backs," G-Man instructed. Calvin and Quick were then led down into the basement.

"Quick who can I send to pick up my money?" G-Man asked.

"Nobody – I have to go myself," Quick replied.

G-Man pushed them onto the hard cement floor. They both tried to turn their heads, but Calvin busted his lip.

"Ron put some plastic under them. I don't want him bleeding on my floor."

Ron placed garage bags underneath both their heads.

"Y'all lucky I got to be going to take care of business and don't have time to torture y'all. I'm going to give you some time to think about my money before I get back," Quick told them.

"Ron stay down here and watch 'em, I'll be back." G-Man said before leaving.

They talked amongst themselves, pleaded with Ron, even cried a little. When G-Man got back about three hours later Ron was so pissed he was damned near ready to shoot G-Man's ass.

"Quick do you know where my money at yet?"

"I swear I can get it if you take me around the way," Quick pleaded.

"Please fellows let me go! I have nothing to do with this!"

G-Man pulled Ron to the side and said, "Fuck this bullshit, put two in their head put some crack bags in their mouth and tie the garbage bags around 'em. We gonna toss they body somewhere."

"Okay, 'cause I'm tired of babysitting these niggas –for real."

That's how their bodies were found the next morning.

When Joy found out her brother was dead with Quick and they both had two shots in the head and crack in their mouths, she knew some baller did it. She vowed to her dead brother that she would make the ballers in Atlanta pay for what they did.

2

Bad Boys

Delores couldn't understand why her relationships always went sour. When she would first met a man he would be falling all over himself for some of her pink pussy, then later on in the relationship he'd be on some Dr. Jekyll, Mr. Hyde shit. And her latest, Rick, wasn't any different. He treated her like a queen when they first started going out. He was always polite, bought her little gifts like a pretty lamp, some porcelain dolls, a nice coat when it started getting cold out and even groceries. He was especially good with Lovely, always taking them places like Stone Mountain, Six Flags, to movies and out to eat.

Delores knew a lot of Georgia men were color struck and wanted a chance to pound away at her near white pussy, but Rick seem like he genuinely liked and respected her. Rick was a milk chocolate colored, clean-shaven brother who had a decent job at Ford Motors and a generous nature (she found that to be true in the bedroom also). He was nothing like that super light pretty-boy motherfucker that fathered Lovely. That pretty nigga could smooth talk his way into a convent and have all the nuns fucking by nightfall. She hadn't seen him since Lovely was eight years old; rumor was that he left town because too many bad dudes were trying to kill him for fucking their women.

Delores just knew she had a winner when she hooked up with Rick. She remembered how she would wake up and he'd be lying beside her fixated on her pretty features. He loved to play in her long black tresses and silky coochie hairs, but she never felt like just another near white conquest. She had her share of those types growing up, she couldn't remember how many times a young black man would be pounding away at her pussy, working hard like John Henry on the rail road and would start saying, *"Call me Mandingo, call me Mandingo warrior you pretty thing you."* Hell-she didn't even know who Mandigo was. She tolerated it and kept giving those guys pussy because she kinda felt she owed them at least that—Roots had just been broadcasted on T.V.

She was sure that Rick would be different, especially after they moved into a house together. Sure it was up the street from the projects, but they were paying a mortgage and not rent. She had been living in low income houses ever since she had been harassed out of Stone Mountain by her own white mother. Her mom said she was mad because Delores became pregnant so young, but Delores knew in her heart that she had been dogged so bad that she had a love/hate feeling towards Black men. Her mother hated the fact that now Delores was fucking black men and was even pregnant by one. Even though her mom had found a white man to marry her and raise her half-black daughter, Delores' mother still had that lustful envy look in her eyes whenever she saw Delores with a black man.

"Girl, he's gonna abuse you," is all she used to say.

"Yeah he loves you now, loves your pretty mixed features. But as soon as life gets a little rough for him he would only see you as a honky, as the white people's daughter and abuse you too." She would go on and on until Delores couldn't take it any more and moved in with her baby's father and then shit started happening just like her mother said.

Her life had been a series of bad relationships since then. She was Queen of the Nile when they wanted to fuck her pretty white features and plump black ass, but she was a Blue-eyed Devil when they got laid off, arrested or made to feel inferior in some way. She couldn't understand how come she kept getting blamed, shit—she didn't even have blue eyes. Then Rick came along and she thought her luck had changed. She really couldn't believe when he asked her to married him. Of course she accepted – wedding proposals didn't come around too often; not even for a pretty woman like herself. Now Rick was kicking her ass for no reason, and she suspected it had something to do with Lovely. Ever since Lovely had gotten a little older there had been a lot of tension between the two of them. It seemed like every time he looked at Lovely he'd get a frustrated look. Maybe he wanted her to leave, but she couldn't throw her only daughter out. She would be glad when Lovely got old enough to live on her own. Maybe then she and Rick could be the way they were.

"Delores we fitting to close up so go ahead and tally up your drawer," her boss broke into her wandering thoughts.

"Okay Frank," Delores worked at the liquor store, it wasn't glamorous but it was steady.

Rick felt like Superman today. He always did after fucking Lovely. When he first started going out with Delores he felt a lot like that. Here was this average looking dude who never had a lot of success with women with this bad near white star and the envy of other men. That's when he was on top. Then he lost his job at Ford Motors, had to get rid of his used Caddy, and found out a lot of men had slept with his near white star. Now he worked at a racist manufacturing plant that made airplane parts. He had been there almost two years and had received no promotions. He had white boys who were younger than him for bosses and all they did was talk to him like he was a kid. Then when he came home he was surrounded by dope boys that made him feel stupid and weak. They had everything: the fancy cars, expensive clothes, big jewelry and exciting lives. All he did was work like a Georgia mule and had nothing to show for it. He worked hard and came home to boring ass Delores. Then he realized he had something every man wanted and couldn't have and that made him feel superior—he had Lovely. Every dope boy around wanted to get between her tenderloins, but only he could. He could take her anytime he wanted and that made him a bigger man than those dope boys and racist crackers at work that looked a lot like her.

"Ha, ha, ha," he laughed, I'm fucking your daughter—I'm *fucking* your daughter."

Plus, he hated the snotty little bitch, who was walking around acting like she better than him. She even thought she was too good to give anybody her pussy. That's why he took it; if he was gonna be miserable, everybody in the house was gonna be miserable. Sometimes he knew he was dead wrong for raping that little girl but he rationalized it. "*She ain't little no more, plus I put clothes on her back, food in her stomach and a roof over her head for two years. Don't that entitle me to something*?"

"Rick stop day dreaming and get your ass over there and oil that machine."

"Yes boss," he was feeling like a weak ass boy again.

"HI LOVELY," hollered Mark.

"Damn, Love, you looking good when you gonna give a nigga a chance?" yelled Steve.

"Lovely when you gonna let me see how lovely you really are under those clothes?" She hated walking down Stanton Road. It was a non-stop hassle, the same guy she ignored yesterday would be cracking again the next day. The dope boys were relentless even though they had tons of easy girls they could fuck.

It was 1987 and Georgia was going through changes. Hip-Hop and the dope boys were taking over. Miami dope dealers flooded the city with coke and the crime rate was escalating. Someone pulled alongside Lovely blasting Too Short, all she could make out is a bunch of bitches and 'hos and if they don't have his money…

"Hey shawty where you going looking all fine as rare wine?" His opening line was a little different so she looked in his direction. *Damn that's a nice car* she thought—it's some kinda gold and green sparkles; candy coated paint job she think they call it.

"Why is you walking in this hot ass sun? Come let me surround you with some air-conditioning." *He's definitely not from Georgia,* she thought.

"Nah that's okay I'm just heading to the store and back," she replied.

"It would be quicker if we rode."

"Nah I'm okay."

"Come on shawty, I ain't the big bad wolf. My name is Big Dre and I'm from that money making Miami."

"Nah I don't ride with people I don't know."

"How you gonna say you don't know me? I just introduced myself."

I gotta go Dre, you have a nice day."

"That's cold shawty." What's your name anyway?"

"Lovely."

"Oh hell yeah, your mama named you exactly what you are." Lovely couldn't help but smile even though she hated her name.

"Lovely how old are you?"

"I'm fourteen."

"Damn, you look a lot older. When do you turn fifteen?"

"July third."

"Well I'm gonna make you my girlfriend after then, but I'll be watching you so don't get involved with no-one else."

"I don't want no boyfriend."

"We'll see after July third You sure you don't want that ride?"

"I'm still okay"

"Well be good shawty 'cause I'll be watching you like Santa," and he pulled off laughing at his own joke.

She saw that his car was a 500 SEL Mercedes Benz, he must be really rolling. She continued her walk, thinking, he was kinda handsome with his dark skin, smooth complexion and thick waves. No kind of sexual attraction was aroused in Lovely, there never was – she just thought some guys looked better than others.

"Hey Lovely wait up, where you going?"

"Oh hey Joy. I was just going to the store."

"So who was that guy you was talking to? I didn't know you like dope boys," she teased Lovely.

"I don't. He just pulled over and started talking to me. His name is Big Dre, he's from Miami."

"Yeah, I heard about him. He sell all these fools they weight," Joy replied."

"I don't know why all these dope boys keep trying to talk to me, I don't like 'em," Lovely answered seriously.

"Yeah, you know I hate 'em."

"I know Joy, I do too, your brother was the nicest guy around here and they had to go and kill 'em."

"I swear Lovely, when I get older I'm gonna make those dope boys pay for what they did."

"You're my best friend and Calvin was the only guy that wasn't trying to have sex with me, so I'ma help you if you need me." Lovely had no idea what Joy could possibly do to dope boys that had guns and stuff.

"Come on Lovely let's steal what you need from the store and keep the money."

They went to the store together, but Lovely paid for the items before Joy got a chance to steal them, she was still scared to get caught.

"Damn, that was stupid Love. We could of kept the money to go to the skating rink tomorrow," Joy scolded her.

"I got money at home, about twenty-dollars."

"Well we coulda had more money, if you stop being so scared." Joy continued.

"Plus girl, how was you gonna steal a loaf of bread, a gallon of milk, and some rice?" Lovely asked.

"Easy, if you distracted him I could of put the stuff in my sweatpants."

"You crazy as hell girl, but that's why I love you," and Lovely put her arm around Joy's shoulder the way best friends do.

"Lovely did you see the way he was staring at you? I swear if you had flirted with him we could have stole the whole damn register."

"You crazy," Lovely laughed and they walked on home.

"Lovely and Joy I'm gonna be back to pick you two up at eleven o'clock, be out front," Delores told them.

The skating rink in Ben Hill was Jelly Bean, and was still a favorite hang-out for teenagers and young adults. It was early May and the young girls were showing off their bodies. Out front looked like a 2 Live Crew video. A lot of guys considered themselves a little too old or busy to come inside. They just parked their nice cars, sat on the hood, let their jewels catch the young girls eyes and then tried to game 'em up. When they saw Lovely hop out the car with Joy about eight of them hopped off their hoods to chase her down, some of 'em even left girls they were talking to. They were a little too slow and Lovely and Joy walked straight into the rink, not giving anyone a chance to speak. Of course, a few of them decided to go in after all.

"Damn these young girls are getting finer and finer," the thirty-year-old cashier thought while staring at Lovely,"she looks like a young Vanessa Williams but lighter and prettier."

Lovely was looking adorable in a pair of pink shorts, pink and white Polo shirt, and white loafers. She made average gear look like it belonged on a runway with her five-feet-eight inch height, youthful firmness and perfect face. Joy was dressed a little tom-boyish with her jeans, baseball jersey, baseball cap and Nike track sneakers.

The skating rink was packed; young horny teenagers crowded the top area where people lounged, some danced, but most tried to hook-up. The skating area was a few steps below the main area and extended the length of the rink. The skating rental area was at one end and the food court and restrooms at the other, admissions and the offices occupied the front middle. Lovely and Joy went and rented skates.

"Ah yo G-Man there go the nigga Calvin sister, the skinny tom-boy looking one," Stan told 'em.

"So and stop talking about that fuckin' boy, that shit's over and done with," G-Man responded angrily.

"Yeah man—a'ight," Stan responded.

"Plus, who the hell is that with her?" G-Man was mesmerized by Lovely.

"Oh that's the baddest little young girl in our school. Her name Lovely, but she ain't fucking. She don't be talking to no niggas at all."

"What is she, some kinda dyke?"

"She's young, I think she scared of dick," Stan responded. Lovely and Joy joined the skate area, the D.J. was playing Miami type bass sound. The kids were skating up a frenzy; criss-crossing in and out of the crowds, spinning, going backwards and flying around the rink full speed. Lovely and Joy wasn't great skaters but both were good enough to keep from falling. Lovely felt no jealousy today, just relief that guys wasn't hounding her.

"Joy can you skate backwards?" Lovely asked her.

"No."

"Well I can," and Lovely turned around and skated backwards all of three seconds.

"Okay if you call that skating backwards, you almost busted your ass," said Joy and they both laughed.

"Lets go get a soda or something, I'm thirsty," Lovely said.

They flew up the stairs, off the skating area. Lovely was in front and when Joy bounded the stairs she ran into another girl, a pretty light brown girl who looked familiar. They grabbed each other to keep from falling and electricity surged through Joy's body. Joy was surprised at her body's reaction to this girl whose body had melted into hers when they held each other against falling. Joy would be turning sixteen in three months and had never had a strong sexual arousal by anyone's touch besides her own.

"Hi, ain't your name Joy?" the girl asked.

"Yeah, how you doing – sorry about almost knocking you over like that."

"Oh it's okay, I'm, alright. Don't you go to Therell?"

"Yeah I do, I knew you looked familiar." Joy smiled at her, intrigued by this girl.

"My name is Candace. I was in your brother's homeroom. I'm really sorry about what happened to him. He was a really nice guy and a great basketball player."

"Thanks, we better move from near these steps before somebody knocks us down. You wanna get a soda with me and my friend Lovely?"

"Sure," and they skated to the food court where Lovely was already in line.

"Hi," Candace greeted Lovely.

Lovely responded with a shy, "Hi."

"I'm buying us a slice of pizza and a soda – want one?" Lovely asked.

Candace answered, "Sure, the next one's on me."

"Okay," Lovely and Joy agreed simultaneously.

The rest of the night the three of them hung together; skating, playing arcade games, and laughing at all the boys going crazy over Lovely. Candace was cute, but her body didn't have that thickness yet so she was overlooked a lot. She didn't seem to mind much and she really enjoyed Joy and Lovely's company. Candace had moved to Atlanta from Philly about a year ago and didn't have too many friends yet.

G-Man watched Lovely a lot that night, but he didn't approach her. He saw all the other guys get turned away and knew she wasn't yet interested in boys, even if her body looked otherwise. G-Man was twenty-one and didn't consider himself too old for Jelly Bean. He didn't skate like he had years ago when he was a clumsy teenager. He saw some of the girls that he could never talk to before still hung out at the rink; girls like Paula and Diana who were queens of the rink back then. Now that he had dough and a reputation he could easily get their interest, but he wasn't interested in them any more.

Long gone were the days when instead of G-Man the kids in his neighborhood had called him Garbage Mouth. Thinking back, he guessed they had reason, he didn't like to brush and he was a nasty joke motherfucker. His favorites were the fuck your mother one; *"I fucked your mother on a red hot heater- missed her pussy and burned my Peter. I fucked your mother on a little red wagon – fucked her so hard her pussy was dragging."* He had about a hundred other ones he used.

G-Man credited jokes for his superior fight game, when you talked about people's mothers all day you had to learn to fight. After kicking a few dozen kids asses they stopped calling him

Garbage Mouth. Now they had no reason; he brushed, got his teeth cleaned every three months, and kept mouth wash in his car. He rarely visited his old neighborhood for reasons other than dough. Growing up at the end of Cambellton Road a couple of blocks from Nabisco in a ragged house with his grandmother was frustrating. She was on a tight budget and they kept necessities but very few extras, and that damn Nabisco plant kept the neighborhood smelling delicious and him hungry as hell. Now he sold drugs in that neighborhood and ate all the sweets he wanted. That's why his five-feet-ten inch frame carried a gut. He was a light-skinned, average looking guy with beady eyes and a stubby little afro. He no longer was into jokes—he was into gunplay, so a lot people feared him. He feared nobody, but he hated the Miami boys and wanted to run their asses out of Atlanta when the time was right. At the present, too many of these Georgia niggas were still fucked up over the *Scarface* movie and acted like those Miami niggas were Tony Montana or The Sosa. He couldn't front, they did have most of the weight, but that didn't mean they didn't bleed just like everybody else.

Some type of commotion near the food court broke his thoughts. He saw Stan going to check it out and knew he would come tell him.

"What was that about"? he asked Stan when he returned.

"That nigga Jay from Sandpiper is with some nigga they call Pistol from New York. He fucked petty ass Darryl from Shamrock apartments up. Pistol slapped the shit out of him and then spit in his face, some thick shit, and told him he bet not touch it, it just slid down his face all slow. The shit was funny as hell 'cause all the girls were just standing there laughing," Stan explained.

"So is Jay hustling?" G asked.

"He been selling a little weed and coke, but I guess he will be selling a lot more now that he hooked up with a New York connect," Stan answered.

"Yeah that's what I don't want. What that nigga Pistol into?"

"I don't know, he just come thru town sometimes in his fancy cars. He supposed to be making a lot of money in New York"

"He needs to keep his ass up in New York. We already got enough problems with the Miami boys trying to run shit down here," G-Man replied.

G-Man saw Pistol and Jay walk by and he decided he would start paying Jay more attention, he didn't need another dope boy with good connections selling in the Ben Hill area or any other area he had work in.

Lovely went back on the rink and Joy and Candace continued to talk.

"So Joy what are you into?" Candace asked.

"The same old boring shit; school and not much else."

"Have you ever boosted?" Candace figured Joy would be a down ass bitch.

"You mean stealing?"

"Yeah, clothes and shit, then sell it to people in the neighborhood."

I only stole small stuff, personal stuff."

"I know it's a lot of hustlers around your way, we could make a killing selling to them," Candace told her.

"Yeah it's a lot of dope boys around my way."

"So is you down or what?"

"Yeah I'm down."

"What about your girlfriend Lovely?"

"She's kinda scared – I don't know about her," Joy replied.

"Shit, as pretty as she is and as much attention she get we could send her into a store to buy one small item and every man in the store will be so busy watching her they wouldn't pay us no attention."

"I don't know. I'ma ask her later," Joy said.

"Okay cool let's go skate," Candace knew they were in.

Eleven came pretty fast and Lovely and Joy were in the parking lot to meet Lovely's mom. Candace decided to leave also, she gave Joy her number and told her to call her. Joy was fascinated by Candace, not only did she seem very street smart for seventeen, but Joy was experiencing a physical attraction towards her. On the rink they skated side by side, and Candace was a lousy skater so Joy held her up a lot, and every time their bodies touched—it was *e-lec-tri-ci-ty*. Outside they saw that Candace had her own car, it was a used Honda Civic, but they were impressed nonetheless. She told them she lived with her moms and that they could come hang out over her crib anytime they wanted. Lovely liked Candace also, but Joy doubted if Lovely liked her like she liked her.

"Did y'all enjoy yourselves?" Delores asked.

"Yeah ma, it was okay. A lot of people were there tonight," Lovely answered.

"Yeah thank you Ms. Delores for driving us and picking us up," Joy said from the backseat.

"Ma can I spend a night at Joy's?"

"Joy did your mom say it was Okay?" Delores asked.

"Yes ma'am, I asked earlier," Joy lied, but doubted her mother would even notice Lovely—she was probably drunk anyway.

"Okay, Lovely come home early tomorrow to help me clean the house."

"Okay mom," Lovely was happy she wouldn't have to be around Rick.

Joy only had one bed in her room and Calvin's room was still as he left it. Joy and Lovely shared a bed. Lovely slept in a large shirt. *Damn she does have a hell of a body*, Joy thought to herself. Joy had a problem getting to sleep as she thought about Candace and the sensation she got when their bodies collided. Then when Lovely's body would rub against hers during the night more sensation surfaced and that night she bought herself to an orgasm, something she had been doing a lot lately.

3

Five Finger Discounts

Summer and school break signaled adventure for Lovely and Joy. The area around Stanton Road was a hotbed of activity: coke consumption was up, drinking was up, and copulation was way up. Skin was the biggest aphrodisiac in western Civilization and Georgia showed more than it's share come summertime. Newly developed body parts were in display by young teenagers, midriff shirts, tennis skirts, cut-offs, short-shorts and daisy dukes had hormones jumping like Kris Kross. The teenage girls and young women were spectacles worthy of the designation *Greatest Show on Earth*, far exceeding anything Ringling Bros. could show you. Their overripe bodies that had been simmering in their own juices waiting for exhibition time were exploding out of their tight clothes. It was a known fact that more sexual exploration, young girls maturation and men's inventive gaming took place during summer; because when the parents were away the children would play. On every block, back road, boulevard and street it was happy hour between 9 A.M. to 5 P.M. So many young girls were at home from school while their parents worked. And no panties were probably more sought after then Lovely Sinclair's. Young boys with no game were ready to get in the game to try and buy her; older men were ready to commit statutory crimes just to ride her.

As Lovely walked to Joy's house, she had to endure, "Lovely when me and you gonna hang out?" Jake hollered from across the street. Lovely just walked faster.

"Lovely when you gonna let me take you for a ride in my new car?" Melvin yelled from the hood of his B.M.W.

"Girl you need a boyfriend that will treat you right and buy you nice things," Junebug said stepping into her path.

"That's okay I'm alright by myself," she replied.

"Hey Shawty, want a free ice cream," the loud ice cream truck with its disgusting driver pulled alongside her.

"No I'm okay" she replied, wondering how many young girls he pulled with that line.

"I told you Skee, they be putting something in the food. Look at Lovely. She only fourteen and already thicker than the Atlanta Hawks' cheerleaders," Dexter tried to explain.

Know everything Barry jumped in. "Yeah I heard they put steroids in the meat so the animals get bigger and they make more money and other stuff too," he tried to explain.

"Then how come you so skinny then, you funny built motherfucker," Skee replied. The crowd broke out laughing.

"Ah fuck you," Barry said, but with a smile on his face because he didn't wanna chance another ass kicking by Skee.

Lovely made it finally to Joy's house, a block and a half away.

"Hi Joy" she said entering the house, I swear you need to see all those fools out there on the corners selling already, and it ain't even ten o'clock yet."

"Yeah I think Fly and some of his workers got locked up by Red Dog last night. They probably trying to claim his corner before someone else get it."

"Joy what the hell is you cooking?"

"Girl, my mother been drunk damn near all week and ... got shit in here to eat, so I'm making doughnuts," Joy dropped another one into the cooking oil.

"Why didn't you tell me to bring some stuff? Want me to go get some stuff out our refrigerator?" that rapist did buy groceries at least, Lovely thought to herself.

"Nah girl this is cool. Calvin taught me how to make this. Here taste one." She handed Lovely a doughnut.

"See first you have to have some canned biscuit dough like this," she explained, showing her a can of No–frill biscuit dough on the refrigerator shelf.

"Then you put some Crisco in the pan and take the dough and make holes in it with a top, those gonna be the munchkins," she said pointing to the little balls from the holes.

"Drop it in the grease, watch it get brown and big, then take it out. Let it cool and cover it with powdered sugar and you got doughnuts.

"You worse than the guy that be saying it's time to make the doughnuts, but they is good," Lovely said laughing.

"So what we gonna do today?"

"Candace gonna come pick us up, so we can hang over at her place in College Park."

"Good, I'm tired of these hounds around here," Lovely replied.

"She should be here in a couple of minutes," Joy said.

Are you gonna give her some of your world-famous doughnuts?" Lovely smiled.

"No, we just met her. She hasn't earned any yet." Both friends started laughing.

Candace arrived shortly afterwards, and honked her car horn and Lovely and Joy left with her. College Park was only a fifteen-minute ride, but much different scenery. Everybody in the

Washington Road area was on the move. There wasn't any idleness or hanging out on corners going on. Candlewood apartments where Candace lived were much nicer than anything on Stanton Road where Joy lived. The apartments were nicer, there were clean streets and walkways, and the complex had a big clubhouse and swimming pool, and even a Gazebo in the middle of the apartments. Both Joy and Lovely liked this new environment.

"Darn it's quiet out here. Where all the people?" Joy sounded like she was complaining, but she really wished she lived here.

"They will be out soon enough—it's still early," Candace said.

"It' looks like it ain't no selling going on around here," Lovely commented.

"Yes it is! But these College Park Police don't play so everybody mostly work off of beepers and have special customers," Candace informed her.

They pulled up in front of Candace's apartment and went in.

"Damn girl. Y'all are living it up in here," Joy blurted out when she saw how decked out Candace's living room was.

There was an expensive burgundy leather wrap-around sofa, a three layered coffee table with separate parts that swiveled, plush cream colored carpet, a large fish tank, a forty inch floor model T.V., top of the line sound system and a large wet bar in the dining area that complimented the cream lacquer dining set.

"Is this your mom?" Lovely said looking at a photo of a beautiful woman who looked too vivacious to have a seventeen-year-old daughter. She was at poolside somewhere with palm trees in the background.

"Yeah that's her at the Bahamas with her old boyfriend."

"Damn, she look like she's in her twenties," Joy said.

" Yeah she had me when she was young. She real cool too," Candace told them. She was used to people being surprised at how young her mother looked.

"Come see my room," Candace said, leading them upstairs. Her bedroom had a large canopy bed, a walk – in closet with enough clothes for a village, its own bathroom with about ten different brand named perfumes in the cabinet. Both Lovely and Joy didn't know what to say, Candace had more gear than both of them three times over, and Lovely had only one bottle of perfume and Joy only had some cheap body sprays.

"Shit, tell your mom she can adopt me right now," Joy said.

"Come on," Candace said with a laugh. They followed her to Candace mother's bedroom where everything was even bigger and better. Her floor model television had to be at least ten inches bigger than Candace's, her bed was circular with lavender silk sheets. She had twice as much perfume as Candace and so many clothes that her closet was overflowing and she had to use a professional clothes rack to hold even more garments. On her nightstand was a photo of Candace and her mother sitting on a new B.M.W. 5 series. She was darker and a little prettier than Candace with a body even surpassing Lovely's. She had on shorts and you can see that she had brought all her ass with her from the motherland. She had nice well-defined legs, big firm breasts and nice thick, long black hair. Now that's what a dark-skinned woman is supposed to look like, Joy thought to herself.

"Girl I just have to be nosy? Where do your mom work at so I can go and apply for a job," Lovely said.

"My mom is a stripper at some exclusive type club."

"For real?" Lovely said.

"She must be getting all those suckers' money," Joy said.

"You cool with that?" Lovely asked.

"Yeah, it's her body not mine, and she gets paid good," Candace said, getting defensive.

"I mean, could you do something like that?" Lovely asked.

"Shit most women get touched and seen for free all day. Why

not? Plus, all she do is strip, ain't no touching or anything."

"No, don't get me wrong. I respect your mom doing her thing. I was just thinking that I would be scared to death to do that," Lovely said. She wanted Candace to know that she didn't look down on stripping.

"Lovely you always being scared of stuff," Joy teased.

"No I'm not. I just don't want to get in trouble – that's all."

"Let's go get something to eat," Candace said. She led them back downstairs into the kitchen. She heated up some lasagna in the microwave, and they ate and watched music videos.

Y'all wanna go swimming?" Candace asked.

"I' didn't bring a suit," Joy said.

"Me either," Lovely replied.

"So lets go to the mall and get some," Candace said with a big smile.

"I don't have money for a suit," Lovely told her.

"You don't need none. Me and Joy will get it for you."

"Okay," Lovely said. After seeing how nice Candace's apartment was, Lovely thought Candace must have money of her own.

"Lovely, at Macy's in the Cumberland Mall they got this young security guard. Go over there and ask him a bunch of questions about store items while me and Joy get some stuff," Candace instructed.

"Hold up, you didn't say anything about stealing."

"Lovely chill. Me and her gonna get a few things. All you doing is talking to the security guard. If we did get caught, we don't know you. You're not with us so you'll be cool." Joy said.

"I don't know Joy." Lovely said.

"Come on Lovely. Use that pretty face and body to help us out," Candace said. Lovely blushed, not use to being complimented sincerely by other females. The thought of her looks being an asset instead of a liability did appeal to Lovely.

At Cumberland everything went perfect. The security guard fell all over himself to help Lovely and with Candace's gadget for removing security tags off clothing they ripped Macy's a new asshole. Candace and Joy wore big shirts and skirts so they tied about six dresses to their bodies and stole bathing suits before leaving the mall.

"Hit one store and leave, then go somewhere else. Next time you come to the mall we'll hit another store," Candace told them. Lovely and Joy now had new bathing suits.

"We can get fifty dollars apiece easy for these dresses. I'm gonna give 'em to my moms to take to the girls at her job. We should have five hundred dollars tomorrow. I'ma give my moms two for free, okay?" Candace asked them.

"That's sounds good to me," Joy said.

"That was kinda fun. The security guard gave me his phone number and everything." Lovely told them.

Later they went to Lenox mall and stole some really fly gear for themselves.

"Oh yeah, y'all gotta spend a night this weekend so we can go to a pool party tomorrow at Park South apartments," Candace told Lovely and Joy. Joy quickly agreed while Lovely said she had to check with her mother.

"The girls went to a movie and returned to Candace's just as her mother was getting ready for work.

"Candace is that you?" Sylvia yelled from upstairs.

"Yeah ma. I got my girlfriends with me, and I want you to meet 'em."

Sylvia came downstairs in a satin robe that grabbed her body, which definitely deserved to be paid for the privilege of viewing. She had a deep chocolate complexion, smooth skin as tight as any teenage girl, and large eyes that radiated a worldly sexiness. Her body was the height of perfection, when she moved, it was like thick mounds of delicious chocolate moved.

"Hi girls," she said giving Joy and Lovely light hugs.

"Hello. You have a beautiful apartment and you are even more beautiful than your photo's," Lovely said, a little intimidated by Candace's mom who radiated a strength that her own mother lacked.

"Thank you," she replied.

"Hello," Joy responded, awed into silence. Candace mother exuded femininity at its maximum. During the hug, Joy felt Sylvia's nakedness under her robe. Her nipples brushed against her ever so lighted and her intoxicating perfume entered Joy's senses and fuddled her brain.

"Ma can they spend a night this weekend?"

"If their mothers say they can. Now y'all have to excuse me while I get ready for work."

Candace excused herself and took the dresses upstairs.

"Ma can you take these dresses to the girls at work?"

"Let me see 'em. Oh, these are nice. How much you want for 'em?"

"Fifty a piece. You can have two for yourself."

Candace sat them on the bed.

"Ay, you be careful out there and watch out for them girls." She said about Lovely and Joy. "They are not as mature as you."

"I will mom. Love you," she kissed her mom and left the room.

Sylvia loved her daughter, but treated her more like a pal. She let her fend for herself mostly, and make her own decisions as well as her own money. She told Candace most of what went on in her life; her ups and downs with men, the goings on at the job, and shared her very materialistic and us–against–the-world attitude with her daughter.

SYLVIA ARRIVED at Dante's Inferno around nine o'clock and the club was filling up already. The Inferno was one of Atlanta's most prestigious strip clubs. It was located in Marietta, Georgia, and catered to professional sports figures, recording artists and record executives, wealthy businessmen, and other affluent patrons. The club contained three floors of the most accommodating and stimulating women in the South. All of them were visually breathtaking, conversationally stimulating, and as classy as New York socialites. Here, conversation was $100 dollars an hour, naked entertainment $300 an hour and outside bedroom dates $1000 dollars an hour. Cristal poured, delicacies (other than the girls) were devoured and money flowed like the Mississippi River. The club contained a four-star restaurant, discotheque, and an Oasis room in which there was a round swimming pool surrounded by sand and women in thongs underneath fake palm trees. Private V.I.P rooms with free drinks, food, computer access, virtual reality machines, massages, saunas and the most exotic women from across the world.

The V.I.P. cost a $100,000 dollar membership fee for two years.

Sylvia went in the women's dressing room/lounge area. About 30 girls were there.

"Okay women, I got some dresses for y'all's pretty bodies for one hundred apiece."

After selling all the dresses Sylvia put on her red and white cowgirl outfit with the ass out, red cowgirl hat and white boots and got her black lasso. Her cowgirl routine was a crowd favorite. The D.J. put on Too Live Crew's "Pop That Coochie," and she went on to the main stage to a crowd of cheering men. Her stage name was "Cleopatra" and she was one of their favorite strippers. Sylvia made about $150 on the stage and about $900 doing private dancing. She paid the house fifty percent of her earnings. She also sold all the dresses including the two Candace gave her. After club deductions and minus Candace's $500, Sylvia had made $1,325 that night; not bad for a Friday – not bad at all. *Soon*

I'll be able to buy a nice house and maybe trade my B.M.W. in for a Benz, Sylvia thought to herself, glad she was able to supplement her stripping with Candace's boosting.

When Lovely arrived home that night, her mother and Rick were already at the table eating dinner.

"Hi mom." Lovely said, barely looking at Rick. He just sucked his teeth and kept eating.

"Did you enjoy yourself over there? What did you do today?" Delores asked." Ma their apartment on Washington Road is real nice, in Candlewood apartments. We hung out there and then went to the movies and stuff," Lovely told her.

"Are you hungry? It's some more chicken and macaroni and cheese in there," Delores told her, already sensing the tension between husband and daughter.

"No I'm okay, I ate already," Lovely answered. "Ma."

"Huh?"

"Can I spend a night at Candace's, me and Joy tomorrow?"

"Okay, as long as Candace's mom don't mind."

"It's okay, we asked her earlier today."

Delores was glad to get Lovely out the house, because Rick was so much more attentive to her when Lovely wasn't around.

I got to start watching her, Rick thought. She's getting too fast. First chance I get I got to make sure she's not giving my pussy away. It's bad enough that I don't have shit now, I be damned if I let those fucking dope boys have her too. Damn, I wished this bitch had to work tonight, Rick thought, sorry that he couldn't get his hands on Lovely tonight.

LOVELY, JOY, AND CANDACE wore new bathing suits under their new gear they stole at Lenox Mall. Lovely and Candace wore short Gucci dresses and Joy wore Polo shorts with a matching top. Park South Apartments was about three quarters of a mile up Washington Road. The one thing it did have out of the ordinary was a swimming pool with high and low diving boards, a very large clubhouse, and a front office that allowed the apartment teens full access. When they got there around ten o'clock the parking lot was full of cars and boys and girls socializing, trying to get a jump on the competition. Park South's makeshift football field next to the pool was full of animated teens, most of the males with a beer in their hand, and lots with reefer joints already lit were being passed to the many young ladies to lower their inhibitions.

"Come on – let's go inside the party," Candace said.

"That will be five dollars," the handsome guy at the door said, smiling in Lovely's direction.

"Would you like to dance?" two boys walked up and asked Lovely at the same time, then looked at each other aggressively.

"No maybe later," she said.

"Okay I'ma come find you later" one said.

Cool, me and you later," the other one said.

They both walked in different directions after giving each other evil looks. The three girls burst out laughing.

"I'm thirsty let's get something to drink," Joy said heading towards the beverage booth. They purchased three wine coolers for three dollars apiece. After about four songs, a popular song by Guy came on and Candace said, "Let's go dance."

They went to the dance area and were immediately surrounded by three very energetic young men. The girls giggled and kept on dancing, and the males started dancing with them. Joy was a little awkward on the dance floor, she moved more like an athlete, but she was having a good time and so did the boy dancing with her. Candace was dancing circles around her companion; she must have been hitting some Philly moves, because teenagers looked like they was taking notes.

"Hi, my name's Rodney. What's yours?" the guy yelled over the music.

"My name's Lovely."

"For real? That's unique and a very good description of you."

Lovely smiled and said "Thanks."

"I go to Lakeshore. I'm the starting quarterback on Varsity. Where you go?"

"I go to Therell," she answered. He was muscular and kind of handsome, but Lovely was only interested in dancing—nothing more.

They had danced for about four songs and Rodney was hoping he could lock her down before someone else did.

"Do you have a boyfriend Lovely?"

"No." She gave short answers hoping he would just dance and not talk. Joy bounced up and grabbed Lovely around her shoulders playfully.

"Come on girl lets go out to the pool, it's hot in here."

"Bye Rodney," Lovely said.

"Oh, I'll see you later," Rodney was mad. *Damn I almost had shawty*. He lied to himself.

Lovely, Candace, and Joy put their clothes in a pile that they could watch. When Lovely came out of her dress and stood there all glorious and stunning in just a bathing suit, all of a sudden the pool deck got crowded. Eyes stared at her so intensely it felt like the suit was getting hot. Lovely jumped in the three feet area hoping that would cut down some of the scrutiny. Candace joined her. Joy saved her though.

"Lovely, Candace watch this!" she yelled.

Joy climbed up the stairs to the high board. She had long athletic legs and small, perky, great breast and looked good in her suit.

"Oh shit—look at her."

Kaboom! Joy's little butt did a cannonball and made a big splash. Some guys got wet, but they just laughed along with everyone else. Candace and Lovely went and dived off the low diving boards and the fellows couldn't of been happier. They got used to Lovely's presence and calmed down a little bit. Candace's thin frame was showcased well by her Donna Karen bathing suit and all three girls enjoyed a lot of male attention that night.

Around midnight a drunken brawl broke out between two guys.

"Come on Joy and Lovely. Let's go before some shooting starts," Candace said.

"I'm hungry," Joy said.

"Me too," Lovely said.

"Let's go to the Waffle House," Candace suggested. They drove up to the Waffle House on Old National Highway and were soon joined by others from the party, including Rodney.

"Hi Lovely, I'm glad we ran into each other–I wanted to get your number so we could go to the movies or something together," Rodney said with beer on his breath.

"That's okay I had a bad break-up recently and I just want to be left alone for a while," Lovely lied.

"Well let me get your number so we can stay in touch–just be friends until you're ready to date," Rodney persisted.

"No not now, but I promise if we run into each other next summer I'll give it to you, Joy and Candace snickered at Lovely's cute little lies.

"Whatever," Rodney said walking away upset.

A grey 500 SEL Benz pulled into the parking lot and out popped Pistol and Jay. Guys stared at the crisp Benz and girls gawked at the two men. As they entered the Waffle House, Pistol's eyes locked on Lovely, and both Candace and Joy knew Lovely had another fan. When they walked to the back and took a booth, Joy said to Candace, "You know him?"

"Not really. I seen him a few times in Candlewood though—that's all," Candace replied.

"I'll be back," Lovely went to the restroom. On her way back Pistol stood up and addressed her.

"How you doing? Lovely's your name right?"

"Yeah, how you doing? What's your name?"

"People call me Pistol."

"You must be a really violent person if they call you Pistol."

"Not at all, I'm just very explosive on the basketball court. Just like your mom knew you would be more beautiful than damn near everybody else and named you Lovely."

"You have a nice car, Pistol," Lovely tried to change the subject. Damn she hated her name and was sick of that line.

"You know Lovely–with your height, your exquisite looks and body–you could be a model. I have friends in the business in New York."

"Oh are you some kind of agent or something?"

"I'm some kinda lots of things, but no I'm not an agent."

"So why you want to help me?" Lovely had a feeling that she knew why.

"Well I'm not gonna lie. I detect that not only are you lovely, but also have a nice personality and learning about you mentally, physically and emotionally would be a journey only fit for a king–and I'ma king.

"Damn, was that some Shakespeare?" Lovely said jokingly but obviously impressed.

"Oh you got jokes huh? That's cool."

"Nah, I'm not interested in modeling–I have plenty of time to try that. Thanks anyway."

"Okay I just like to see women fulfill their potential. How about me and you getting to know each other better," Pistol said.

"You seem really nice and I enjoyed our conversation, but I'm not interested in a man right now.

"That's cool Lovely. Looking into your eyes and hearing your voice was worth the conversation alone." Pistol smiled and sat back down and started eating.

"Damn, that's the longest I've seen you conversate with a guy and you was all smiles," Joy commented when Lovely made it back to her table.

"He was real nice, he said I should model and wanted to get to know me better."

"Did you get the number at least?" Candace asked.

"Nah, I told him I wasn't looking for a man."

"Girl go get his beeper number at least. Shit we could sell that nigga a ton of stuff in the future," Candace told her.

"Yeah go ahead Lovely," Joy added on.

Lovely reluctantly got up and went over to Pistol's table.

"Pistol can I get your number, in case I change my mind?" Lovely asked him.

"Here's my skypager number. Instructions are on the card. You can reach me anywhere in the country."

"Okay, maybe I'll be talking to you soon," Lovely said walking away.

After they ate the girls went to Candace's apartment.

"Who wants the sofa downstairs?" Candace asked.

"Me, I'll sleep downstairs," Lovely said.

"Okay Joy you can sleep with me in my bed. There's some sheets and a blanket in that closet right there," Candace instructed Lovely.

Joy was happy to be sleeping in the bed with Candace. Nothing happened, but while Candace slept, Joy couldn't help but let her hands caress Candace's body "accidentally." Candace never awakened during the stolen caresses and Joy eventually fell asleep happy and wet with one hand across the meaty part of Candace's thigh.

4

Gifts and Trips

July third was just another day for Lovely who planned on hanging out with Joy and Candace like she been doing everyday since school break.

"Happy birthday, sleepy head," her mother sang barging into her room.

"Ma, it's too early." Lovely pulled the covers over her head. Delores snatched the blanket from atop her head.

"Stop acting silly. I want to give you your birthday gifts before I go to work." Delores left the bedroom and came back with a mini stereo system and a nice outfit for Lovely.

"Here this is from Rick," she said handing Lovely an envelope.

Lovely opened the envelope; it was a bullshit birthday card and $50 dollars.

"Thank you Ma–I really like my gifts." Delores leaned down and hugged her daughter. "Oh yeah–tell Rick thanks," Lovely added with very little enthusiasm.

AFTER HER MOTHER and Rick left for work Lovely caught another hour of sleep, then she got up and really examined her gifts. This is a nice system for my room, she thought plugging it in. The outfit was a beautiful skirt and blouse that was a little immature for Lovely. *If that motherfucker really wanted to give me a gift then he should of committed suicide*, she thought while pocketing the fifty-dollar bill. I know that piece of shit is mad he hasn't been able to catch me alone all summer, Lovely thought pleased with herself. Now I have to keep avoiding him until I can figure out how to get away from him. Joy came over about 10:30 that morning holding a garment bag.

"Happy birthday old lady," she said, giving Lovely a big hug.

"You gonna be an older lady next month when your birthday comes," Lovely replied.

"Here Love, me and Candace got this for you."

"Lovely had been wondering what was in the garment bag. She opened it and pulled out a butter soft black and red, light leather jacket. Therell High School colors.

"This is fly, I'm gonna save this until we go back to school, thank you."

"So what else did you get?" Joy asked.

"My mom's got me a real nice mini stereo system and a nice outfit. Rick gave me a birthday card and fifty dollars."

"Let's go see the stereo," Joy said bolting up the stairs.

Joy was fingering all the buttons trying to figure out the features when they heard a car's horn beep twice. Joy looked out the window and in a shocked voice said, "Lovely you is not going to believe who is out there."

"Who?" Lovely said as she walked to the window. Oh shit what is he doing out there? "Joy do me a favor and ask him what he wants while I get dressed."

"Okay, but hurry up! You don't want these petty gossiping motherfuckers seeing one of the biggest dope boys in front of your house."

Joy hurried outside, and Lovely quickly threw on a short set, washed her face, brushed her teeth and brushed her hair.

"Hi, who you looking for," Joy asked Big Dre who was now driving a convertible Saab.

"I'm looking for your friend Lovely. Where she at?"

"She was getting dressed. She wanted to know what you want?"

"Tell her I got something for her."

"Okay, I'll see what's up," Joy said leaving to fetch Lovely.

"What did he want?" Lovely said, now dressed and anxious.

"He said he got something to give you."

"Come with me," Lovely said, and they headed outside. Joy stood watch in the front lawn while Lovely went up to the car to find out what Big Dre wanted.

"Happy birthday, Lovely."

"How you doing Dre? It is okay if I just call you Dre right?"

"Of course."

"So what brings you around here, Dre?"

"You didn't think I was gonna forget it's your birthday did you?"

"I guess not," Lovely answered, uncomfortable with a major drug dealer being parked in front of her house.

"Here—I bought you a birthday gift," he said as he extended a long jewelry box towards her.

"Why you do that?" she asked.

"Because I enjoyed our conversation and I would really like us to be friends—no strings attached."

"Dre, you seem like a really nice guy, but I'm still not interested in a boyfriend."

"I understand and really you're still kinda young to have a boyfriend. I just want you and me to be able to talk sometimes, maybe go out sometimes–nothing sexual. I like you because you aren't a money hungry skeezer. Now can you please take the box—my arm is getting tired," he said smiling. Joy just stood back there fascinated by Lovely's magnetism. She believed that because so many of these young men came in contact with so much ugliness and malice, that a beautiful and innocent young girl like Lovely represented everything good missing in their lives. Joy fancied herself a bit of a sociologist.

Lovely opened the box and couldn't believe her eyes: there was a gold bracelet made out of three link bracelets, one white gold, one pink gold and one yellow gold. In the center of the bracelet was Lovely's name spelled out in diamonds.

"I can't take this, this is *way* too expensive."

"What you mean you can't take it? You have to take it—I don't know anyone else named Lovely," Dre said, his smile putting her completely at ease. She noticed that four of his teeth had diamond-filled caps. *That's fly as shit*, she thought to herself.

"Dre this is too expensive," she protested.

"Don't worry about it. That cost me almost nothing. A jeweler owed me a favor."

Lovely didn't believe him but decided not to press the issue.

"Friend, I got to go take care of some business. Enjoy your birthday and call when you get a chance tonight. He handed her a piece of paper with his beeper number on it.

"Okay, thank you for the bracelet. It's the nicest bracelet I ever saw," Lovely said still awed by the jewelry.

Big Dre drove off thinking he was one step closer to making Lovely his woman.

When Lovely showed Joy the bracelet she said, "Damn you got his nose open like 7-11."

Lovely couldn't believe Dre had been that nice to her, that he remembered her birthday and everything. Joy thought about the power Lovely had over one of the biggest dope boys in the city and men in general. Joy knew what they wanted, it was just like with Calvin; these dirty niggas hated to see somebody clean and innocent trying to rise. Soon as they do, they want to get their grimy little hands on 'em and bring them down to their level. Joy knew that those men, including Big Dre wanted to steal Lovely's innocence and that made her feel more protective of her friend. While Lovely was in the bathroom Joy made a bowl of cereal. She looked at the wallpaper on the wall, the tile on the floor, the magnets on the refrigerator and the full pantry and thought this looks like a real home, but Lovely prefers to be at my ghetto ass apartment. Something must really be wrong in here.

"So what you gonna do with the bracelet?" Joy asked when Lovely got out of the bathroom.

"I guess I'ma keep it, I tried to give it back, but he wouldn't take it. Said he don't know any more Lovelys."

"You know he gonna want some."

"I told him I wasn't looking for a man, and he said we could be friends—nothing sexual."

"They'll say anything," Joy warned her.

"I know. What should I do?" Lovely asked.

"Just don't get in his car or go anywhere with him alone."

"Okay. I told him I would beep him tonight. Plus, I better hide this. I don't want my mother or Rick to see it."

"What's up with Rick?" Joy tried to get Lovely to open up.

"Nothing–I just don't like him, because he bosses my mom around a lot." Lovely was too embarrassed to say more.

"You sure that's it?" Joy said, trying to dig deeper.

"Yes," Lovely replied, slightly annoyed.

"Okay. I'ma call Candace and see if she's coming to pick us up."

Joy suspected that there was more, but until Lovely opened up there was nothing she could do. *I swear if a nigga was doing me or my mom wrong I would set his ass on fire while he slept*, Joy thought to herself.

THAT EVENING DRE was busy preparing some work for his buddy Gator to handle until he got back from Pittsburgh.

"While I'm gone, tell niggas we low so they can only cop ounces. It's fifty-two ounces ready–charge $800 and don't accept less than $700 and that's only if they get a lot. There's five hundred twenties already bagged up for Techwood and another five hundred twenties if that run out. I should be back in less than three days—can you handle this shit," Big Dre asked.

"Yeah nigga, I been handling shit right," Gator responded, annoyed with Big Dre for talking to him like a kid.

"And nigga stay out the shaker booty clubs and handle *bizness*."

"I got this nigga—stop tripping."

Dre's beeper started vibrating and he called the number back. "Yeah who this?"

"Hi. It's me Lovely. You wanted me to call right?"

"Of course, I'm glad you did, 'cause I'm going home for a few days and wanted to tell you. How was your birthday?"

"Fine —me and my girlfriends went to Six Flags."

"Good make sure you beep me in three days, talk to you then," and he hung up.

Big Dre was twenty-four years old and getting rich. He felt about Atlanta, the way Scarface had felt about Miami: "The city is just one big pussy waiting to be fucked." He had the money, the power and the women; so many that sometimes he worried that he could be the first nigga to O.D. on too *much* good pussy. But like so many men that enjoyed a hedonistic lifestyle he craved someone clean, wholesome, untouched—someone worthy of deep feelings and pampering. It had never been difficult for Dre to get women; his tall stature, handsome youthful good looks, charming personality and ghetto stardom was an irresistible combination. In Lovely he saw what he wanted. He knew that she hadn't been involved with any of the men that approached her on a regular basis. And like the best packages she was still uncut, undiluted and untouched and he wanted to be her first and only handler. But his uncle down in Miami wanted him to take care of some business for him in Pittsburgh, P.A.

Dre's uncle Ranell had bricks like the Columbians down Miami. For as long as Dre could remember Ranell been up. Uncle Ranell always looked out for Dre and his other cousin who was also called Dre. His name was Andre Sparks and his cousin was Dreyfuss Sparks but he was taller and soon became Big Dre. Little Dre was locked up now in Dade County Jail without bond for two homicides. Uncle Ranell was always there for him. When he was little, his cousin Dre and he worked at Ranell's supermarket and got paid. When he was in high school Ranell bought him a car and let him and Dreyfuss work in his clothing store. And when he decided to hustle in Atlanta, it was Uncle Ranell that gave him half a key to start off with, and later fronted him five keys at a very good price. Now Uncle Ranell needed a favor and he was more than happy to oblige.

His uncle called him the night before and said, "Get to a pay phone and call me back."

"Yeah Uncle, what's up?" Dre asked after driving to a phone booth a couple of miles from a restaurant he was eating at.

"You remember Squid from Opa Locka?"

"Yeah, real dark skin ugly nigga?" Dre replied.

"Yeah that's him. He calls himself Samson now. He's been hustling in Pittsburgh, P.A. for like two years now. I started frontin' him joints about nine months ago. Now he owes me a hundred and twenty G's for two months and he's not answering my beeps. Walt already up there. Meet him, find that nigga, get what you can, and make him disappear.

Make it neat, 'cause I might let Walt stay up there and move work if he handle himself okay. Can you handle that?" Ranell asked.

"Sure Uncle. Do Walt know his way around, and do he have some iron?"

"Yeah he knows his way around a little and he got heat up there. Try and catch a plane tomorrow; he's waiting. Here's his pager number—got a pencil?"

"Yeah go ahead."

"1-800-Skypager code 5012."

"Okay, uncle, I'll be out tomorrow."

"A'ight be safe, and make it quiet."

DRE HATED AIRPLANES and was glad when he finally arrived at Pittsburgh International. He beeped Walt and went into a sports bar to wait. A couple of real thick women walked in and out of the bar but he was determined to focus on the job at hand and be gone. *Oh Squid, now he was the man huh? Oh well almost everyone gets a chance to dance at least once in the dope game*, he thought to himself. He remembered Squid as being a scrawny, acne–prone dirty guy that girls used to run from. *Now he called himself Samson huh*? Big Dre thought. *I wonder how strong he gonna act when I catch up to him*. Dre hoped this favor wouldn't be complicated, he wanted to get back to Atlanta.

Pittsburgh's airport was large, but nowhere as enormous as Atlanta's with their moving stairs and trains to different gates. Two heavily tattooed thugs walked by with visible gang colors. *So they on it like that here? Good. Gang activity always keeps police busy so less manpower can be assigned to hustling*, Dre thought.

Finally Walt arrived and they acknowledged each other with the street recognized nods. Walt walked ahead out the exit, past the cabstand towards the parking lot. Dre followed him discreetly to an Astrovan with tinted windows. No one else was around at the moment.

"Damn, my nigga, what's up? I ain't seen your ass in years," they gave each other a gangster hug.

"Ah–a nigga just been earning and learning that's all," Walt replied. "So you ready to go find this nigga, or what?"

"Yeah, but what's up with the van?" Dre asked.

"I didn't know if we was gonna have to snatch his ass off the streets, plus this won't trace back to nobody if we have to dump it."

"Do it have all the paperwork in case po-po pull us over?" Dre asked.

"Yeah my nigga–insurance and everything."

"A'ight let's get the fuck out of here then," Dre said, noticing two white men in Steelers caps heading towards cars near them.

The highway to Pittsburgh was bordered by boring looking towns.

"So how long you been looking for Squid, I mean Samson?" Dre asked.

"For about a week now. He pops up here and there, but mostly he be on the low."

"So how he get his money?"

"He sell weight around town to a select few, mostly cats moving major coke. I know he be supplying those niggas on Center Street and Wylie Ave. on the Hill District, and those niggas on the North Side on Federal Street."

"How they reach him?" Dre asked.

"They beep him, he call back and takes they order and meets them somewhere of his choosing."

"Did you find out anywhere we might can snatch his ass up?"

"I know two places: one is this club called The Name of The Game, he goes there some weekends, but a lot of people he's cool with be there. And I found out where he live from this girl named Kim who used to be friends with a girl he was fucking.

It's big as hell, with alarms on all the doors and windows. She took me by there."

"What's up with Kim?" Dre asked.

"She's cool, she from Homewood where I'm staying, I was fucking her for a while. She thinks I was looking for Samson to buy some coke."

"What the fuck kinda shit is that?" Dre asked. He had never seen a highway that went right through the middle of a mountain.

"Dog they got a bunch of weird shit in the mountains. Once we come out this tunnel we'll be there."

"Shit, it's about time nigga, I was starting to think you was lost." Dre estimated that they had been driving about forty minutes.

"I need a hotel room, and we gonna need some guns," Dre told him.

"You can get a room at the Vista Hotel, and I got two nines at the crib."

They drove through the tunnel and came out onto a bridge that led right into the city. Dre was surprised by the vastness and beauty of the city. It wasn't too hard for him to imagine that plenty money could be made there.

Dre checked into the Vista and then he and Walt toured the town a little. Walt showed him various locations where major drugs were being moved, mostly coke and heroine. They drove thru some projects on the Hill.

"Yeah Dog, those right there is Francis, those are Robinson Court, that's Whiteside and that's Sugar Top."

"Damn, they put all the projects near each other?" Dre commented.

"Yeah, I know some bad bitches out there too."

"We ain't got time for that bullshit. I'm trying to handle business and be out," Dre told him. "Yo! I'm hungry, lets go get something to eat."

"Okay, let's go to The Colonial Inn, they got decent food," Walt responded.

After they ate Big Dre said, "Now take me past this nigga crib."

They were driving for a nice while. "Big Dre, this nigga live in some rich suburbia type, exclusive shit called Fox Chapel."

"Is there a lot of police around?"

Nah, it's real quiet out there; your neighbors be way on up the road," Walt explained.

They watched the house from a safe distance. "Did you go up close last time?" Dre asked.

"Yeah I had the girl knock, nobody answered."

"How you know it was alarmed?"

"It had alarm security stickers everywhere; on the door and on the windows."

"Okay. I got an idea. Drive me to a hardware store. We'll come back real late tonight when that nigga sleeping."

Dre shared his plan on the way to the hardware store and as they arrived, Walt said, "That's the craziest idea I ever heard, but it should work. I know this crack head in Homewood that would be perfect; his name is Stretch—you should see how skinny this nigga is."

They went inside and purchased the various things they needed for the job. They paid for the stuff, carried it to the van, and started driving towards the hotel.

"Drop me off so I can rest up; plane rides always get me tired. Get Stretch, keep him with you, pay him anything you have to pay him and pick me up at two o'clock tonight out front."

"Okay, bring the guns right?" Walt asked.

"Of course bring the guns," Dre forgot that even though Walt had him by about ten years, he wasn't as smart as he was. Dre went to his room, got comfortable and called downstairs to the desk to ask for a 1:30 wake up call. He fell asleep wondering what Lovely was doing.

LOVELY AND JOY were spending the night at Candace's crib. Her mother was at work, and they were upstairs discussing sex. "Candace, did you have a boyfriend in Philly?" Lovely asked.

"Not really, I did give a couple of guys some pussy: the ones that deserved it," she replied.

"What did they do to deserve it?" Joy asked.

"Well the first guy, we use to go to Gratz High School together and he use to give me rides home. He was hustling so he bought me lunch a lot. His name was Steve but everyone called him Hoagie. One day I felt like leaving early, he drove me home and I was already curious so we did it in the house."

"Did you like it the first time?" Joy asked.

"It mostly hurt the first time, but I played hooky from school a lot and sometimes we would have sex. It got a lot better and he started buying me nicer things like sneakers, gear, paying for my hair and nails to get done, and giving me money—so it was cool."

"Who else?" Joy asked. Lovely was just soaking everything in.

"Oh yeah, it was this other guy on my block name Cal. He was ugly, but he kept telling me he would eat the shit out of my pussy 'til I talked in tongues. So after a few weeks of him saying this and Hoagie never putting his tongue down there, which was kinda surprising since he was a fat greedy motherfucker that seemed to eat everything else..." They all chuckled at that.

"Anyway, I let him eat me and he did a damn good job. It felt much better than Hoagie's dick. So I started letting him eat it regularly and have some pussy," Candace told them.

"Did he have you talking in tongues?" Joy asked.

"Nah, but my speech was slurred." They started laughing harder now.

"Lovely, why you so quiet," Candace asked.

"Sex gets her nervous," Joy said.

"No it don't, I just don't see what's the big deal," Lovely answered.

"If you was doing it right, especially being eaten right, you would know what the big deal is," Candace told her.

"Shit, my mom's is always with a man and she don't never seem happy."

"Yeah that's the bad part: with sex the man comes with it and they are mostly assholes."

"Too bad we can't get good sex without the man," Joy said.

"They got a lot gadgets for that, but it ain't the same as a real person," Candace said to them.

"You used vibrators before?" Lovely asked, shocked.

"Yeah, my moms bought me one last year. She said it felt just as good as the real thing and it wouldn't give me a baby or diseases," Candace said.

"Your moms is a trip," Lovely responded.

"Can I see it?" Joy asked.

"Sure, hold on," Candace went in her closet and came back with a sock, from out the sock she pulled out a pale plastic vibrator that looked quite large, but was only a medium size.

"You be sticking that inside you? Is it electric?" Lovely asked.

"Yeah I put it inside me. It's operated by batteries. Catch!" Candace tossed it towards Lovely.

"Augh," she refused to touch it and just let it hit the bed.

"Girl, don't treat my boyfriend like that. Touch it—don't be scared. It's clean and it won't hurt you unless you want it to."

Lovely picked it up. Why is it white?"

"My mom said the black ones are usually bigger and I need to work my way up to those."

Joy and Lovely giggled. Lovely was thinking how harmless it looked.

"Let me see," Joy got it from Lovely. She turned it on and it started vibrating.

"Look at me I'm Superdick, da–da–daah," she had it up high, waving it around the room like it was a toy airplane.

"Girl stop playing with him before you hurt his feelings." Candace retrieved her vibrator and put it back on the dresser inside the sock.

"I'm tired, and I'm going to sleep. If one of y'all want to borrow my boyfriend tonight go ahead–I won't get jealous," Candace then got in bed. Joy slept with her and Lovely slept on an inflatable mattress they bought with their boosting money. It was 1:45 A.M., Candace went right to sleep, and Joy soon feel asleep languishing over how good it felt to be so close to Candace. Lovely stayed up for a considerable amount of time wondering how sex felt when it wasn't being forced on you. She also thought about Dre. He had rushed off the phone last time, and she wondered what that was about. I hope he don't think I'm going to sweat him because he bought me a bracelet. She looked down at it. *It is fly as hell though*, she thought before she fell asleep.

AT 1:45 A.M. BIG DRE was just getting out the shower, throwing on his boxers, black jeans, and hoody and black Nikes. He was rushing to make it out front before two o'clock when Walt and Stretch was suppose to arrive.

The menacing looking van arrived at 2:03. Big Dre climbed in and took a look at Stretch. Yeah, he was a lanky motherfucker, obviously a smoker, but not totally gone like some men that no longer bathed, worked, pursued sex, or possessed any self-respect.

"Stretch, you sure you can do this, right?" Big Dre asked him.

"Yes Sir, I went to PITT for electronics and I've worked around that kinda stuff for eight years."

"Okay, whatever Walt promised you I'm gonna pay you double that 'cause I want this done right, done quiet, and I want you to keep your mouth closed afterwards."

"I told him a thousand," Walt said.

"Okay, I'm gonna pay you two thousand instead."

"Thank you–it will be done right and I'll never mention it again," Stretch told him.

It was 2:21 when they got to Samson's house. They parked down the street, off the road where the car wouldn't be detected. All three of them approached the house, and a new burgundy Maxima was parked out front.

"That's his girl car," Walt whispered.

The lights were out, the house looked asleep, and the woods were alive with owls and crickets and other night dwellers. Both Big Dre and Walt were armed with nice Smith and Wesson nine-millimeters. Dre would have preferred them attached with silencers, but no neighboring houses were even visible.

Stretch approached the front window and with a large magnet was able to manipulate the lock. Then he took a stick of chewing gum and stuck it in his mouth. When the piece was sufficiently moist he took it out.

"See, what you have to do is put something between the contacts to make them think they're still connected," Stretch explained.

"We got us a real live fucking McGyver," Big Dre whispered to Walt.

Stretch used the gum to hold the silver wrapper in place and lifted the window. No alarm went off, and Big Dre and Walt sighed in relief. Stretch then went in and disabled the alarm system while Big Dre and Walt climbed into the open window. No one stirred in the house and they proceeded up the stairs. All three crept around on some real cat burglar type shit, which Stretch had been led to believe it was. They entered the master bedroom and were greeted by a beautiful sight. Stretched out on the bed was an Amazon of a woman with legs thick as a tree trunk, ass fat enough to break a young child's fall. She was lying there sexy like, asleep with a red teddy on. Big Dre felt a yearning in his groin area.

"Hold her down," Dre whispered to Walt and Stretch. Dre cut a piece of tape off the roll and duct-taped her mouth. She struggled as he tied her spread eagle on her stomach to the four bedposts.

"Walt go watch the front of the house and let me know when a car is pulling up. Make sure he can't see you. Try a window," Dre told him.

"Stand at the door so you can hear him," he told Stretch. Stretch was visibly nervous. He was shaking like a fiend that sold his coat in winter. Dre ran his hand along his captive's beautiful body; up her chocolate fit legs, between the crack of her plentiful ass, and up her back.

"Do you know where your boyfriend keeps his money?" he asked her.

She nodded her head yes, vigorously.

"We just here for his dough, behave yourself and you will live thru this okay?" he said this while touching her shoulders tenderly. She was still shaking her head yes, enthusiastically.

"I'm gonna remove the tape, if you make noise it will go back on and make me angry. You don't wanna see me angry right?"

She shook her head no, sternly.

He snatched the tape off and she winced from the pain, but didn't make a sound.

"It's in the safe inside the closet," she told him.

Dre opened the closet and in the back was a nice size, sturdy safe.

"Do you know the combination?" Dre asked.

"No I wish I did. I would have been robbed him and left," she said with a serious look on her face.

Dre chuckled and told Stretch, "Come here."

"Can you get into that?" he asked Stretch motioning towards the safe.

Stretch looked it over and said, "That would take hours and the right tools."

"Fuck that. Dude should be here soon. Go wait in front of this door in the hallway so you can hear when he's coming," Dre told Stretch.

"Is your boyfriend carrying a gun on him?"

"Probably not, he usually don't pack," she replied.

"What's your name?"

"Tenisha."

"Tenisha you have a beautiful body, do you mind if I take your teddy off?"

"Go ahead."

He ripped it off exposing enough woman to service a block of angry inmates.

Dre's dick was harder than robbing Fort Knox.

"Tenisha, we might be a while. Are you down for a little fun?"

"Sure baby."

Dre laid his dick along the side of her face and started receiving an expertly executed blowjob. Tenisha sucked his dick like her life depended on it, because to her—it did. Stretch peeped in, enviously. This angel faced Amazon sucked dick devilishly, she did a trick where she licked his nuts when her mouth reached the bottom of his shaft. He wished he could take her with him, at least her mouth.

"Baby you taste so good and you're so big," she said with so much sincerity between gobbles of Dre's dick. After the blowjob Dre put a pillow underneath Tenisha's stomach and started pounding her from the back. She was still tied down and loving the hammering her pussy was receiving, moans like that couldn't be faked. Dre had just shot his load when Stretch said, "a car is coming up the driveway."

Big Dre stuck his wet dick in his pants, buttoned them up, and then slapped the duct tape on her pleasurable mouth. Walt and Stretch was already in the foyer waiting downstairs. Dre was about four feet from the door. When it opened, he leveled his firearm at Samson's forehead. Walt closed the door behind him.

"Squid, what's up bitch-ass nigga, remember me?" Dre asked.

Squid tried to reach for something and Walt slapped him in the back of his head with his gun and it discharged. Squid fell to the floor and so did Stretch, shot close range in the chest.

"Damn, my bad," Walt said staring at Stretch.

"Fuck him, if he wasn't so fucking tall you might of missed," Dre said since he would have killed Stretch later on anyway. You can't trust a neighborhood smoker to not tell anything. Squid aka Samson was still on the floor looking like the same old dirty nigga from Opa Locka; just a lot bigger and a lot better dressed.

"Lift his bitch ass up and take him up stairs," Big Dre commanded Walt.

"What about him?" he asked looking down at Stretch who lay motionless in the floor.

"What about him? Leave him the fuck there," Dre said, irritated.

Dre followed behind them, his nine at attention, Squid's .38 in his pocket. When they opened the bedroom door and Squid saw his girl butt naked and tied down tears burst from his wig.

"Yo, you ain't have to do my girl like that," Squid had the nerve to say as if there was etiquette to home invasions.

"Pussy, keep talking and I'll have your stupid ass butt naked, tied up just like that. Now sit your stupid ass in that chair," Dre told him.

"Walt tie his ass up and tight," Dre told him. Squid was tied to a floral loveseat in his bedroom.

"Yo, go downstairs in the kitchen and bring that iron up," Dre told Walt.

"Turn it on at the highest level," he told him when he got back.

"Pussy, my uncle wants his 120 thousand you owe him, where it at?" when Samson didn't answer, Dre pressed the iron down on Tenisha's beautiful ass and her cooked flesh smelled nothing like bacon.

"Okay man, I got what's left in the safe in my closet, I swear Big Dre—that's all I got. The combination is left twice twelve, right once around twenty-four and straight left to thirty-six."

"Get that out of there," he told Walt.

"How much is it," he asked Squid.

"About $75,000."

Walt tossed lots of bundles of cash out the closet.

"Count it," Dre told Walt.

Dre then dropped the iron on Tenisha's other ass cheek and left it there. "Is that all you got?" he asked Squid.

"Yeah man I swear, please stop," Squid was crying like a cheerleader after a championship lost.

Sexy Tenisha's muffled screams could be heard through the duct tape. Dre taped Squids mouth next.

"I'ma give you a chance to tell me where some more money is, or I'm gonna keep torturing you."

Skin was stuck on the iron and still cooking. Tenisha's ass looked like Jeffrey Dahmer was dining there, and the iron was super hot, Dre felt the heat's radiance. *I know he wish he hadn't bought such a nice iron*, Dre thought to himself, with a smile.

"It's seventy-six thousand," Walt said.

"Okay. Find a bag and put it in." Dre said.

Then Dre pressed the hot iron atop Squid's baldhead for what had to seem like an eternity.

"Is you gonna tell me where some more money is?" Dre asked.

Squid definitely wasn't Samson no more; he peed on himself and cried more tears than Dre thought was possible. It sounded like he said through the tape, "That's it–I swear to God," Dre had to be sure so he burned him again, this time even longer. *Yeah that's what he had said*, Dre thought.

Dre was done with the interrogation so he pulled a shorter piece of rope from his pocket and strangled Squid. He strangled him for far longer than Walt thought was necessary, even though he didn't voice his opinion. Afterwards he kissed the back of Tenisha's neck and strangled her too.

"Take those bodies downstairs next to Stretch's," he told Walt.

Dre went into the kitchen and got the items he purchased from the hardware store.

"Start cleaning that blood up. Use some ammonia from out the kitchen," he told Walt.

Dre then placed a funnel inside each corpse's mouth and poured lye down their insides. After he filled their mouths, he applied new pieces of duct tape. He hoped the lye would totally decompose their bodies from the inside out within a couple of weeks. He then put them inside industrial-size garbage bags.

"Go get the van," he told Walt. While Walt was gone he searched the house, but found nothing else worth taking. They carried the bodies and placed them inside the van, not concerned with fingerprints 'cause all three entered the home wearing gloves.

"How far is this place?" Dre asked.

"It's fifteen to twenty minutes away," Walt responded.

"And their bodies should go unnoticed for at least a month?"

"Yeah, it's a garbage dump. Nobody will smell nothing and we can throw some garbage on 'em."

"Yeah a'ight," Dre responded.

Dre was now ready to be out of Pittsburgh. His errand had taken only a day but he was exhausted and ready to get back to Atlanta. The bodies were left on Pickle Hill, a dump behind Lemington Heights Projects. Dre had Walt cover the bodies with garbage and debris for extra precaution.

It was 4:27 when Walt dropped Big Dre back off at the Vista Hotel.

"Yo, you did good and that's what I'm gonna tell my uncle. Don't worry about shooting the smoker, we was gonna have to kill him anyway."

"You want me to pick you up tomorrow?"

"Yeah at three o'clock in the afternoon, and not in this van, here."

Dre gave him $5,000. The next day Dre got up around twelve o'clock and purchased a T.V. and a Phillips head screwdriver. He opened the T.V., and placed the money inside and closed it back. He then found UPS in the yellow pages, went there and sent the T.V. to an address him and his Uncle used in Dade County, Florida. At three o'clock Walt drove him back to the airport where he boarded a plane back to Georgia and his operation.

I hope my young girl Lovely ain't mad we didn't hang out on her birthday, was one of his last thoughts before nodding off on the airplane.

5

Home Horrible Home

It was too hot to be outside on the sixth of July, so Lovely and Joy sat around Candace's house watching videos, talking shit, and enjoying the A.C. They were downstairs trying not to wake Candace mother who was still asleep at two o'clock in the afternoon. She had endured a long night of shaking her ass.

The girls heard her when she got in at 6:30 in the morning sounding slightly drunk and talking to herself.

"I swear if one more motherfucker try and stick their nasty ass finger in my coochie—I'ma cut that shit off."

She then banged around in the kitchen making herself some coffee or something else that required a commotion. Candace told them it was best to stay out of her way and leave her alone when she was like this.

"And if I see that blond hair blue eyed bitch Jessie try and steal another one of my customers, I'ma beat that bitch back to Indiana." The tirade continued. It was quiet for a minute.

"Candace, Candace," she now stood in the doorway.

"Yes."

"Make sure you clean that downstairs up today," she demanded, then went to her room and slammed the door.

Candace wasn't upset with her mom or embarrassed, she figured stripping all night was enough to make anyone drink and act mean from time to time. Lovely was a little frightened by Ms. Sylvia's mood. She exuded so much strength and power, and had such a physical presence that Lovely was a little intimidated by her even when she wasn't in a bad mood. Joy was transfixed by Candace's mother, and when she stood in the doorway she looked like a damp Goddess to her. Her body was showcased in a tight mini-strapless dress, wet from what Joy thought was sexual sweat secreted during her many lap dances and exhibitions. Joy wished she could go watch women dance and bend the weak men to their will. Joy knew Ms. Sylvia had to be a dominating figure in the world of men and she admired her for that, because she held men in nothing but contempt.

The girls had finished cleaning downstairs together. They were bored and getting tired of videos.

"Lovely, why don't you beep that guy that gave you the bracelet," Candace suggested.

"Yeah. It's been three days, he's probably back by now." Joy said. Lovely dug in her Coach purse, one of her many boosted accessories, and found Dre's beeper number. She beeped him and waited for his returned call. The phone rang and when Lovely answered the phone she heard "Yeah, did someone beep me?"

"Hi, this is Lovely."

"Hi Shawty, I was waiting for you to call. I got back a little early. Sorry I was in such a rush on your birthday."

"It's okay, um–I was just calling to say hi and tell you the bracelet is really pretty," she said shyly.

"So what are you doing now? Let's hang out."

I'm with my girlfriends. Could you hold on one minute I got

to do something."

"Yeah a'ight," Dre responded.

Lovely sat the phone down on a pillow so he couldn't hear her and told Candace and Joy. "He wanna hang out."

"Tell him you and your girlfriends are going to get something to eat and to meet you at the Denny's on Old National," said Candace.

"You want to?" Lovely asked Joy.

"I don't care," Joy said.

"Come on, I wanna meet him and see if he got real dough," Candace said.

"Okay," Lovely agreed and returned to the phone.

"Me and my girlfriends were going to Denny's on Old National. You wanna meet us there?"

"Yeah I ain't doing nothing, but it's gonna take me about thirty minutes to get there," Dre answered.

"That's cool, we'll meet you there," she said.

"See you soon Love-ly," he said her name playfully and hung up.

The girls got there first, went in found seats and ordered. Soon Dre arrived in his Benz. He stepped out the car and for the first time Lovely noticed how tall he was: at least six-feet-two she estimated. He was impeccably dressed in what Candace immediately recognized as expensive linen pants and shirt and Gucci loafers. His jewelry wasn't over-sized, but it was expensive. *His braids look so nice and neat*, Lovely thought to herself.

"Damn, this nigga here is good for a grip, I wonder how *we* can get some," Candace said.

This nigga thinks he's the shit, huh. If I was a man I would take his shit, Joy thought to herself.

Young girls always wanna show you off to their little friends. That's cool. I'll have her all to myself eventually, Dre thought when he saw Lovely sitting and eating with her two friends.

"Hi ladies," he said, but he was smiling at Lovely, who he noticed was wearing the bracelet.

Sitting there relaxed with her girlfriends, taking small bites of chicken Parmesan, she looked even more beautiful than she did before. Her tan gave her an exotic Brazilian look and her hazel eyes made you want to pamper and protect her. This girl was no dime, she was a quarter.

"Hi." Joy and Candace said in unison.

"Hi Dre," Lovely said.

"Have a seat," Candace said.

He did and Lovely said, "That's my friend Candace, and you met my friend Joy."

"How you doing ladies? Is the food here any good?" he asked to break the ice.

"It's pretty good," Candace answered.

"Order something," Lovely suggested.

"I can't—I'm still full off of some buffalo wings I had right before you beeped me," he told Lovely.

"I just came to see how you was doing and watch you eat—see if you ate like a pig," he said jokingly.

Lovely covered her mouth and laughed. Dre laughed too. Joy and Candace just watched the interaction. After they finished eating Dre paid for their meals and left a large tip, displaying a monster knot of mostly fifties and hundreds.

"Dre I sell men's clothes, and I got some shirts your size," Candace told him.

"Yeah? Let me check 'em out."

In the parking lot Dre purchased all the 2X shirts Candace had in her trunk and gave up 550 dollars, the knot barely decreased in size.

He offered to take them bowling, and they accepted. The girls followed behind him in Candace's car.

"Lovely, he's cute and the nigga is paid," Candace said, " Joy ain't he cute?" Candace asked.

"He's alright," she responded.

"Lovely he really like you, and you can get some real dough out of him," Candace said.

"Nah, I ain't into that," she replied.

"You ain't into what? Girl you better get some of that nigga's paper – that's what ballers are for," Candace said.

"Dope boys just wanna fuck you, then fuck your life up," Joy interjected.

"That's why you get they ass first. My homeboys in Philly would kidnap his ass; make him tell them where his dough is stashed. I know that nigga right there is probably worth a half a million," Candace said.

"Why females can't do what men do?" Joy asked.

"They can, in Philly it's girls that hustle like men, do stick-ups like men, even bust they guns like men," Candace replied.

"Y'all tripping–he done spent 550 dollars with us, what else y'all want?" Lovely asked.

"A half a million," Candace replied and her and Joy started laughing.

Dre parked in front of the bowling alley. Inside they had a good time, but Dre's eyes and attention stayed fixed on Lovely. Her very developed ass and hips were the center of attention every time she had to bowl. Lovely and Big Dre were really enjoying each others company; their conversation flowed smoothly and Lovely found herself becoming fond of a man for the first time. Joy asked Candace about how Philly guys be snatching dope boys, wishing she could do something like that and move her and her mother off Stanton Road for good. Day quickly turned to night and Dre and the girls parted company, Lovely promised him she would beep him soon and meant it.

When Lovely got home that night Rick was the only one there.

"Where's my mom at?" she asked, scared to be alone with him.

"She went to the store," he replied.

She went upstairs to her room and tried to close the door behind her, but Rick was right behind her.

"Where you been, huh?" he asked.

"Out with my girlfriends."

"Nah–you probably been with some boys letting them feel you up like this," he grabbed her ass real rough with two hands.

"Stop," she swatted his hands.

He pushed her on the bed and climbed on top of her backside and reached around and grabbed her breast. He was instantly hard and his privates being pressed up against her disgusted her.

"Stop Rick, I swear I'm gonna call the police," she said very frightened now.

"Bitch if you ever call the police on me I swear I will come back and stab you and your mother in y'all's sleep," he said angrily. "Now pull those fucking pants down."

That's when they heard a horn blast. Lovely's mom signaling Rick to come help her carry the groceries in.

"You lucky, but real soon and I bet not find out you been with anybody else" he told Lovely before heading outside to help his wife.

A couple of weeks later Lovely woke up to the smell of bacon, so she dragged her weary self down to the kitchen. She had been up late the night before celebrating Joy's birthday with the two girls at Candace's. When she got downstairs bacon, pancakes, eggs, and biscuits were sitting on the counter and her mother looked ready to leave the house.

"I have to go see your grandmother about something."

"Morning," just then Rick came into the kitchen. Lovely knew this was exactly what Rick was waiting for. She had successfully avoided him for two months.

"Ma, can I come?"

"Nah stay and eat your breakfast."

Lovely knew Rick was smiling inside.

"Please," Lovely pleaded," I haven't seen Grandma all summer." She honestly disliked going over there but anything was better than being alone with Rick.

"I'm just going and coming right back," Delores didn't want her daughter around when she asked for money.

"Please it won't take me but a minute to get dressed."

"You ought to leave her here so you can hurry up and go and comeback," Rick said almost like a command.

"Please ma, let me ride with you!"

Delores natural instinct was to do as Rick said, but she saw desperation in her daughter's eyes. Her little bit of mother's instinct took over. "Okay, hurry up and get dressed."

Lovely dashed up the stairs, a survivor's relief giving her new energy.

Rick looked at his wife real evil in a way that made her want to run and hide. He snatched a plate of food and headed back to their bedroom. He passed Lovely in the hallway, and said, "You think you slick, but I'ma get you, little pale bitch."

She was terrified of her familiar rapist and hugged her side of the hall like he was contaminated with the Ebola Virus or something. She knew she had to figure out a way to stay away from him.

Lovely and her mom rode mostly in silence. Delores knew something was seriously wrong between her daughter and her husband, and even though she loved her daughter she didn't want to hear anything that would force her into a confrontation with her husband.

Delores stole a look at herself in the rearview mirror. She admitted to herself her beauty was fading *fast. I probably couldn't even get another man if Rick left me*, she thought to herself.

Rick will change soon. He's just being mean lately 'cause he had a string of bad luck, soon everything will be like it use to be, Delores kidded herself. She looked over at Lovely whose eyes were closed and she looked a thousand times more relaxed then she did around Rick. She thought to herself, Lovely is a big girl now; she can take care of herself. Plus whatever problems her and Rick have they will work it out. It's probably some type of father-daughter thing. She liked to think of Rick as Lovely's father so she wouldn't think of her first love. Her subconscious told her she was in denial about a lot of things and didn't want to face the fact that her marriage was a complete failure and her daughter was in danger. Every time her subconscious would try and speak up, she would beat it down viciously, similar to how Rick did her.

Pulling up in front of her grandmother's large expensive home, Lovely couldn't help but feel like her and her mother had been ostracized like a couple of Lepers. Her grandmother's neighborhood, home and lifestyle was in stark contrast to the piece of shit house in the middle of a hardened ghetto that she lived in with a negligent mother and a perverse stepfather.

Delores hated being here; she hated being reminded that she had been cast out of a white Eden for committing one sin; having an interracial daughter. The same fucking sin her mother had committed, *old hypocrite bitch*, she thought to herself.

Damn, I hope Henry doesn't wake up. Kate hated when her daughter and granddaughter came around. Kate didn't want to remind her husband or her neighbors that she had a half-nigger daughter. And her daughter was so stupid she went and made the same mistake, now she had a half- nigger granddaughter. Lovely seemed nice enough, but Kate knew she would also start fucking niggers, having their babies, eating their food, listening to their music, so she never got emotionally close to her granddaughter, because she didn't want her heart broken by her like Delores had done.

It was easy to tell that her grandmother didn't want them there. She kept them in the living room area and spoke in hushed tones. Delores wanted some privacy so she gently led Kate into the dining room alone.

"Mom can I get the money so I can go?"

"How come you ain't got no money gal? Why that husband of yours didn't give you none?' Kate said husband like it tasted funny in her mouth.

"Ma I told you an emergency came up and things are a little tight right now."

"Huh, a $1,000 sounds like a pretty big emergency."

"Ma, can you stop giving me a hard time? It's not like a thousand is gonna hurt you or nothing."

Delores knew her mother wanted her to grovel and to make her feel like less than dirt for disobeying her and getting involved with a black man. She didn't want to tell her the truth, but that would ensure that she got the money.

"Ma I need it for an abortion."

Kate just shook her head like that was the saddest thing she ever heard.

"Here," she handed Delores an envelope that was tucked in her satin bathrobe.

Lovely looked around the living room at all the antiques her grandmother possessed and thought how just a small amount could move them off Stanton Road, maybe away from Rick. She also knew her grandmother resented her mother for being with black men and her because she was interracial. It was another reason Lovely hated her racial mixture.

On the way home both mother and daughter were quiet, feeling a lot smaller than they had when they awakened this morning. Lovely thought about the time when she was in

Underground Atlanta window-shopping and heard two white women call a young white girl a white nigger because she was with a black guy. That was the way Lovely felt every time she left her grandmothers house, and she knew her mother felt the same way too.

That night Lovely spent the night over Candace's house and Delores and Rick were alone. He had a hard time sleeping wondering where Lovely was, if she was fucking anybody, and how long would it be before he could catch her. He tried to fuck Delores that night, but it wasn't that exciting.

"Bitch how come you haven't been listening to me lately?" he woke her from her sleep.

"What is you talking about? I do be listening."

"This morning I told you to leave Lovely here."

"But, but she wanted to see her grandmother."

"She didn't want to see that mean old bitch, she just wanted to be hard headed, and you too," his anger at Lovely successfully avoiding him increased.

"Rick it ain't nothing. I be listening to you," Delores tried to rub him softly on his chest which use to get him in a sexual mood.

"Shut up bitch," he said, and then kicked her off the bed.

She hit the floor hard, whimpered and got to her feet.

"Where you going bitch?"

"To sleep downstairs on the sofa."

"Bitch sleep right there on the floor, beside the bed and you bet not move."

Delores slept on the side of the bed and for a long time Rick could hear her crying and that made him feel better.

6

Police Involvement

"Yo! My nigga, what kind is this?" Stan asked.

"Nigga that right there is a Bull pup. It's a semi-automatic shotgun. That's for when we finally go to war with those bitch ass Miami boys," G-Man replied.

"Yo! This some new shit ain't it?"

"Yeah, yeah! Those are Mac 12s they like baby Mac 11's but they shoot .38's," G-Man replied.

"Damn, these joints fit right in a holster. You can walk right up on niggas with like thirty rounds," Stan said checking out G-Man's arsenal.

There was the Bull pup, the two Mac 12s, two nine-millimeter Glocks, one with an infrared beam, and Taurus .38 auto. Like most up and coming drug dealers, G-Man was given a sense of power and security by guns.

"Man, we ought to slump that Miami nigga Big Dre, or better yet Bullshit Dre," Stan laughed, sounding a lot tougher than he really was.

"His time coming, I'ma run his bitch ass out of town or put some of these in 'em," G-Man said holding the Bull pup the way Tony Montana did in the last scene of *Scarface*. The Bull pup reminded him of the M60 Tony Montana had.

"I thought you was suppose to get a AK like that nigga Barry got," Stan inquired.

"Yeah I ain't caught up with him yet, but I suppose to get this AR-15 from the Bullet Stop out Marietta."

"You getting a lot of guns for those Miami boys," Stan said, practically insinuating that G-Man was scared of them.

That pissed G-Man off, "Yo wasn't you fittin' to take Rico that four-and-a-half?"

"Yeah."

"Then go ahead, what you wasting time for?"

Stan was thinking, *ah nigga don't get mad at me 'cause those Miami niggas got you scared like a little bitch*, but of course he kept that to himself. Not only was Stan scared of the Miami boys, but he was scared of G-Man too.

G-Man called Ron, "What's going on?"

"That stuff we had out Apple Tree is already gone. We got enough for two this time."

"I'ma call my man and see what's up. Bring what you got by the crib."

"A'ight, later," Ron said.

"Later," and G-Man hung up.

He called his connect in Pensecola, Florida, "Yo! What's going on, it's G."

"G what's up my man?" his Latin friend replied.

"Yo! My man's coming soon. We need parts for two Chevy Novas."

"Okay, we got that. Tell him to come on down."

"A'ight, I'll tell him. Later," G-Man said.

"Later," said the Latino before he hung up.

In the middle of the night when most people were getting their beauty sleep, Ron and a woman took off for Pensecola. He took a woman with him because he thought it helped to keep the police off your ass, and he was right.

Nobody liked a female witness against them, not even the police, because women were emotional and good at persuading a jury. They drove through Georgia, skirted across Alabama and arrived in Florida early the next morning. After a three-hour sleep, they drove to Juan's Junk Yard.

"Ron whad-up ome boy?" the bronze guy with bad pronunciation said.

Ron recognized him from his last visit. "I need two of those things."

"Two! Ju moving up huh? Good-good," he said smiling, happy to see progress.

"In your car, you follow me. We move stuff, mucho caliente here – very hot," he climbed into a suped-up Datsun and drove to Ron's car and waited.

They arrived at a rundown miniature farm with chickens running around and pit bulls chained to trees.

"Come, come," he motioned to Ron.

They went inside a barn filled with what looked like fighting roosters in pens, and Ron was glad 'cause they looked upset with the world. The stench assaulted his senses; it smelled like shit, piss, and ammonia. After a couple of seconds Ron's head cleared up and his senses adjusted.

"Here ju go. That be twenty-four for ju," he said giving Ron a big smile.

Ron cracked a key open and examined it. It showed no additives and appeared to be just straight Bolivian coke.

"It look good," Ron told him.

"Ju know we only have good thuff for ju."

It was around noon when Ron headed back to Atlanta with

two keys stashed in the back panel of a very conservative Cadillac Seville. They were coming up. With two keys him and G-Man could start making some serious dough, especially if they could cut into the Miami-boys' business.

BIG DRE SAT in his restaurant eating barbecue ribs, baked macaroni, and buttermilk biscuits, listening to Gator.

"Like I was saying, somebody done opened up another spot in King Ridge, and we starting to make a lot less money.

"How much we make over there this week?" Dre asked.

We made twenty-three and last week we made almost thirty thousand."

"Yeah that's a big difference. We gonna have to close 'em down."

"How you want me to do it?" Gator asked.

"Smoke them niggas out the way we did the ones on Martin Luther King Drive,"

"That will definitely work."

"And don't forget to get the sand and screws from the hardware store," Dre told him.

"Yeah I got you. Later," and Gator left.

That evening Gary and Rodney was in the spot getting their dick sucked by a smoker for a twenty rock.

"Damn girl slow up. Suck my dick slower, that rock ain't going no-where," Gary told her.

"Shit, if you wasn't so fucking skinny I would fuck you from the back, but I'm scared I might hit a bone and break my dick," Rodney said.

"Ha, ha- ah - ha - ah," Gary tried to laughed.

Rodney had mixed some coke in a blunt and was feeling hella good.

"Don't tell me, don't tell me, I bet you use to be the prom queen, but now, you just the prom fiend. Ha,ha,ha,ha,ha,"

Rodney was really enjoying himself.

"Stop, before you make her laugh and she, oh yeah" then Gary resumed his sentence, "before you make her bite my dick or something."

"Hurry up bitch, I want some licky licky, some lic..." Rodney said when two flying objects crashed through the living room window, followed by loud blinding heat when the Molotov cocktails exploded. Rodney tried to run towards the bedroom for protection and felt his back being ripped apart by the screws that became dangerous projectiles destroying anything in it's path. He lay on the floor while miniature fires started all around him. The female was caught totally off guard, slow to make the transition from sucking to protecting.

Screws punctured her lungs and earlier smoke escaped, her face was shredded and her eyeballs ruptured; she died in agonizing pain. *I ain't even get my rock*, was her last thought before dying. Gary had escaped the bullet-like projectiles and was crawling towards the door.

Fuck, all these damn locks in my way, he thought. Gary had one more lock left, and then he felt the flames licking his back, caressing his neck. He tried to remove his clothing, but the gasoline had soaked through and his clothes stuck to his body. Now his hair was on fire and he patted it out, but the smoke had long since invaded his lungs and he started to succumb.

"All those fucking locks," Gary cursed before he too lost consciousness.

Earlier that day Gator had prepared the Molotov cocktails the way Big Dre had showed him. He took two liter soda bottles and filled them halfway with gasoline. Then he added about a quarter bottle of sand and a quarter screws, and stuffed a rag halfway in the bottle. He knew from experience that the screw would act like bullets and a new fire would develop from everything the sand touched. He and a lieutenant firebombed the apartment together. He didn't care that three people died—they shouldn't have trespassed on their turf.

Detective Hutchins and Greenlee were the two homicide detectives assigned the deaths at Kings Ridge Apartments.

"What we got here Steve?" Hutchins asked.

"It look like somebody made a fancy pipe bomb Sir," Steve Phillips the crime scene expert knew he shouldn't have said sir if he wanted to be thought of as a peer, but he was in awe of and a little afraid of the six-feet-four, massive red-head detective and couldn't help himself.

"What about the bodies, any identification?"

"No Sir, not yet, but it looked like they was running a dope house. We found some crack, a scale and loaded firearm in the backroom."

"Well make sure you get their fingerprints."

"Yes Sir," Steve responded to Detective Hutchins.

Detective Greenlee quietly looked for clues and allowed Hutchins to be the vocal one. Detective Greenlee knew Hutchins came from a long line of very prejudiced rednecks. Hutchins felt that the good old Southern white folks owned the whole South and any crimes committed by Blacks in Atlanta were a personal affront to him. Detective Greenlee, a transport from Alabama and graduate from Tuskegee wasn't hindered by Hutchins's attitude. He just quietly solved homicides and worked towards his goal of becoming the youngest black police chief of Atlanta and later on maybe even the mayor.

"I hope these dope dealing animals aren't starting up turf wars like they have up North," Hutchins said.

"We need to solve this one quick before that's exactly what we have," Greenlee responded.

"Shit, it looks like we'll have to work late to finish all this paperwork," Hutchins said disgusted.

"I'll go see if any neighbors seen anything." Greenlee told

him.

They had silently agreed a long time ago that Greenlee was better at questioning potential black witnesses. His five-feet-eleven inch frame, sympathetic eyes, chocolate colored skin and laid back demeanor usually got other blacks to relax and let their tongues flap.

THE CHROMED-OUT brown and gold Caddy with the brown ragtop and gold Daytons came gliding down Auburn Avenue blasting N.W.A. and headed for Charles' Disco. Then G-Man switched to a Too Short tape, his favorite rapper and one he resembled.

"Charlotte don't spill none of that cooler on my seats."

"I won't and the way you got your two tone leather seats is nice."

G-Man and Stan looked at each other and gave a quiet little laugh, both figured these girls probably never been in a car this pimped-out before. They had met the two caramel-colored cousins that afternoon at Greenbriar Mall. Both looked like they just had stepped out a music video wearing not much fabric on top of too much package. The just-off-the-porch girls were going to be juniors at Mays High when school started. They saw the gold, saw the beepers, and they were looking for adventure. It was an easy sell getting them to go to Charles' Disco that night. Stan was smoking a joint and passed it to Tameka. She took a pull; coughed a little and giggled, "here Charlotte." Charlotte looked a little more experienced and handled her puff expertly.

"Is this Ses? It's good," she said. The men in the front of the car looked impressed. Charlotte was glad she remembered some rap terminology. This was her first time smoking too.

Lovely, Candace and Joy arrived in the parking lot of Charles' Disco two minutes before G-Man and were heading inside when he parked. Charles' Disco was dark, a little dangerous and full of sexual excitement; just the way horny southern teenagers and young adults liked it. The décor was Early American Ghetto; mirrors partially covered the old fashion burgundy velvet wallpaper. The worn strobe lights barely illuminated the dance floor full of gyrating bodies, unsolicited caresses, and heavy eyelids not quite concealing good weed and lustful invites. The three girls wore Gucci sneakers, Lovely wore a short red and white Gucci summer dress, Joy wore a Gucci sweat suit and Candace had on a pair of white shorts and a white Gucci shirt. Lovely wasn't wearing the bracelet given to her by Big Dre; Charles' Disco was thuggish, and larcenous.

"Stan, ain't that that Lovely over there?" G-Man asked.

"Where?"

"Over there by the bar."

"Yep- that's her and damn she's looking good. She look like a young Vanessa Williams," Stan said.

"Better," G-Man replied.

They both stared at her nice ass bouncing around like it had a mind of its own and teasing the shit out of all the males and maybe a few women. They were standing near the bar trying to place an order and bopping to the music meanwhile.

"You know who she look like? She look like that girl that played in *Flashdance* but better and with a better body," Stan remarked.

"I don't know, all I know is I want to fuck that young girl, "G-Man answered.

"Man I'm fittin' to go over there and holla at her," Stan had forgotten all about Tameka and Charlotte who was seated at a table waiting for Stan and G-Man to bring them drinks.

"Go head my nigga, put your mack down," G-Man said half mockingly, not expecting Stan to have any success. Stan walked over to the ladies.

"Could I buy y'all drinks," Stan asked.

"Thanks, but we got 'em," Lovely answered.

"Lovely right. You go to Therell."

"Yeah I do."

"Well hi Lovely, my name is Stan and that's my partner G-Man over there," he was hoping G-Man's name was at least recognized and he would get some props for being his partner. Lovely looked Stan over: he was slim, around five-feet-eleven inch, neat, nicely dressed and somewhat handsome, but nothing exciting. She noticed his so-called partner's unwavering eyes on her and was a little uncomfortable. The image of a hyena watching a potential victim popped into her head.

"So what's up?" Lovely asked with a bored expression.

"Me and my partner got a table and we wanted y'all to come chill with us."

"Thank you but we gonna walk around a little bit. Bye."

"Here Lovely," Joy handed her a drink and all three girls walked off. Lovely noticed the partner still staring after her. G-Man was standing there thinking, I'ma find a way to fuck that little bitch. Stan came back dejected.

"I probably would have pulled her if she wasn't with her friends."

"You couldn't pull her with a tow truck. Stop sweating that and let's go handle these young girls," G-Man told him.

"Yeah," Stan brightened up remembering that they were there with Tameka and Charlotte.

All night the trio was asked to dance or offered drinks. Joy had started to fill out a little more during the summer, but still had a tomboyish quality. Candace was cute and stylish so she turned a few heads. Lovely was causing even more of a frenzy; her honey-roasted tan gave her an exotic Brazilian look and her natural soft, long curly hair made you want to run your hands through it. Those still innocent hazel eyes were hypnotic. She grew a couple of more inches and her body got way more attention than she wanted. They accepted dances together, drunk Champale, didn't slow drag and left before the usual closing ceremonies of gunfights in the parking lot.

G-Man and Stan took the girls home around 2:30. They couldn't stay out all night, but promised if they came to their house during the week when their mother was at work, intimacy would jump off. Tameka was staying over Charlotte's house. G-Man and Stan were definitely going after those drawers sometime during the week.

The next day Candace and Joy were arrested trying to boost some Nautica gear. Lovely occupied one security guard but another plainclothes security officer spotted them. Lovely was not connected to the two shoplifters and was able to leave the store without incident. Candace was eventually taken to Fulton County Jail, and Joy taken to the juvenile facility next to the stadium. Lovely was unfamiliar with judicial systems so she called Joy's mom. Ms. Murphy was drunk and didn't sound like she could be much help. Lovely couldn't reach Candace mom who may have already left for the strip club.

She felt an enormous amount of guilt. Watching for security had been her responsibility. She had watched Joy and Candace be escorted to the police cars. They didn't shed a tear even though the dismay on their faces couldn't be masked. How they were able to hold back tears was a mystery to Lovely, she had immediately went into the Mall restroom and cried. After being embarrassed by the discomfort she caused two older women in the restroom she left, first declining their help. She hoped Joy and Candace wouldn't be upset with her or worse yet, blame her for their being caught.

7

Bend Over and Spread 'em

Nothing was more miserable than confinement, and Candace was experiencing it first hand at the Fulton County Jail. *I hope they don't find out I'm using an alias*, she was thinking when the butch looking muscle-built C.O. said, "Bend over and spread 'em."

"Bend over more," Candace stood naked in a mildewed group shower area, having her anus inspected.

"Lean up against the chair." Now the C.O. was probing Candace's vagina with two latexed fingers like she was looking for a missing family of refugees.

"Now pour this over your head and take a shower." The C.O. handed Candace some weak antiseptic fluid in a Dixie cup that was suppose to kill lice. Candace was also given a bar of green soap that made you ashier than Somalians and itch all day and night. Lotion was a precious commodity for the first couple of weeks of incarceration. Candace couldn't imagine that far, she only had been in jail for four hours.

After Candace finished showering she climbed into the oversized tan, formless and dreary prison issued pants and top.

"Miss when can I get a phone call?" Candace asked.

"When I give you one. Now go sit back over there on that bench."

"Stinking bitch," Candace mumbled in a low tone on her way to the bench. The C.O. heard it, but was used to it and didn't respond.

It was almost obscene the way people in processing dragged their ass around consuming time. Candace had been fingerprinted then made to wait, photographed then made to wait, showered then made to wait, asked a dozen questions and made to wait. The most troubling question had been: "Where would you like your body sent if something happened to you?" She was almost afraid to say her mother. She imagined the doorbell ringing, her mother answering, tired from dancing the night before.

"Yes, can I help you?"

"Are you Sylvia Atkins?"

"Yes I am."

"I have a package for you if you will sign right here."

Then the UPS driver would go into the back of the truck and toss her dead body on her mother's welcome mat.

She was served a cold bologna and cheese sandwich with almost spoiled milk and a rotting apple. The main holding cell stank; it was crowded and a lot of women gave her either menacing or lascivious looks. In nine hours she went from fearing a cell to craving a cell. She wanted to sleep, get out of the holding cell and get some space her own.

She had wolfed down the cheese and bologna sandwich. Hunger had been kicking the inside of her stomach. Now her stomach bubbled and she feared that she had to shit, because there was no way she was using that lowly commode they had festering in the corner.

It was after 2 A.M. when she was finally allowed a phone call.

Good thing her mother worked late hours.

"Hello. Dante's Inferno. Can I help you?" someone answered the phone.

"Yes, this is Sylvia's daughter and it's an emergency. Can you please put her on the phone?" Candace said with rapid-fire urgency.

"Okay, hold on." About ninety-seconds later the girl returned to the phone. "I'm sorry she's in the middle of something and asked me to take a message."

"Tell her, her daughter is locked up at Fulton County Jail under the name Sherrie Miller, S-h-e-r-r-i-e Miller, and I need her to come get me out."

"Ms. Miller time to go," a different butch looking C.O. said.

"Okay sweetie I'll tell her. You hang in there I'm sure she'll get you out real soon."

"Thank you. Bye," Candace had to relinquish her lifeline. She was then finally led out of processing.

"Damn C.O. we don't get our own cells?" Candace asked.

"Nope, the whole jail is over crowded." The C.O. opened another larger cell. Candace carried her thin plastic mattress, two sheets, and one pillowcase with no pillow, toothpaste, toothbrush and soap. She had a plastic cup, a small comb, and a disgusted look. About 30 people were packed in an area about the size of two small bedrooms. One bedroom had eight bunk beds, all fully occupied. The eating area had four tables, three of them fully occupied. Candace laid the painfully thin mattress atop a table and tried to fall asleep. She vowed that the next day she would get one of those bunks or die trying.

Candace tossed and turned most of the night. Sleeping in the open air atop a table surrounded by other incarcerated women was not conducive to a good night's sleep. She hated it, but deep into night her stomach won the war. She found some toilet paper and cleaned the commode like a lab technician after an Ebola outbreak. After her shit, her stomach was settled and she was able to fall into a more natural sleep.

When she woke the next morning, motherfuckers were scurrying around like a bunch of roaches after the lights go out, moving to and fro aimlessly with miserable and defeated looks in their eyes. They temporarily brightened up when the breakfast carts arrived. Candace didn't see why; the breakfast made her more depressed. They were served lumpy lukewarm oatmeal, two hardboiled eggs, a small container of milk, and coffee that would probably make a good insecticide. Everyone ate silently and purposefully like they had just left a famined country.

After everyone was finished eating there were three trays left. Most of the women kept eyeing them like they were Christmas gifts, but no one dared touched them. *I wonder whose trays those are*, Candace thought, If these other bitches ain't gonna touch 'em, then fuck it. Candace took two eggs off the top tray, cracked them, and started eating. The other girls stared at her wide-eyed like she had slapped Jesus.

Candace had just finished eating the second egg when the most intimidating female specimen she ever seen walked out the sleeping area. And Candace was from Philly where they don't intimidate easily, but Ox wasn't your normal female. She was about five-feet-ten, 180 pounds, with hair shorter than project's grass. She also sported a scar on her face that looked like it was put there by Jason himself. This woman looked like she wouldn't back down from anyone. Ox was from Brooklyn originally, Red Hook Projects, and had stomped down her fair share of niggas and bitches. She was locked up in Fulton County Jail for robbing females near the West End Mall area.

A person would think she earned the name Ox by her looks and obvious strength, but that wasn't it. Ever since her face had been cut on Riker's Island with a razor, she carried a razor blade, usually in her mouth. Ox was a slang term for a small razor carried in a person's mouth.

Ox looked at the top tray and asked, "Who the fuck ate my eggs?"

Candace was scared, but she wasn't going to cower to no female not even one that looked like Al Capone.

"I ate 'em," She step forward prepared for whatever.

"Why the fuck did you eat my eggs?"

" 'Cause I was hungry," she answered steadily.

Ox looked her up and down and Candace stood her ground.

"Was they worth you getting your ass whipped?"

"The shits were cold and nasty, and I don't plan on getting my ass whipped. Ox just stared at her for a few seconds real evil like and then busted out laughing.

"I like you. Where you from?"

"I'm from Philly."

"Philly come sit with me while I eat my breakfast and let's talk. It was like the whole room breathed a sigh of relief. Maybe they thought Ox would whip all their asses for letting Candace eat the eggs.

While Ox ate, they discussed New York and Philly. They talked about how pretty Atlanta was and how nice the people were. They also discussed how easy it was to make money, which was kinda ironic since they were only meeting because they both got caught trying to make money. After breakfast, Ox made someone vacate her bunk. Her and Candace talked most of the day and were on their way to becoming good friends.

LOVELY WENT home and waited for Joy to call. Lovely heard the downstairs door open. "Oh shit," she said and tried to gather her things to leave. Someone was home early.

Rick had took to leaving work early and popping up at different times, trying to catch Lovely home.

"Where do you think you are going?"

"Leave me alone Rick I gotta go take care of something important."

"Get your ass in there," he said pushing her back into her room.

"Leave me the fuck alone, Rick."

"Who the *fuck* do you think you're talking to?" he said, crossing the room with the quickness of an experienced predator. He smacked her so hard she almost did a 360-degree spin. After she regained her equilibrium, she said, "You fucking bastard," and grabbed a pair of scissors off the dresser and stabbed at him. No scissors were gonna keep him from his prey. He sidestepped the blade and received one deep jab to his arm for the effort. He then faked left and charged forward, catching her with a vicious slap that sent her crashing into a wall. Her left cheek instantly started to bruise and the corner of her lip split open.

He forced her on to the bed and snatched her clothes off. He took what he wanted, trying to hurt her as much as possible in the progress. Lovely cried through the whole ordeal.

"I knew I was going to catch that bitch," Rick said, very pleased with himself. As hard as I be working, as much bullshit I have to put up with, I deserve some affection when I come home. He stood in front of his bathroom mirror bare-chested feeling victorious as he talked to his reflection.

Rick knew he was losing possession of Lovely. Today was the hardest she ever fought back. He wanted to savor his feeling of triumph as long as possible. He walked back to her bedroom and said, "See what you made me do?" Lovely now had on a thick layer of clothes and lay there on her bed curled up like a wounded animal, sobbing.

"And you better get yourself together before your mother comes home, 'cause if I get any shit out of her I'ma beat the bullshit out of her. Then I'ma come back in here, and I won't be so nice next time." He went back to his room to bandage his arm and savor his victory. Lovely lay there unresponsive, swearing to herself that she would find a way to get rid of his ass.

"SPREAD YOUR CHEEKS wider baby. That's right. Girl you got fat pussy lips on you. Now let me see the booty talk. Bounce it baby—bounce it."

Now that major ballers were starting to frequent Dante's, Sylvia had to work harder. They wanted her to open further and spread it wider, bend over more, make the butt cheeks bounce. The white businessmen were usually satisfied with just seeing some good pussy and a fat ass.

"Now come sit on it and feel how big my dick got for you." She had to admit, she did enjoy grinding on a big black dick more then most of those little white peckers. A lot of times it was hard to tell if they were even hard.

"You feel all that dick girl? Imagine if we didn't have these pants between us. How 'bout it?"

She ignored his last remark, concentrating on her grind, wishing this shit would be over already. This was his third song, and his country ass was getting on her nerves. Everybody wanted a skeet and usually kept paying until they soiled their pants. The white men came early and demanded much more friction. Both added up to plenty dough, but she hated feeling their sticky goo on her ass and legs.

"Oh baby that felt good. Here's two hundred dollars. Buy yourself something nice. Big Daddy will be back to see you in a couple of days."

"Okay, Big Daddy. You make sure you hurry up and come back. You know you my favorite customer," Sylvia said in her most appreciative and innocent voice. She had found out that was the voice they liked best when they handed her their money.

She knew she had to change out of her red thong, it was sticking to her ass crack, and the adhesive had been supplied by

Big Daddy. She needed a shower, but didn't want to lose any money in the time it would take to clean up. She was trying to get $4,000 more for a new Benz.

The lights dimmed and the D.J. announced "And now for your voyeuristic pleasures, little Bo Peep and her sheep." At that moment two dancers came from behind the curtain. One was a statuesque blond, five-feet-ten, thin legs, with pubic hair shaped into a heart, green eyes and gigantic breasts that God couldn't have made all by himself. She had a small blond woman in tow on her hands and knees, covered with pink fluorescent foam to give her a sheep-like appearance. Sylvia observed the performance for a couple of minutes.

Little Bo-Peep sat on a bench looking sad crying and the sheep rubbed against her in an attempt to comfort. The more the sheep rubbed, the wider Bo peep's legs parted until the sheep was between her thighs. Bo-Peep pushed forward on her bench and the blond-haired sheep licked her to an orgasm. Afterwards the sheep mounted Bo-Peep and fucked her out of her depression with a strap-on. The crowd was in a trance, customers and fellow strippers alike stood around the stage salivating. Sylvia headed to the back to get a shower and a new outfit.

Jessie and Trisha came out of the dressing room together. "Sylvia your daughter called from Fulton Country Jail and said she needed you to come get her. She's locked up under… hold on, hold on, here go the paper right here. She sounded really sad. Are you gonna go get her?" Jessie purred in her Southern twang.

"Thanks for the message. Aren't you on your way somewhere?" Sylvia said; she was not about to give the nosey bitch more to talk about.

Sylvia looked at the clock and saw it was almost midnight and thought there's nothing I can do now; she can wait 'til morning. She went to take her shower, knowing the D.J. would be announcing Cleopatra to take the stage, and she would have to go dance.

THE PROCESSING AT the Juvenile facility was a lot quicker than in Fulton County jail.

After calling her mother who was drunk and incoherent, she called Lovely. The juvenile facility allowed you a whole ten minutes to call whoever you wanted before they locked you down.

"Hello," Lovely sounded like she had been crying.

"What's wrong?" Joy asked.

"Nothing I was just worried about you," Lovely said. Joy suspected Rick had something to do with it, but let it pass.

"I called my mom, but she was drunk and didn't understand shit I said."

"What you need? I got about $1200 saved up," Lovely said.

"Can you come visit me tomorrow and bring me five pairs of white cotton panties and bras, cosmetics, slippers, a cartoon of cigarettes, and money for my account, Joy answered.

"Sure I'll be down there around eleven, but don't you have bail or something?"

"Nope, 'cause I was already on probation for shoplifting."

"Do you need a lawyer or something?"

"Yeah, a lawyer might get me out or at least get me less time."

"Okay I'ma beep that guy Dre and see if he know a good lawyer I can afford."

"If you need it, I got another $1,400 hidden in a pair of Calvin's old Reeboks in his room," Joy told her.

"I haven't heard from Candace yet," Lovely told her.

"She probably called her mom to get her out."

"Yeah, I'm sure her mom has plenty dough save up."

"I know I would if I had that body," Joy said.

"You better worry about protecting your own body," Lovely told her.

"Girl, you know I can handle myself. What about you? Are you gonna be alright?"

"Yeah I'll be alright, I just will be glad when you get out of there." Their friendship had reached a sisterly level.

"Lovely, be careful with that guy Dre and don't give him no pussy. As soon as they get what they want they start dogging you."

" Joy you are still a virgin yourself, so how come you know so much about boys?"

"Lovely you don't have to fuck 'em to know they ain't shit, and that guy Dre ain't no boy; he's a grown ass man chasin' you."

"Ms. Murphy time to go," the administrator told Joy.

"Love I got to go, I'll see you tomorrow. Stay safe."

"You too, and I'll see you tomorrow, Luv you."

"Luv you too, bye," Joy responded.

After Joy hung up Lovely felt so alone.

8

Battery Operated

Dre helped Lovely find an attorney, but it didn't help much.

Joy was given six months jail time for her probation violation. Lovely visited her once a week, but Joy's mother had made only one short visit.

Candace sat in Fulton County Jail four days; the time it took the lawyer to petition the court for bail, Sylvia had been upset that some of her "buy a new Benz money" had to be used for a lawyer and bail. Candace repaid her $1,800 of it and was back to boosting. School would be starting in a week and she and Lovely were making a killing. That is whenever she could convince Lovely that is, who had become even more scared to participate.

When school started, not only was Lovely the best-looking girl at Therell High, she was now one of the best dressed. Niggas followed her like a float at the Christmas Parade. She had blossomed over the summer. She was now five-feet-nine a sultry 135 lbs, with a full heart-shaped ass, smooth as glass with big thighs and hips to match. She maintained her quiet shy ways, got excellent grades and had the whole school wrapped around her finger. Even the females couldn't hate for long, she was so perfect without even trying and without acting like she was better than anyone else.

Dre thought she was better than everyone else though, and he showed it by buying her gifts, picking her up from school, and being patient. She still hadn't given him any pussy. They kissed, he touched, but nothing more. He was okay with it, as long as she wasn't giving anyone else anything.

On the weekdays when he wasn't busy he drove her home from school. The men around Stanton Road assumed that Big Dre was now her boyfriend. They made sly remarks, but mostly backed off. Dre's reputation was so large in Atlanta that Lovely was almost off limits.

Now that Joy's apartment was no longer a refuge, Lovely went to drama, singing, and dance classes after school. Dre had paid for them and even came to her performances. She made sure her moms was home before she went anywhere near Rick-the-rapist. She spent her weekends either at Candace's house or visiting Joy. Candace went a few times to see Joy though she said she hated visiting people in jail. She had obviously had some visiting experience in Philly. In return Lovely went with Candace a couple of times to visit Ox. Lovely thought Ox looked a lot like one of the WWF Wrestlers and didn't like the way Ox looked at her. Candace laughed when she told her that.

G-Man knew Big Dre was responsible for burning him out of his new spot in Kings Ridge, but he hadn't struck back yet.

"Damn my nigga, when we gonna take it to Big Dre and 'em?" Stan asked.

"Looked stupid they got more ones, more guns, and more soldiers than us, so we gotta plan a sneak attack."

Stan did not appreciate G-Man calling him stupid, but he didn't point that out. "Why don't we try and hook up with Jay and his partner Pistol from New York? I bet they got lots of ones, guns, and soldiers." Stan said.

"Nah, that ain't how you war with someone, by bringing another more powerful enemy into your camp. Have you ever read *The Prince* by Machiavelli?"

"By Mack-a-who?"

"By Machiavelli, he was a great strategist a long time ago in Italy."

"You *read* that?" Stan asked with doubt in his voice.

"Yeah I read that nigga. What you think I can't read or something?"

"I just ain't never see you read no book."

"Anyway, Machiavelli said if you invite a powerful foreign power to help you fight battle, then eventually you will have to fight them or they will take over."

"Was Machiavelli some great General or something?"

"No, he was a politician that became poor when new people took charge of Italy around the 1400's. He tried to get a job or get on the new rulers good side by writing a book describing how government should be run and wars fought. That book is called The Prince by Machiavelli."

"How you find out about that book?" Stan asked.

"My cousin that goes to Morehouse gave it to me."

"Yeah, your cousin goes to Morehouse?"

"Yeah, motherfucker, niggas in my family do be going to college," G-Man said losing patience with Stan.

"Is he a Que-Dogg?"

"I don't fucking know! Did you understand the point I was making?"

"Yeah I understood you I ain't stupid," Stan replied.

"Plus, Jay and Pistol is helping without even knowing it. By them warring with The Miami boys near Techwood, it's showing the rest of Atlanta that the Miami boys can be done up just like anybody else," G-Man continued.

"Yeah, but what about oh fuckboy Dre?"

"I got something planned for his ass real soon. You said he be picking up that girl Lovely from Therell right."

"Yeah, about three times a week," Stan replied.

"What time do school let out?"

"Around 3:15. Why what you gonna do?"

"You'll see. Now come on let's go past the mall," G-Man said.

They left the apartment to go see what action they could find at Greenbriar mall. Stan was still wondering what G-Man had planned, and he hoped it wouldn't affect Lovely. Stan liked Lovely even though they never had any real communication.

Damn, I got to get me some smarter friends, G-Man was thinking, but smarter friends are dangerous too. He wished he had Machiavelli on his team to help him with all these out-of-towners. So that little stuck-up bitch is fucking with that nigga Big Dre. That's cool—when I get rid of him, her ass will be mine, G thought while his head bopped to some Rakeem the Dream.

Dre was starting to pressure Lovely for sex, and she knew it was just a matter of time. She enjoyed his company, being treated like a princess and feeling protected around him. But that didn't make her want to have sex with him or anybody else. It was Saturday night and they had gone to a nice dinner and movie. He was his usually sweet and generous self, but she felt expectations changing.

"Why don't you spend a night with me, we don't have to do anything, I just want you near, Dre asked.

"Dre I'm not ready for that yet."

"Lovely after all this time you mean to tell me you still don't trust me?"

"It ain't that, I'm just not ready to get serious yet."

She looked in his direction to try and get a reading on his

true feelings, but his face was unreadable. After a few long minutes he finally said, "You right, I am moving too fast, I'm sorry I pressed you." Dre was not about to drop the ball when he was so close to scoring the basket. He knew he would be the first one in that pussy and it would be more than worth the wait. He now owned the baddest young virgin in all of Georgia, and he wasn't about to scare her off by pressuring for the goodies before she was ready.

"Dre, I'll call you tomorrow," and she gave him a quick kiss and bounced for Candace's door. He was getting her nervous with the quietness and she couldn't help but think of Rick.

Candace wasn't home yet so Lovely let herself in with a key Candace had given her. She then went upstairs to lie down. She removed her leather skirt and silk shirt. She took off her bra and lay on the bed in her panties and an oversized shirt she retrieved from Candace's closet.

I know he gonna get more and more impatient Lovely thought to herself, and I don't want to lose him, but I don't know if I can have sex with him.

Maybe if..., nah that's nasty. But maybe I can get myself used to sex if I do it myself. She rummaged through Candace's closet till she found the vibrator she had first seen a few months ago.

She removed it from its sock and held it in her hand, intrigued by it's sleek and sly demeanor. Could this innocent looking piece of plastic change the way she felt about sex? She doubted it. When she flicked a switch it jumped to life, hopping around in her hand like an animal trying to be freed.

She looked around the bedroom. It seemed too big, too public for what she had in mind. She went into the bathroom, turned on the faucet, put the toilet seat down, stood again and rinsed it off, then sat on the toilet seat. With the door locked she became more adventurous, she pulled her panties down and held the vibrator to her opening. She liked the sensation and moved it around. She felt a warm, heightened pleasure that she never felt before. She tried to penetrate herself, but a nauseous feeling overcame her and she couldn't. The outside manipulations felt pleasurable, but any penetration brought feelings of violation and her body rejected it.

Candace had went to a house party with Randy, a football player from Lakeshore High. Shortly after arriving he proceeded to get drunk with his homies and act silly. After a hour of being turned off by his new characteristics Candace told him she was leaving. That's when he decided they should fuck for the fist time, in a room full of coats—of all places. After fighting him off a little, she got her coat and drove herself home. She was glad she never gave him none and glad she wasn't emotional over him.

When she entered her room she heard the sound of running water and knew Lovely was in the bathroom. Then she heard the undeniable humming of the vibrator and smiled to herself, glad Lovely was coming out of her shy and reserved ways. The humming soon stopped and the water ceased. Lovely walked out the bathroom and embarrassment registered on her face when she saw Candace.

"Hi Lovely. Did you enjoy yourself?" Candace said teasingly.

"Hi Candace," Lovely said in a low voice.

"Girl ain't no reason to feel shame, that's what it's here for. Did you *enjoy* yourself?"

"Well it felt okay when I rubbed it against myself, but I couldn't put it in me."

"Are you serious? Well did you at least have an orgasm?"

"I don't think so," Lovely replied.

"Well you must not or you would definitely know. You never had one huh?"

"I don't think so," Lovely knew she sounded dumb but couldn't help it.

"Hand it to me. Let me show you."

Lovely handed her the vibrator and remained standing near the bathroom door while Candace removed her black lace panties and lifted up her skirt. Lovely knew she shouldn't watch but couldn't force herself to look away.

Candace started off slowly, rubbing it along the opening, and around her clit and hood. Then she slid the vibrator in.

"Ah, that feels good." She leaned back on the bed and moved the object smoothly in and out of her. Lovely was wide-eyed and excited by the exhibition. And when Candace came, Lovely could feel some of it rush thru her and an excitement engulfed her like never before.

After the seconds it took Candace to get herself together she asked, "You wanna try it again?"

"No, I don't like the feel of it in me," Lovely said looking at Candace's nicely trimmed and pretty pink pussy, surprised that she found another girls privates good looking.

"There are other ways to have an orgasm. Come sit and let me show you," Candace commanded.

Lovely did as she was ordered.

"Lay back," Candace said gently and pushed her back on the mattress. She removed Lovely's silk pink panties and tucked her large shirt around her waist. With her fingers she bought Lovely pleasure that surpassed the vibrator. Lovely felt like she was on a roller coaster—The Scream Machine—going higher and higher into ecstasy. Then the sensation changed, got more intense, more intimate. Lovely felt like she was in a dream full of a million-nerve ending sent to please her. She couldn't believe Candace had her mouth on her—it felt so unbelievably good. Then she felt the roller coaster start racing down hill at 200 miles an hour towards the ultimate pleasure and she exploded and screamed. Her explosion washed through her body like a fifty-foot wave. If she had known how to count it, she would have known she had three orgasms in rapid succession. She never felt so weak and exhausted, yet so satisfied and fulfilled. She fell asleep just like that: her shirt up, a wet orgasmic puddle underneath her, and Candace looking down at her beautiful face, pleased with the job she had done.

Lovely slept off her first good—very, very good sexual experience—well into the afternoon.

9

I'm Burning Up

Candace knew she wasn't a true lesbian. What she did to Lovely wasn't about attraction or affection; it was about control. Her mother had told her, "Sex *is* a woman's most powerful weapon. If used right, it can get you anything you want and control anybody you want."

Candace needed to control Lovely. She was the key to real prosperity. Lovely's wicked body, beautiful face, and innocent ways, Candace knew she could get some major hustlers to let their guard down. Candace had no intentions of boosting the rest of her life or dancing like her mother. She knew if she could get one of those suckers with their nose wide-open for their stash, she could go back to Philly in style, pushing an exotic whip, buy her a house out Wynnfield, open a couple businesses and never have to boost again. Shit, she could get her gear custom-made if she wanted. But that scary bitch was the key to everything. Candace watched her sleep, knowing she almost had her.

Lovely felt awkward around Candace the first day after their sexual encounter but they soon settled back into their comfortable friendship. Neither one of them talked about that night, but Lovely often found herself staring at Candace, wondering how she knew so much about so many things. They grow up real fast up north, was her only conclusion.

Lovely had taken to pleasuring herself a lot more since her episode with Candace. She had even found her g-spot after three hours of searching. She wished that vaginas came with maps and instructions. No matter how she tried, her orgasms by herself didn't feel anything as good as what Candace gave her.

She knew she wasn't attracted to Candace in a romantic way, but she was attracted to what she could do to her. Even thinking of the pulsating waves of ecstasy she experienced got her panties soaked.

It had happened twice since then. With no provocation or warning. Lovely would be sleeping over and in the middle of the night Candace would go down on her. The orgasms would be so fulfilling that she would just purr like a cat while multiple orgasms swept over her. Candace never indicated she wanted anything in return. They never kissed or hugged and the next day they acted like it never happened. Lovely knew she was starting to look forward to the late night interludes, even crave them.

Lovely's physical adventures bought her more mental anguish. She was so confused; was she now gay because she let a girl go down on her? She knew she liked Dre's company, but she didn't want him putting anything inside of her. She knew she didn't want to be Candace's girlfriend or be a couple, but she didn't want her to stop giving her orgasms either. So what did this all mean? Why wasn't she normal?

"Lovely you ready to go?" Candace hollered from upstairs breaking her chain of thought.

"Yeah I'm ready." Lovely really didn't want to go boosting, but she seemed unable to tell Candace no since that first orgasm.

G-MAN AND RON was cruising Atlanta's smooth streets, sucking up the view. The streets were clean, crime stayed hidden out of sight, and the people looked relaxed. The black mothers with children in tow looked happy, more buoyant then anywhere else in the country. The black men still had those hungry eyes, but looked less oppressed, more oblivious of the low survival rate for black males. All in all, Atlanta was a great place to live; a real city of brotherly and sisterly love. Yet all Edens have their serpents and Atlanta was an oasis cascading towards calamity.

As G-Man and Ron neared the corner of Campbellton Road and Delow the smell of the greasy goodness of The Barbecue Pit invaded the car. It didn't make them hungry, it made them angry that Big Dre had a thriving legit business and they didn't. They saw Big Dre's red convertible Saab. G-Man looked at his watch and formulated a plan. Minutes later at the mini mart G-Man purchased the necessary supplies to Ron's dismay.

"G, this is the dumbest idea you ever came up with." Ron was one of the few men who wasn't afraid to speak his mind to G-Man.

"Would you stop bitching? I'm telling you this shit will work."

"If anything, why not blast his ass."

"Fuck that, I want him to suffer like my cousin in Kings Ridge suffered. I want to hear his bitch ass scream," G-Man said getting excited and spraying spittle on Ron's hand.

Ron wiped it on his pants leg and kept on talking.

"It's daytime. People are gonna see us."

"C'mon Ron, stop sounding like Stan. I'm telling you I used to stand up there when I was young and nobody could see me."

They parked in Apple Tree apartments near one of the exits and went to seek out a suitable location. They found a spot that provided good cover. The apartments closest seemed empty and they ducked out of sight.

"YO GATOR I'ma bout to go pick my young girl up from school and drive her to dance class. I'll be back in about a hour," Big Dre said as he got up to leave The Barbeque Pit.

"Damn dog, I ain't never seen'd you chase a pair of panties this strong. That baby milk on her breath must got you wide-open."

"Nigga don't be jealous 'cause I got the baddest young girl you ever saw on my hip."

"Yeah, but when you gonna get that bad ass young girl to sit on your dick?"

"It's coming my nigga, it's coming."

"It ain't coming, and that's the problem," Gator responded jovially.

"Man you silly as hell," Dre said laughing as he left The Barbecue Pit.

It was the end of September but the Atlanta weather held summer in a headlock. Big Dre climbed into his red convertible Saab feeling good. He loved Atlanta weather, always nice and not as hot as Miami. *It is about time she started sharing all that fucking body she got*, Dre was thinking. He felt confident any day now. He knew virgins were hard to crack, but once you did, you could lock 'em down for as long as you wanted. They had discussed sex a few times, and she was always uncomfortable with the subject. She told him she never had a boyfriend.

"I never gave anybody none," were her exact words. He checked around and nobody he knew of had got any or knew anybody else who had.

Dre was passing Apple Tree Apartments, looking to the right of him to see if he could see any golfers. None was this far on the course, he thought that maybe one day he would...

He heard a loud crash as something hit the side of his car. *What the fuck*!. He thought somebody was throwing rocks.

Another object crashed into the dashboard and shattered. He smelled gasoline before he felt heat surround him. Flames licked his face and engulfed his hair. Fire scorched his skin, his nerves, his muscles, and tendons. He ran his car into a stop sign, and had the sense to get out the car and run. He looked like a large human match running on fire. He ran into the first establishment he came upon, a restaurant, and collapsed in their foyer. A quick thinking waiter had the presence of mind to spray him with the fire extinguisher. That waiter may have saved his life, but his face was another matter. Big Dre would never be considered handsome again. He had suffered severe burns to his upper thighs, his groin area, his torso, and his arms and worst of all – his face, neck and head.

"Ha-ha-ha-ha-ha, did you hear that nigga scream? Great balls of fire – that nigga was running fast as shit. Ha-ha –ha-ha," G-Man could barely contain himself.

Ron laugh along with G-Man jokes but his mind was on escape and a possible war. He wished they had shot him instead of setting him on fire with Molotov cocktails. Ron looked at The Barbeque Pit as they turned down Delow Road and headed further away from Campbellton Road. He hoped G-Man hadn't just signed their death certificate.

Dre was taken to The Burn Unit at Grady Memorial Hospital in downtown Atlanta. Doctors worked arduously trying to save Dre's life. He had first, second and third degree burns on sixty-five percent of his body. Half of his face was disfigured and he would probably never grow hair on his head again.

Lovely found out what happened the next day from Gator when she called The Barbeque Pit looking for Dre. After school she caught the bus to Grady Hospital. She was told she couldn't see him because he had just come out of surgery and was still in critical condition. The next day she arrived after school and was told she couldn't see him because of weakened condition. On the third try she was informed that he had been upgraded from critical to stable condition and that she could visit for ten minutes only.

It was a good thing Dre's eyes were closed when Lovely first walked in the room. Her eyes were full of horror, then pity. He was in a plastic bubble, not only burned up, but also shriveled. He was a smaller, sadder version of his once vibrant self. By the time she whispered his name, her beautiful hazel eyes had nothing but sympathy in them.

"Dre, Dre baby it's me – Lovely," she spoke softly. He looked at her with wonderment and gratitude. She gave him a 300-watt smile, and he knew she was the best thing in his life right now. He couldn't talk because of his breathing tube, so she did all the talking.

"Baby, the doctor said you gonna be just fine and I'm gonna be here for you."

He gave her a lopsided smile that would have been comical under different circumstances.

"Baby this is my third time coming to see you, but they just let me in today. I talked to your cousin Gator. He said he'll be by tomorrow an that he got everything under control." He gave her another smile.

"Miss, it's about time to go," a nurse stuck her head in to say.

"Okay"

"Dre Baby, I'ma come see you tomorrow after school. Don't worry about nothing – just get better."

Lovely kissed the bubble wishing it was Dre and left. When she left the room a single tear fell down his cheek maybe his first in ten years.

Dre was in a bubbled world of silence, but his thoughts were loud. Wondering who did this to him was foremost on his mind. Whoever did it, they gonna die, they squad gonna die and maybe their family too. Then his thoughts switched to more pleasantries. *Damn my young girl was looking so good, and she act like she really care for a nigga. I gotta lock her down, maybe give her some babies. She too valuable to let get away*. He was nodding off, the medication made him drowsy. I hope Gator don't fuck up business was his last thought before falling into a deep sleep.

Back at the police station, Detectives Hutchins and Greenlee's frustration with the King Ridge case was reaching a boiling point.

"How the hell could there be a full fledge dope spot out there and nobody knows who owns it? Usually those dumb ass dope boys can't wait to advertise to the whole world that they are now selling drugs," Detective Hutchins exclaimed.

"Man, you know how it is," when crime is involved people inherit Stevie Wonders' eyesight," Greenlee replied.

"Ain't that the truth."

They both relaxed, sipped the nasty hot coffee, neither anxious to return to that above average temperature outside.

A freckled face rookie with a sallow complexion and a bad haircut informed them that the Captain wanted to see them in his office.

"Yeah Captain, what going on?" Detective Greenlee asked.

Neither detective took a seat. They didn't want to be there long or provoke a long drawn-out conversation.

"Have you come up with any leads on those homicides in Kings Ridge Apartments?"

"Not yet, but it's still early," Detective Hutchins replied.

"Well it looks like some more gas bombs were used yesterday, this time on a motorist in a convertible. He was driving down Campbellton Road in front of Apple Tree Apartments. Here's the police report."

"We will get right on top of this Captain," Hutchins replied and they left his office.

"It says here our victim was taken to Grady Memorial, let's

call and check on him," Detective Hutchins said.

After being told that the witness couldn't talk yet they decided to go check out the crime scene.

"We'll go talk to our witness tomorrow," Hutchins said.

"Yeah, I guess he won't be moving no time soon," Detective Greenlee replied.

They left the precinct in good spirits, happy to finally have some possible leads on their triple homicide.

10

Solitude

The girl came at Joy with a shank; her self-made knife was about six inches long with wrapped tape as a handle. Joy had done the unthinkable in her eyes: interfered in the shakedown of a weaker juvenile.

Joy snatched a wool sweater off the back of a chair and used it to shield herself. Her attacker lunged and Joy jumped left, the sweater was used to confuse. Joy was like a matador at a bullfight. The attacker lunged again and this time the knife caught in the sweater. Joy grabbed her arm and ran her into a table. They both fell over it, but Joy was on her feet first. Joy grabbed a plastic green chair and started beating the girl across her back, shoulders, and head with it. The sharp edge of the plastic ripped a four-inch gash in the girl's head that bled profusely. When the Juvenile Facility guards finally reached Joy, she was on her fourteenth hit. Joy was tackled like she was trying to score the game-winning touchdown at the Super bowl.

Joy was immediately taken to isolation. Her unfortunate attacker was taken to medical for x-rays and bandages. This was

Joy's third fighting incident in the month and a half she'd been there. In a boring juvenile detention facility, there was plenty of bullying, plundering, rumbles, and sometimes rape.

Joy's latest ruckus was caused by her willingness to help her roommate keep her new sneakers. Joy shared a room with Belinda: a shy, introverted sixteen year-old with pockmarked skin. Belinda had a juvenile life sentence. She was in the facility until she turned eighteen for stabbing a schoolmate who picked on her incessantly. Good thing the girl hadn't died or Belinda would have been heading to Atlanta's state penitentiary after juvenile.

Joy learned all about Belinda's dismal past during their nightly conversations.

"I hate my moms, all she wanna do is get high." Belinda's mom was one of Auborn Avenue's most faithful customers.

"The bitch never bought me school clothes or any food. If it wasn't for my grandmother, I mighta starved."

"So how did you catch your case?" Joy asked her.

"This girl Carla saw me and me moms together and went and told everybody my moms was a dope fiend and I was a welfare baby. Everybody would tease me and call me "Pork-and-Beans." They said we was so poor we eat pork-and-beans for breakfast, lunch and dinner, and use the bean juice to make Kool-aid with. Joy had to struggle not to laugh.

"Then one day we was on the school bus. My grandmother had bought me a nice jacket, and Carla kept trying to take it. She said I had to have stole it, because we were so broke I only get rocks for Christmas. I pushed her, then her and her girlfriends acted like they was gonna jump me so I stabbed her, but I really didn't mean to."

Joy felt sorry for Belinda even though her own life was also pretty fucked-up.

After a couple of weeks of confiding, Joy told Belinda about the death of her brother Calvin. Belinda had heard about him and by the time Joy finished detailing the tragedy they were both crying.

Belinda caught all kinds of hell from other girls in the facility. The meager possessions her grandmother brought her were stolen. She had also been sexually assaulted by some of the girls there. Belinda had been retreating more and more into herself. With no friends she barely talked or even lifted up her head. That was until Joy came along. Now that they were such good friends, she was starting to act like a normal teenager again.

One night Joy was awakened by Belinda crying in her sleep. Joy woke her up and while she sat on Belinda's bed holding her, and listening to her rehash her nightmare, old feelings started to resurface. Joy became acutely aware of Belinda's perky little breast on her arm, and her tender nipples could be felt through her cotton nightgown. Her thin, hard legs made Joy's own legs burn at the contact and her innocent aroma of budding womanhood, ivory soap, and cheap perfume filled Joy with a longing. Joy kissed her. There was much hesitation in Belinda's mouth, but when she finally gave in – it was completely. They kissed, touched, licked and sucked on each other until dawn, then retreated to their own beds feeling great. Now Belinda was all alone again and scared until Joy got out of isolation.

LOVELY TRIED TO ignore the middle-aged man in the business suit that had been staring at her for much too long. He acted like he could see through her clothes and made her feel naked and vulnerable. She hated riding MARTA'S hot-ass bus. Even though it was early December, the temperature remained a pleasant mid sixty degrees, but inside the bus felt like eighty degrees.

"Shit," she tried to move but her new Prada shoes were glued to the floor. She snatched her foot up to find a dirty wad of green gum as the culprit. X-ray eyes smiled and she gave him her most evil look, but he only smiled harder.

Good, she thought when she saw Grady Memorial looming ahead. Three seconds after getting off the bus she was approached.

"Hi sweet thing – need some help with your bag?"

"No thank you," she answered dismissively.

Another few seconds later and, "Hi sweet thing, can I walk with you?" another man asked. She just ignored him and kept walking.

"Honk, Honk, Honk."

Somebody was holding traffic at the red light staring at the bounce of Lovely's ass and the soft sway of her hips. It was a relief to finally enter Grady's lobby. Of course the attention didn't stop there: a white man who looked like he worked for the hospital asked if he could give her a physical. She glared at him in response.

When she reached Dre's room on the third floor his buddy Gator was with him. In three months time Dre had been given numerous skin grafts and was expected to remain in the hospital at least two more months. Lovely had been visiting him religiously. It wasn't that she was in love or felt anything more than they were very good friends, but she felt needed. Him needing her gave her a feeling of worthiness. Plus, it was good to talk with a man for hours without any sexual pressure.

"Hi sweetheart. Why you look so mean today?" Dre asked.

"Cause some guy just stared at me damn near the whole bus ride. And look, I got gum on my shoes."

"Poor baby," Dre said.

"Gator, don't we still have that little red Mustang we took back from Smitty?" Dre asked.

"Yeah, it's parked at the crib,"

"Yo Dawg, let Lovely get that so she don't have to keep catching the bus everywhere."

"A'ight, I can drive her to get it when we leave here," Gator responded.

"That's cool with you?" Dre asked her.

"Sure, me and walking will not miss each other."

His generosity almost made Lovely cry happy tears, because genuine kindness rarely came her way.

"Shit, anything would miss you. Don't I get a kiss or something? You don't have to be shy 'cause Gator here."

Lovely moved closer and gave him a big kiss, tasting barbeque and ice cream in his mouth. It tasted pretty good so it couldn't have come from Grady's.

"Y'all didn't save me something to eat?" she asked.

"Gator, I do have the taste for some Buffalo wings. Why don't you go get us some eats. dawg."

"Yeah a'ight I'll be right back. You want anything special Lovely?"

"Buffalo wings is cool and some curly fries."

After Gator left, Lovely sat next to Dre on his bed. The room was spacious. Dre paid extra for a private room, phone, color T.V., and special care and attention from the doctors and nurses. Gator had also bought him a mini stereo system and a video game system with tons of cartridges. Dre also had orderlies he paid to buy him meals from the various restaurants and fast food places in the vicinity.

In his three hundred dollar slippers, silk pajamas, and robes, Dre was the king of the third floor.

"So how do my face look?

"A whole lot better," she replied.

"You sure?"

"Yeah, they doing a real good job."

"So I still got a shot at being your boyfriend?"

Dre faced was heavily scarred but much improved from a month ago.

"Of course," she smiled, "when I'm ready to have a real boyfriend."

"If I'm not your boyfriend, how come you still come see me everyday?"

"Cause you are my really good friend and friends are supposed to stand by each other, right?"

"Right. Come here," he said as he moved in for a kiss.

He could feel himself stiffening and longed to be inside her like a convict longed for freedom. Most of the time he had been in the hospital he was filled with so much pain that sex had been the farthest thing from his mind. Now that his body was healing his sexual appetite was returning. He was appeasing his carnal desires in the afternoons with other lady visitors while Lovely was in school. Even though his body wasn't as picky, his mind wanted Lovely for sex, for companionship, maybe even for love.

"I'ma have Gator put the car in your name. You do know how to drive don't you?"

"Real good. Candace taught me," she replied.

"Why don't you go get your learner's permit? This way if you get pulled over you'll only get a ticket."

"I'ma do that, but first I got to get the book and study."

After Gator returned with the food they ate, laughed and played video games until around seven o'clock. Lovely kissed Dre goodbye as she and Gator left to pick up her Mustang.

Lovely felt relaxed, maybe more relaxed then she ever felt before. As she accelerated and felt the power of the engine, she felt powerful and sophisticated. She felt she could go anywhere at anytime. This was her first time driving by herself, and her newfound independence was like a stimulant.

Gator had washed the car and Armor All-ed it down; the seats, the dashboard and the tires that were already on black five stars rims. The Armor All and green tree fresheners mixed well together and the bucket seats felt good underneath her. She searched through a large variety of tapes; from old to new, from hip-hop to pop to rock to R&B and Jazz. Someone had been very eclectic, Lovely selected her favorite rapper and cruised the Ben Hill Section, then East Point, then College Park. She was determined to take the longest, most scenic route, ignoring any possible highway entries.

"Ah look at me, look at me," Lovely said aloud as she looked at herself in the rearview mirror and for one of the few times saw what everyone else did. She was beautiful when she was happy and soon she started nodding her head to "all the way to heaven, heaven, heaven," with Dougie Fresh.

Before heading home, Lovely stopped by The International House Of Pancakes for some chocolate chip pancakes. When she got to Candace's house it was 1:34 A.M., and the house was quiet. When she got upstairs Candace was asleep with a very serene look on her face. Lovely showered and put on an over-sized shirt to sleep in. Candace was still sleep and Lovely climbed in bed with her. Her new car still had her feeling amped up and she wanted to share some of her energy. That night Lovely initiated sex for the first time in her life. She went to sleep feeling good about herself, thinking I ain't no scaredy cat. I'ma take charge woman with her own ride. She fell asleep with a lovely smile on her face.

11

Younger and Younger

Delores looked into Lovely's empty bedroom on her way to the kitchen. A wave of loneliness and emptiness engulfed her. She was hurt that her daughter no longer wanted to sleep under the same roof as her. She hardly saw Lovely, now that she spent most nights at Candace's house. Her maternal instincts told her to refuse to let Lovely stay over at Candace's especially on school nights, but her love-starved, selfish feminine instincts told her that her daughter's absence would improve relations with Rick. Plus, Lovely told her that she had a good job in College Park and didn't want to drive all the way back to Stanton Road every night. She even had a nice looking red car to prove it. Although Delores suspected this wasn't quite the truth. But Lovely had never lied to her before, so she accepted her story.

Unfortunately, her and Rick's relationship hadn't improved and Rick's treatment of her was even worse. Rick was even more sullen and ill-tempered. Delores walked around on egg-shells, always fearful of verbal assault or worse yet—a physical attack.

Her most recent beating occurred for running out of coffee.

She had meant to go to the store that day, but her new job at a car dealership had kept her busy. Even Rick's sexual appetite had become more perverse and abusive. He only wanted either oral sex or rough and painful anal sex. He no longer kissed, caressed, held or complimented her about anything. He also stayed out late at night and once she even detected scratches on his back that she hadn't made.

Delores went to the kitchen to make Rick's breakfast, even though he probably wouldn't wake up for another hour or two. It was Saturday and she had to go to work; today was a car dealer's busiest day. She loved her new job even though her boss had twelve strands of hair laid sideways across his sunburned scalp, a beer belly that strained his tight polyester pants and breath that smelled like an assortment of snack foods and gingivitis.

He was super nice to her though, something she craved. He even told her, "Darling any car you want just let me know and I'll let you have it half price with no money down." She hadn't taken him up on his offer, but a used yellow Corvette was calling her. It was like the car was saying "Come on Delores, buy me, drive me, I'll make you happy. I'll never hurt you the way men do." She laughed, thinking of having a car that was possessed like Christine in the movie, but instead of killing people, it only flirted with her all day.

Maybe she would call Lovely and see if they could hang out together on Sunday. A movie, lunch, and some shopping with her daughter would be nice. The distance between them was getting wider and wider, and she feared a relationship like the one she had with her own evil mother.

Just then the doorbell rang and she hurried to answer it, fearful Rick would wake up in a foul mood and take it out on her. At first glance the disheveled woman on her welcome mat was unrecognizable.

"HI DELORES, um, I need to ask for a favor." The woman's voice was familiar and then Delores realized who it was. Oh my God, I can't believe how bad Joy's mom is looking, Delores thought but she said, "Sure Brenda come in."

It was easy to tell from her bloodshot eyes, tattered clothes, and yellow teeth that Brenda had been trying to drink herself into oblivion. Delores knew the woman had taken her son's murder hard, but didn't know Brenda had damn near given up on life.

"So how you been Brenda? Lovely told me about Joy."

"Well that's what I came over here for. I wanted to go visit her today, but I'm broke. Um-um, could you lend me a few dollars for a little while?"

If Delores had thought that this broken mother was really interested in visiting her daughter she would have offered her a ride to the Juvenile Facility and wouldn't have minded being late for work in the process. Delores could tell Brenda was in no shape to visit Joy or had no inclination. So she handed her a twenty-dollar bill from her purse, knowing it would purchase the strongest cheap liquor. She wasn't angered, just saddened by the predicament of this tormented woman. She wished she could help her more, not financially but emotionally. Then she taught, shit I'm an emotional wreck with a crazy husband and daughter that hates it here for some reason, so who am I to help someone.

"Thank you Delores. Thanks, I'll tell Joy you said hi and I'll give this back soon."

"Don't worry about it" Delores said to Brenda's rapidly fleeing back.

Brenda was in a hurry to get to her destination, like the ghetto would ever run out of liquor.

Delores hurried off to her job, her only solace of late. In her eight-year-old car that was nearing a 100,000 miles, she thought about the yellow corvette. Maybe I will get it, I bet I will get a lot of attention in that.

When Rick finally got out of bed the house was empty. In his boxers and feeling frisky he went and checked Lovely's room.

Little bitch been avoiding me. That wore-out whore of a mother just let her do what she wants. When I catch that little bitch I'm going to fuck the shit out of her. I'm gonna make her asshole bleed," he laughed at that. Most of Lovely 's clothes were still there. He ran his hands through her underwear drawer. His sick mind thought about how good she must of felt when she was younger and un-tampered. Now he wished Delores was around to sexually abuse.

Maybe tonight I'll find someone new, he thought. He had taken to cruising the streets trying to pick up young girls. He paid them for sex, the younger the better.

A big smile crossed his face when he thought of the fifteen-year-old he picked up near The Martin Luther King Youth Center. He took her to a seedy motel and tried to brutalize her. After he had went limp, he punished her with an oversized dildo he took with him on these misadventures. He had left her crying and hurt, but he left her $20, so he figured they were even.

Delores called from her job.

"Hi Lovely, how you been baby?"

"I've been okay How you doing mom? Is everything alright?" Lovely said, a trace of panic was in her voice.

Lovely worried about her mom in the house all alone with her sick bastard of a husband.

"Baby, I called to see if you wanted to hang out with your mom. I was thinking we could go out to eat, see a movie together, and do some shopping tomorrow."

"Ma I would really like to, but I promised one of Candace's friends we would both come to her baby shower. We can do it next weekend if you want."

"Okay baby, next Sunday. I got to go now, I see a new customer."

"Okay bye ma."

"Bye baby, call me," and Delores hung-up.

Lovely could not understand how a seventeen-year-old girl could want a baby. Candace's friend Tangie acted like she was happy to be eight months and looking like a pregnant porpoise. Worst of all, her baby's father was a thuggish knucklehead named Darryl who had no job, sold garbage weed that he smoked half of, and cheated on her blatantly. Oh well, it was Candace's friend and she had promised. Of course, Candace took it as an excuse to do some major boosting. Maternity clothes, baby clothes, accessories, and new outfits for them were flying out of department stores. With Dre's help, Lovely could afford nice things for her and Candace, but the girl didn't believe in paying for anything. So Lovely went along when she couldn't avoid it and started saving her money.

They arrived at the baby shower around four p.m. it was in Tangie's mother's cramped two-bedroom apartment out in the Red Oak projects. The apartment was filled with cackling, physically grown girls with too much energy and not enough options. Most would be contemplating a situation similar to Tangie's very soon.

They arrived just in time to enjoy a humorous man bashing conversation. It would have been more appropriately thought of as a boy bashing conversation, but in the ghetto the distinguishing lines between man and boy were very blurred.

"Girls, I don't even be wanting to give Randy none this good pussy until he takes me out or buy me stuff," some girl in a tight yellow pantsuit said.

"Shu – I have to keep Warren on a diet. He always wants to put his face down there. It wouldn't be so bad if he knew what he was doing: instead of feeling good – the shit tickles," another girl in a tight outfit said.

"Now that I'm fucking Steve and Keith ain't hardly getting none, he always asking me why I got to twist your arm just for some pussy," a pretty light-skinned girl with bumps on her neck from cheap jewelry said.

"Shit, I wish Rodney would twist my arm, pull my hair, fuck it – the nigga could whistle all I care. Anything so the shit wouldn't be so boring. That shit's worse than watching paint dry, even worse than listening to my history teacher explain the French Revolution."

The other girls including Lovely and Candace laughed at the pretty, articulate girl with skin the color of dark, rich soil.

Soon the bashing died down, nobody really wanted to inadvertently remind Tangie of the trifling boy she was pregnant by. When gift opening time came around, Lovely and Candace had to take two trips to the car to retrieve all the gifts they had stole for Tangie and the baby. The other girls looked jealous and impressed all at the same time. They all ate and bull-shitted for a couple of hours, then the shower broke–up. Nobody that didn't live there really wanted to be in Red Oak when it got dark.

Lovely and Candace had become more sexually active with each other since Lovely started staying over on a more permanent basis. As Lovely drove them home, Candace fingered her on the deserted street leading from Red Oak. Lovely swerved a little, but not too bad. That's the way it was: Candace never asked, she just initiated a sensation and Lovely's body responded. It was just a short tease to get Lovely's undivided attention.

"Did you have fun?" Candace asked.

"Yeah I had fun, but I still don't see how she could want a baby."

"Stupid and in love, that's how," Candace responded.

"Better her than me."

"Yeah, so what's up with you and Big Dre?"

"Why you ask that?"

"I was wondering if you found out if he was really 'Big' or not," Candace said in a distasteful way.

"No, we ain't never had sex," Lovely responded defensively.

"I was just teasing you," she slapped Lovely's thigh playfully. "You have been spending a lot of time with him," Candace continued.

"Cause he in the hospital and I feel sorry for him and he's a nice guy."

"Girl you suppose to spend time with him if he's giving you cars and giving you money. But we could probably get him for a whole lot more," Candace's voice took on a serious quality.

"What you mean?"

"You don't know where he keep his dough?"

"No," Lovely answered quickly.

"You need to find out. We could be rich."

"You bugging. He would kill us if we stole his money," Lovely answered.

"He didn't kill those niggas that burned him up, plus he wouldn't know we did it."

Candace could tell by how tight Lovely's mouth was that she was upset and didn't want to discuss Dre any more. Candace would drop the subject for now, but not forever. Lovely just didn't see opportunities before them. She didn't understand no man could be trusted or counted on. A bitch had to get her own dough to live good in this world. Lovely was upset now, but Candace knew after she bought her to multiple orgasms tonight she would be all right.

12

Change is Coming

When Lovely got to the hospital, Dre was in his room looking cheerful and anxious. He looked like an average B-boy in his new Nike sneakers, black jeans, red Hugo Boss sweatshirt and red baseball cap. Lovely had left school early for this special occasion: after five months Dre was finally leaving the hospital for good.

He had endured numerous skin grafts and reconstructive surgeries. Over sixty percent of his body had been severely burned, and his hospitalization had cost more than 200,000 dollars. He had the best doctors and the newest developments in burn treatment and rehabilitation. He no longer had his youthful good looks, thick braids and muscular body. The right side of his face was extremely dry and darker than his left. His hair wouldn't grow so he wore a baldy and his chest and abdomen bore the heavy scar tissue from his heated hell. Now he was a slightly below average-looking guy with an interesting history and a large amount of cash stashed away.

He had asked Lovely to come pick him up today from the

hospital. She was glad to, besides – it was the car that he had given her that made her transportation possible.

Lovely drove Dre to The Towers—a luxury high-rise apartment building on the outskirts of downtown Atlanta. Before going upstairs they toured the downstairs amenities. The building's first two floors contained a grocery store, a laundry room, and dry cleaners, a fully equipped gym with racket ball and basketball courses, swimming pool, sauna, and a masseuse for hire. There was a doorman and a security guard in the foyer.

"Wow, this is a nice apartment building. It must cost a whole lot to live up in here," Lovely said wide-eyed.

"It does, I'm paying $1,200 a month for my two bedroom. Come on let's go upstairs so I can show it to you." Dre led her towards the elevator. They got off on the twenty-eight floor onto deep burgundy carpeting that led to six different apartments. Dre opened the door to 28-D and the sight was breathtaking.

"Let's take our shoes off," Dre told Lovely.

There was a small mat along the wall to place their shoes. The carpet was a three-inch deep, cream-colored foot pamperer. The living room was expensively furnished with Italian-styled blood red octagon shaped leather sofa and a wall-sized window with a panoramic view of downtown Atlanta. The dining room was also elegantly furnished, and the kitchen was fully stocked. The bathroom contained a double shower and large sunken Jacuzzi tub.

"Let me show you the bedroom," Dre said, leading Lovely down spiral stairs to the bottom level of the apartment. There were two large bedrooms. One was furnished with a large bed encased in a black lacquer frame that was mirrored on the back and right side. The only other items in the room were a large floor model T.V. and a top-of-the-line music system. This room was obviously for fucking. The other room was empty but spacious and with a great view.

"I left this one empty because I didn't know what you wanted in it," Dre told Lovely.

"What you mean, what I want in it?"

"I want you to move in here with me. We don't have to be on some Romeo, Juliet type shit. We can still remain just friends, but I don't want to live here by myself and you're the only person I trust."

"I don't know if it will work, what if you get tired of having me around? Plus any other lady friends ain't gonna like it," Lovely said. His offer had caught her by surprise.

"I haven't brought anybody up here. You are the first visitor. And you took such good care of me in the hospital that I have become spoiled. I need you to continue to take care of me. Plus, it will be strictly friends – no sexual obligations at all."

"Are you sure?" she asked.

"Sure about the sexual obligations?" he kidded.

"About everything."

"Yeah I'm sure. Didn't I have a long time to think about it?"

"Yeah, I guess you did," the offer was looking more and more attractive.

"Oh yeah, there is one rule: No visitors and don't give out the number, let people beep you."

Lovely thought moving in with Dre would free her from rape by Rick and her sex acts with Candace.

"Okay I'll move in. This is way better than anywhere else I lived."

"Good, let's go shopping for your bedroom furniture and get you a key and parking space in the garage."

Lovely had just taken a very big step in her life. Her and Big Dre would be living together, and for better or worse things were about to change.

Damn I'm moving up in the world, Lovely thought to herself after spending almost $6,000 dollars of Dre's money on a bedroom set, T.V., and sound system. How Candace would take this was nagging at her all that day, but she was having too much fun to let it get in the way.

"Hello, can I speak to Lovely?"

"Do you know when she might be back?" Joy asked Rick.

"Lovely don't stay here no more," Rick said, slamming down the phone.

"Fucking evil bastard," Joy said.

She called Candace, "Hello?"

"Hi Candy, it's me. What's up with you?"

"Hey girl what's going on? Why you haven't called in a while?"

"I was in the hole again for fighting."

"Damn Mike Tyson, what you trying to do, stay there?" Candace asked

"No, but they gave me six more months to do."

"Girl that's fucked-up, I miss you out here," Candace said sincerely.

"I miss you too Candy. Where's Lovely?"

"Oh girl done blown up. She has a new red Mustang and living in some expensive shit with Big Dre."

"Get the fuck outta here! They on some serious shit like that?" Joy asked.

"Lovely only been staying with him for two weeks, and she said they haven't had sex yet, but that nigga already got her on some prisoner bullshit."

"What you mean?"

"I hardly seen her in the last two weeks, even though she did give me a couple of hundred dollars. And she can't have no visitors or phone calls, you can only beep her."

"You know how niggas is, always trying to lock a woman down soon as they get her. She came by this weekend but I was still in the hole and couldn't have visitors. She left three hundred on my books though. So have you been going out doing your thing at the stores?" Joy asked.

"Not with Love. I got a girlfriend I met at Fulton County that just came home, me and her go on runs together now."

"Yeah, well, bring me some gear."

"Okay I will. Size five-to-six right?"

"Girl I'm getting big in here, I now wear seven-to-eight. I even got titties now."

"Go ahead girl, with your big titty self."

"Candy, I got to go. My fifteen minutes are up."

"Okay I'll tell Lovely you called looking for her and to come see you. Bye."

"Bye girl I love you," and they both hung up.

Candace liked the fact Lovely would be living with Dre, it would make robbing him easier when the time came.

WITH BIG DRE incapacitated, G-Man business expanded. Big Dre's replacement, Gator, wasn't as good a businessman or intimidating on the streets. G-Man's name, influence, and drugs had spread thru Ben Hill, Southwest Atlanta, East Point, and College Park like an out of control wildfire.

G-Man and Stan were now cruising in G-Man's new 735 BMW.

"G, I think that nigga Big Dre getting ready to make a move. He's been hiring a lot of workers and bringing more people up from Miami."

"Stan don't you ever get tired of worrying about everything like a little bitch? That burned-up nigga don't want no more problems, and so many niggas hate him, he don't know who set his dumb ass on fire."

"Now he don't even be at the restaurant on Cambellton that much and I heard the new Benz he be driving is supposed to be bulletproof," Stan said as he continued to try and get G-Man to take the situation seriously.

"I don't give a fuck about no armor car rumors started by a bunch of bitch-ass niggas. I got more guns, more soldiers, and more heart than him. This is my city. If Dre make any kinda move I'll bury his ass for good this time."

Stan said fuck it to himself, when the shit hit the fan he would be smart enough to stay out the way.

"G, did you her about The Miami Boys out in Techwood and Pistol and Jay?"

"Yeah, I heard The Miami Boys shots some of Pistol and Jay's workers and closed down their spot in Edgewood Apartments."

"So do you think Pistol and Jay gonna go at 'em?"

"You fucking right. Everybody ain't scared of Miami like you, " G-Man said.

Stan was tired of G-Man saying he didn't have heart; he was just careful. He decided to change subjects and fuck with G-Man a little.

"Yo! G, I heard that girl Lovely lives with Big Dre now. He suppose to have her on lock."

"Fuck that gold-digging bitch; she just like all the rest of these hoes out here."

Stan disagreed, but remained quiet knowing G-Man wished he could have her, anyway he could get her, even if it meant spending large sums of money on her.

"I'm dropping you off, I got some things to do. Where you going?" G-Man asked angrily.

"Drop me off in Sand Piper, my car is out there," Stan answered pleased to have gotten G-Man upset.

IT WAS LATE AFTERNOON and Sonya's mind was on what she would wear that night to The Phoenix nightclub. She worked at the Ramada Inn near the airport, and this Friday was particularly hectic. She had been checking people in since 10 A.M. and had forty-five minutes to go 'till six o'clock quitting time, when the Miami Boys walked in. Sonja hung with a bunch of girls that prided themselves on knowing who was who in Atlanta, especially the serious money getters, and Sonya was no different.

The short, stocky one was the boss of the large crew that dominated the Techwood area. The tall, slim one was his right-hand man and they always traveled together. Sonya's girlfriends had pointed them out at a Hawk's basketball game. The girls were about twelve rows up and these Miami bosses were floor side and hadn't seen them.

"How are you gentlemen doing today? Can I help you?" she said in her most professional tone.

"Yes, we would like two rooms until Monday. Are there any suites available," the short, stocky one replied.

"Yes, we have two business suites available on the fifteenth and sixteenth floors. They both have a large bedroom with a large living room area with a desk."

"Thanks. We will take both of those."

"Here you go, fill out these forms. Will that be cash or credit card?"

"Cash," the tall one said pulling a knot form his pocket.

The short one finished filling out the form and she handed them keys. They both had large black leather carry-on bags, and she wondered if they had drugs or money in them. Probably neither, she thought. The bosses usually tried not to be the one carrying the evidence.

Sonja kept abreast of the street news and was familiar with the escalating beef between The Miami Boys and Pistol and Jay. She and her girlfriend had spent a night with Pistol and Jay about two months ago. They had met at The Phoenix one Saturday night and had spent the night together at the Hyatt Regency.

The sex was good but their status was better. Sonya and her girl had wished for a relationship, but only got beeper numbers, wet asses, and a few hours of those high-powered hustlers' time.

Sonya beeped Jay and hoped her information would get her some of his time. After five minutes her beep was returned and she provided him information. He promised the four of them would get together soon and thanked her for looking out.

Friday night in the hood was payday for drug dealers all across America and Atlanta was no different. If anything, it was an even bigger payoff in Atlanta: with unemployment consistently down, and it's high concentration of people wanting to feel good and have fun from Friday to Monday. There was plenty of money to be spent, and Pistol and Jay were in a position to make a lot of it.

The recent shootings by The Miami Boys had caused a lot of anxiety amongst their workers. That was soon rectified with another trip to the gun stores. Now all six of their locations kept at least two men armed with bulletproof vests and Mac-11's on post during operational hours. The $250 vests and $229 Mac-11's went a long way towards making the workers feel safe. The armed men now had a swagger like: can't nobody fuck with us—we gangsters. Especially Rock and Bud, who were stationed near Techwood because they expressed the most animosity towards The Miami Boys and least amount of fear.

They had just left Rock and Bud when Jay got the beep. The number was unfamiliar and him and Pistol was in conversation, so he called the number. He listened to Sonya, who he only vaguely remembered, attentively. After she surrendered her information, he told her what she wanted to hear: that she and her girlfriend would be hooking up with him and Pistol soon and hung up.

"That right there was that chick Sonya, who we took with her girlfriend to the Hyatt Regency," Jay told Pistol.

"The one we met at the Phoenix?"

"Yeah that's her. She works at the Ramada Inn near the Airport and guess who checked in there a little while ago?" Pistol remained silent—he wasn't into guessing games.

"Them bitch-ass Miami Boys and they boss is there. The short dark skin dude with the process and the tall dude he always be with." He said excitement in his voice.

"Is she sure?"

"She said she was positive."

"Stupid motherfuckers. They must think it's a joke. They must think they skin made out of Teflon. That's good. I love stupid, brave motherfuckers, 'cause they easily become sleep-in-grave motherfuckers." Pistol said with a sinister smile.

Jay gave him a few minutes to gather his thoughts then asked, "So how we gonna do them niggas?"

"I was thinking that this would be a good opportunity for Rock and Bud to prove themselves."

"You want me to turn around?" Jay asked.

"Yeah, lets go talk to them," Pistol was already planning his and Jay's alibi.

ROCK AND BUD waited in the Ramada's parking lot for their intended victims to show. Nervous tension weighed heavy in the car like fog. They were unsure which of the three remaining cars were Miami's or if they were using cab service, so they waited, watching the exit.

"There they go! There they go!" Bud nervousness raised his voice an octave.

"Calm down, I see them. We gonna follow them 'till we get a good spot," Rock said in a soothing voice that was meant to relax Bud.

The grey Mazda was a rent-a-car. It was after 9:30 P.M. and dark outside, but Old National Highway was well lit so they followed a discrete distance behind.

"I'm telling you these Georgia niggas are starting to get more heart. We can't take them too lightly." The conversation inside the Mazda was lively.

"For sure. We gonna have to hire some more guns and set a few examples," his right-hand man replied.

"And we need to deal with that buster from New York, Pistol, or before you know it there will be a thousand of 'em getting in our way."

Yeah we have to find a good place where him and his man Jay be and ice 'em. I wished we could carry they ass to the Florida swamps and feed 'em to a gator alive.

"That would be cool as hell. One time I seen a gator in Key West eat a wild pig—that shit was ill."

They turned off Old National onto a back street that led to Washington Road. They were so busy talking that they didn't see that they weren't alone.

Rock and Bud were in an old Caddy they had rented from a neighborhood friend for the weekend. The rental had to stop at the railroad crossing for an old cargo train. The gate was down and the Miami Boys waited and talked.

"We got 'em. You take the passenger side and I'll get the driver side. Come on," Rock ordered Bud. The Caddy closed the rental in with nowhere to go. The Miami Boys tried to flee the car, but was too late. They were met with semi-automatic gunfire. They tried to take cover, but there was nowhere to hide. The Mac-11's were hollering loudly and so were those boys. Bullets hit everywhere: severing fingers, rupturing eyeballs, nuts got bust, lungs were filled, and stomachs were intruded. How unfortunate that they protected their heads so well, because their brains were able to register sixteen, hot, torturing bullet entries for one and twenty-one entries for the other.

The train was no longer an obstacle, but it didn't matter—

only one car would be leaving that scene.

Lovely and Dre lay in bed together, something they had been doing since her third week there. When, after arriving home late from a movie and dinner and lighting up some killer weed, Dre finally tasted and sampled some of lovely's sacred stuff.

Wow, I'm finally in this, he thought as he ate her pussy like it was the last meal. Then when he was inside her it was better than Christmas for his dick. The wait made the pussy feel unbelievably good and he was on cloud nine, but something was nagging at his subconscious. It wasn't until later while she slept beautifully in the nude that he figured it out. He checked the sheet for blood to make sure. "Damn sneaky bitch wasn't a virgin." He had no intentions of letting her go nowhere, but he thought about her differently after that. Rape wasn't having sex to Lovely, but Dre knew nothing of her history of sexual abuse.

Now they were in bed watching the late news when the beautiful mocha-colored news lady announced that two men had been found murdered. She went on to announce it was a grisly scene with both victims shot multiple times. She said the victims were in a rental car and both were identified as Miami natives.

Lovely could see that Dre's interest intensified as soon as he heard, "Miami." He got up and started reaching for his clothes. "I gotta go check some things out. I'll be back later." He said as he hurried off.

She was glad he was going out, now she could pretend to be sleeping when he got back and not have to give him none. She regretted giving him some three weeks ago. Now he wanted it all the time. He was rough and even ate her rough. He felt nowhere as fantastic as Candace. Whenever she knew it was coming, she would try to drink a little first, she still crave Candace's mouth and hands, but with him starting to become more and more possessive it was harder to spend time with her. She had heard that men started acting like they own you eventually, but she didn't expect that from Dre, especially after only three weeks of sleeping together. She swore to herself that she would not allow herself to be in a relationship like her Mom's. Her attitude towards Big Dre was starting to change. At the same time Atlanta hustlers attitudes towards The Miami Boys was also changing.

Part Two

And underneath it all,
No one had seen her claws…

13

Things Done Changed

Even something as sweet as a peach can become sour, and the Peach State had become just that for Pistol and Jay. They had been on the run for sixteen months, just ever since Rock and Bud spilled their guts. The careless motherfuckers had been pulled over for speeding by the College Park police miles away from the carnage. Even though they only received a ticket and were allowed to leave, that incident would eventually lead them to their downfall. Their Caddy had been spotted leaving the scene of the crime by a half sleep, old geezer with glaucoma in one eye who told the police he saw a white late model Cadillac leaving the scene. A high-strung rookie officer then remembered pulling over two overly anxious young men for speeding. The car was traced back to a spineless friend who took less than thirty minutes to remember he had rented his Caddy to Rock and Bud on the day in question.

Rock and Bud had lasted all of three months before copping out to double homicide, which led to double life sentences for both of them, which made them eligible for parole in ten years.

Now their mouths had chased Pistol and Jay out of Georgia and into Brooklyn's seedy underground. Pistol had figured where better to hide than among New York's millions of residents.

With Pistol and Jay's absence, and the Miami Boys' veil of invulnerability pierced, Georgia's own hustlers emerged as the kings of their dominion. G-Man and his team were at the forefront of a drug renaissance, but Lovely, Joy, and Candace weren't far behind. No game is played or gains parlayed without women involved, and Lovely, Joy, and Candace were more than your average women.

"Girl, I can't stand that nigga Dre; I hate when he touches me and everything. I'm glad he bought himself a house outside Atlanta, and I don't have to see him but a few times a week," Lovely vented to Candace.

"Why don't you leave him then? You know you can move in here. There's plenty of room since my mom moved out, Candace said.

"Are you serious? You think I should just up and leave?"

"Fuck no!" Candace replied. "I was just teasing you. You need to fuck him till we get our hands on his stash. Plus he owe you for a year and a half of pussy—some brand new, nobody had any before pussy."

Even Candace didn't know about all the sexual abuse Lovely had suffered.

"I definitely ain't ready to give up my apartment and new car." Lovely said. She still stayed at The Towers, mostly alone, when Dre wasn't there which she preferred and now drove a raspberry-colored new BMW compliments of Dre.

"If I can come up with a way for us to rob him of his dough, are you with it?"

"I don't know. I gotta hear the plan first."

"You *still* a scaredy cat?"

"Whatever," Lovely said dismissively.

Candace got up nude from her bed and walked into the bathroom. They hadn't had sex in a while, and Lovely felt a gush of wetness thinking about it. She was uncertain about why Candace stopped being sexually interested in her, all Lovely knew was that she missed Candace's mouth. Her own fingers were a weak substitute, and only Candace's mouth would bring that sweet satisfaction she craved at that moment.

Candace knew how bad Lovely wanted her. That morning Lovely had tried to put her hands between her legs, and Candace had to stop her. Now Lovely was in there probably horny as hell. Candace hoped that Lovely's lust would make her more controllable. Candace was coming up with a plan for taking Dre's money, but she wanted to wait until Joy came home.

Candace showered her body, fully aware of it's beauty. She was now fucking with the big dogs. One of her men recently had inherited a chain of restaurants from his father, and Candace was helping him spend all his cream. Another was an older guy who had an office cleaning company. Candace was taking his ass to the cleaners. Candace had been a good student of her mother's and she now used what she had to get what she wanted.

Her mother had moved on to bigger things, she still worked at Dante's Inferno, but she was also trying to start an escort service. She brought a new house out Marietta, and had a new Benz in the driveway. Candace was happy for her, plus it left her the Candlewood apartment and even more freedom.

She heard Lovely try the door and smiled to herself. Candace knew exactly what Lovely wanted but she couldn't allow that. Candace needed to control everybody around her.

Candace stepped out the bathroom still nude, her thick body wet from the shower.

"Lovely, dry my back for me."

"Sure."

"Lovely dried her off with soft tender strokes, then tried

kissing the back of her neck.

"Stop Love, I got to get dressed and go somewhere."

Lovely sucked her teeth, stopped drying Candace off and sat back down on the bed. Candace smiled to herself.

"Candy, what we gonna do for Joy's coming home? She gets out in three weeks."

"Yeah I know. How about a party here?"

"Yeah that would be hot."

"Okay, we'll have a party here, but we have to plan it right—you know how Joy is," Candace said.

"Yeah we'll hook it up. She'll like it." Just the thought of Joy finally coming home lifted Lovely's spirit.

"We have to get her some nice things for her birthday and homecoming gift." Candace said as she finished getting dressed, ready to leave the house.

"Yeah I got something in mind," Lovely replied, picking up the keys to her new ride.

They left driving in opposite directions.

Lovely sat at the red light, lost in thought, wondering why Candace was acting funny towards her. Maybe it was because they hadn't spent much time together. Lovely had been busy finishing up school, going to acting classes, dancing classes, and being a prisoner to Dre's jealous and controlling ways. She was late for acting class, which was starting to pay off. She had appeared in a commercial recently for a tampon company. She had been approached to model, but had declined because she wanted to prove she had value beyond her looks, so concentrated on acting and dance.

She didn't want to see Dre, but she needed him for Joy's gift so she beeped him.

"Yeah what's up?"

"I was wondering if you were coming home tonight?"

"Why, was you trying to sneak off with one of your

boyfriends or something?"

"No! Dre you know I don't mess with nobody else. I just wanted to know if you was coming over so I can make you dinner."

"Where you at?"

"On my way to acting class, damn," Lovely answered.

"Why you late?"

"I was hanging with my friend Candace."

"I thought I told you I don't want you out College Park."

"Dre you is not my father. I can go hang out with my friends if I want."

"Lovely I will talk to your smart-mouth ass tonight, and I bet not catch you talking to that faggot Al B. Sure-looking nigga in your acting class again."

"Whatever."

"Whatever, bitch!" Dre cursed out while slamming the phone down.

I'ma have to teach that ungrateful bitch some manners soon, Dre thought to himself.

Lovely laughed. That jealous ass-hole stay tripping. If I was fucking somebody it wouldn't be some pretty motherfucker looking for more dick than me, Lovely said to herself, thinking about the absurdity of Dre's misplaced jealousy of her fucking with gay Jermaine. She sped up not wanting to be too late for today's rehearsals. They were rehearsing for a play, *A Streetcar Called Desire*, and she and Jermaine were in the leading roles.

14

He Hit Me

Big Dre was late for his so-called meeting with Stan, but so what, Stan wasn't nobody but a small time punk that worked for G-Man. Stan had been sending word for about a week that he wanted to talk to Big Dre, and finally Dre's curiosity won out. Dre knew G-Man's organization was on the rise; they had just taken over the old Mr. V's nightclub and renamed it G-spot, and it was doing good. Dre had also heard that a couple of their spots were making good money. Maybe, they wanted to get their weight from him. He could definitely use the business. Lately a lot of his customers had found other sources or traveled to Florida for themselves.

Dre spent a lot of time at his furniture store near Five Points station in Down-town Atlanta. He hated to admit to himself that he felt safer amongst the crowds of people and heavy police presence downtown. The fire had taken a lot out of him, even some of his heart, although he'd never admit that.

When Dre walked in he spotted Stan in the back of the showroom sitting on an ugly green crushed-velvet sofa they had been trying to get rid of all month. To Stan, Dre looked diminished in size and spirit. *Damn, that fire really done him in* Stan thought to himself.

"So what's up? I hope you came to buy something, like that nice sofa you sitting on," Dre stood over him without offering a handshake.

"Nah player, not today. I came to give you some important info. If we can work out a deal first," Stan remained seated like the weak underling he was.

Three of Dre's flunkies from Miami were in the store so he felt secure. Plus, he had never heard anything even remotely threatening about Stan.

"Follow me. Let's go talk in the office," Dre said leading the way further back into the store.

So far, so good, Stan was thinking. Soon I should have my own coke and my own connection without that fucking G-Man.

Dre reached into the refrigerator and pulled out flavored ice tea for himself and Stan.

"So what kind of info do you think I might be interested in?" Dre said taking a seat behind his desk. Stan looked uncomfortable seated in front of the desk.

"First player, I want to know if I help you, you can help me. I'm trying to get fronted something nice so I can do my own thing."

"That ain't a problem. Let me hear what you got to say," Dre was becoming impatient.

"Okay, you know the nigga G-Man I be working for?"

"Yeah, I heard about him. Go ahead," Dre demanded.

"Well, it was that nigga G-Man that had the spot out at King Ridge apartments and when it got burned down he got mad. It was him and his partner Ron that set you on fire in front of Apple Tree apartments."

"You sure it was them?" Dre said as he struggled to contain

his anger. He removed his baseball cap and started scratching his bald scarred scalp.

"Yeah I'm positive, G-Man told me about it himself. Plus, he wants to run you the fuck out of Atlanta."

"Yeah, then what is he waiting for?"

"He told me he was building his arsenal, his soldiers, and his money up to run all you Miami niggas out of Atlanta."

"Ha, ha, ha," Dre gave a half-hearted laugh. "He ain't built like that."

"Listen Player, he might not seem like much, but he puts in his work. You remember those two basketball stars from Therell—Quick and Calvin," Stan asked.

"Yeah, I remember them. They got smoked."

"Well G-Man is the one that did that."

"Damn, he did that. Yo, you telling me a lot of stuff. Why? I know it ain't all about some blow." Dre knew a bitch when he saw one and a telling bitch was dangerous.

"Nah, I hate that nigga. He think it's all about him, like he tougher than everybody else. And he's a greedy motherfucker. Don't want nobody to get money but him," G-Man was also fucking Stan's baby momma, but Dre didn't need to know about that.

Dre sat there awhile without responding. Lost in thought, he was angry with himself for underestimating G-Man who he had dismissed as a small time hustler. He thought that only another Miami hustler would have the balls to take him out. There were at least five independent Miami crews getting large sums of money in Atlanta. He had even made some moves against a crew that originated from Broward County in Miami that he suspected had been involved in the attack against him because there had been tension between them for years. Now he would have to shift his attention to the Atlanta hustlers, who had become more willing to fight for their territory. It was like the killing of those

Miami hustlers by Pistol and Jay had awakened a sleeping giant, now they all acted like they wanted to stand up to the Miami hustlers.

"So how much you gonna give me?" Stan said impatiently.

"Oh yeah. I'm gonna hit you off with a brick. When you start buying them up front I'll charge eighteen-five. When I front you-it's twenty-one. Okay?"

"That's cool. I should be done in about two weeks."

"Stan, don't fuck my money up."

"Nah my nigga, I know how to take care business," Stan was full of smiles; he would be the man now.

"Beep this number tomorrow around noon, and one of my people will meet you with it," Dre was ready to get this coward out his presence.

"Okay, okay. Thanks a lot and everything I told you is the truth—that nigga G-Man is crazy."

After Stan left, Dre sat in his office for long time thinking of the right way to kill G-Man. Dre hated having to engage in some more gangster shit. He wished he could just sit back relax and let the money come to him, but G-Man deserved the most tortuous death he could think of. When he finally thought of a death worthy of the occasion, he just sat back and smiled.

"Them bitch-ass niggas are gonna wish they had never been born when I get done with them," Dre said out loud while checking himself out in the mirror. After pulling his baseball cap further down on his head and adjusting his Armani shirt and octagon-shaped Armani shades, Big Dre decided to go check on Lovely.

"LOVELY, LOVELY SINCLAIR. Focus. This is a love scene and you are hugging him like he's your cousin. Embrace him. Kiss him like every cell in your body is longing for him."

"Yes, Madame Denwa," Lovely said. She knew she was

fucking up rehearsal today. She needed to get shit together before the legend in her own mind, her acting coach, Madame Denwa gave her leading role to one of the many hungry bitches that wanted to take her place, kissing and hugging gay Jermaine. She did have to admit he did look good today, all rugged looking with jeans and a tight t-shirt on. His acting abilities, looks, and style had the other acting students calling him Billy Dee Williams.

"Places, everyone. Places!" Madame Denwa yelled, ready to direct Lovely and Jermaine's passionate love scene all over again.

Big Dre took a seat in the back row of the acting school's auditorium just before the scene started.

Lovely was focused now and so was Jermaine. The scene was intense, passionate, and sparks could be felt at the back row. Dre's blood boiled, his head itched, and he cursed under his breath. "I knew that sneaky bitch liked that nigga." He watched a little more of the scene and left before Lovely could see him. Rehearsals ended around 6:30 P.M., and Lovely headed straight home to fix Dre and herself a nice dinner.

When Lovely arrived home, she was surprised to find Dre in the living room, sitting in the dark like some kind of intruder.

"Hi baby, you're home early. I didn't even get a chance to cook yet. You want steak, potato and broccoli with cheese? Why you sitting in the dark?" she was determined to be nice. She turned on the lamp and Dre looked like he was bothered by something.

"What's wrong baby?" Lovely sat in his lap and put her arm around his neck. He pushed her off him and asked, "Why you just getting in? Where the fuck you been?"

"Come on Dre. Don't start that bullshit. You know I go to acting class today."

"Was you with that nigga you like there?"

"I do not like anybody there, Dre," Lovely was exasperated

by Dre's reoccurring accusations.

"Bitch you must think I'm stupid. I was there today, and I saw the way you was all over him like a little whore."

"Fuck you Dre, you are stupid as hell. That was acting—what I pay to learn—and that guy is gay, so can you please cut the bullshit?" she went into the kitchen to cook.

He followed her still unsatisfied with her answer, "So what is it you wanted? Why was you so concerned about whether or not I was coming over?"

"It was nothing Dre."

"Don't give me that bullshit. What was it?"

She was trying to busy herself in the kitchen, hoping he would get tired of arguing like she was tired of his ass.

"What was it?" his voice left her no option.

"I wanted to know if you still had that old Mustang."

"Well, you know my best friend Joy? She gets out of Juvenile soon, and it's her birthday."

"So?" he interrupted.

"I wanted to know if we could give her that old Mustang as a coming home/birthday gift."

"Wasn't that basketball player Calvin her brother?" he asked.

"Yeah, that was her brother."

"Fuck no she can't have it, but I do have another gift for her. Today I found out that G-Man is the one that killed him."

"How you know?" Dre had Lovely's undivided attention.

"Fuck how I know. I know." Dre wasn't about to tell her his source or that he knew who set his ass on fire. He didn't want to remind her that his attack still went unpunished.

"Oh shit, wait until I tell her this. It's been bothering her ever since it happened."

Lovely hadn't thought about Calvin in a long time, but now anger and sorrow over came her. He had been her best friend's brother and the nicest guy she ever met. When Dre saw that her eyes were moist, he jumped to the wrong conclusion.

"What you getting all sad about? Was you fucking him?"

"No Dre... I wasn't fucking him," Lovely said, tears falling down her cheeks.

In the past Dre asked her about any relations she had before him and she had always insisted that she never gave anybody some but him. Of course he didn't believe her, but he never pressed her. Tonight would be different: the gloves off. He no longer cared about her feelings; not tonight at least.

"What about the rest of those guys around Stanton Road? You mean to tell me you never gave them none either?"

"No Dre, I never gave any guys any before you or since you."

"Bitch, you *must* think I'm stupid," he walked up to her. "You wasn't no virgin when I fucked you, you sneaky 'ho."

Lovely stood her ground and yelled, "Get out of my face Dre. You are one stupid, insecure ass nigga, and if you want to believe I was fucking them then yeah, I fucked all those niggas on Stanton Road, and it was better-way better than yours!"

"*What* bitch?" Dre slapped her with a force that sent her flying into the $800 Frigidaire.

"You better remember who the fuck you talking to, and who pays your bills."

The back of her head hit the icemaker on the fridge causing a gash that trickled blood and the release of about twelve ice-cubes. She just lay there and cried. Dre exited the apartment, not wanting to see the outcome of his temper.

Lovely remained on the kitchen floor, leaning against the refrigerator, rubbing the back of her head. She was seething with hatred for the burnt, insecure ass-hole who paid her bills.

After gathering her strength and dignity, she dried her eyes with the front of her polo shirt. She then got off the floor, put the food she was gonna prepare back into the fridge, and went to the bathroom. She wet a washcloth with alcohol and wiped the blood off her wound. It stung and she frowned as she noticed the pink hand print on her face and swollen left ear. He had slapped her so hard that she feared her eardrum might be busted. She yelled, "I hate him, I hate him, I hate him!"

Both ears seemed to be working fine. She didn't want to be there, just in case he came back tonight so she called Candace. To her dismay Candace wasn't home, so she beeped her 911. When the phone rang she hurried and answered it but it was Dre.

"I didn't mean to…"

"*Fuck you!*" she yelled, hanging up on him.

The phone rang again and this time it was Candace.

"What's up? Why the 911?"

"That bastard hit me, and I want to come spend the night with you."

"Sure, I'll be there in about fifteen minutes. Meet me at my apartment," Candace heard vulnerability in her voice and thought, this is what I've been waiting for.

Candace rushed home to get the ambience perfect. If everything went right, she could well be on her way to reaching her goals. Lovely arrived twenty minutes after Candace.

"Oh, damn Boo, that corny motherfucker is gonna pay for this," was Candace's reaction upon seeing Lovely's face which started to swell. They hugged for a long time, and Lovely let the tears fall freely. Candace removed Lovely's jacket and led her to a chair.

"So what happened sweetie?" Candace could tell Lovely needed some babying.

"I was trying to cook us dinner and he started an argument about me liking this gay guy I told you was in my acting class.

"I told you men are stupid and insecure. They are just like kids with toys around Christmas time. They cry and plead, act all good to get you, then don't want nobody else near you, then break you up and throw you away," Candace reminded her.

"I hate him. I hope somebody burns the rest of his ass up." Candace had to suppress a laugh; Lovely sounded so twelve year old.

Candace retrieved some Chinese food from the microwave and proceeded to feed Lovely like she was a tender lover. Afterwards she said, "Come on Love lets go upstairs."

Candace used the dimmer to turn the lights down and placed a Sade cassette in her bedside sound system.

"I was about to take a shower. Come on, take one with me." Candace invited her.

Lovely walked towards the bathroom helpless and defeated.

Candace kissed her cheek and said, "It's gonna be okay Love," and she started undressing her. She adjusted the water, led Lovely into the shower, and then undressed herself. Candace stood behind Lovely and washed her whole body. She washed her hair, then her neck, under her arms, and softly across her firm breasts. She ran the sponge across her stomach, down her back and all over her ample ass. She then dropped the sponge and lathered Lovely's pubic area with her hand, tenderly massaging the silky patch of hair, feeling Lovely's clitoris stiffen in her hand and her lips reach out for her touch. She ran her soapy hands between the crack of Lovely's ass and over her asshole, feeling the hard muscles in Lovely's ass and thighs from dance classes. She then sat on the edge of the tub, turned Lovely towards her and pulled her vagina to her mouth. Soap, water, and pussy juice mixed in her mouth, but she kept on sucking Lovely's clit, then expertly used her tongue, found her G-Spot with her finger and brought Lovely to a quivering orgasm.

After they rinsed and dried off, Candace laid Lovely on her bed, flipped the tape over and got her strawberry-flavored massage oil out the drawer. Candace was determined to give Lovely the greatest night of pleasure she ever experienced. She fully oiled and massaged the back of her body, stopping to tease

Lovely's asshole with her tongue. By the time Candace turned Lovely over she was already wetter than an Olympic-sized pool.

First she massaged her temples, kissing her eyelids, then she massaged her earlobes, her neck, the length of her shoulders and down her arms. She massaged oil across Lovely's whole torso, then concentrated on her breasts, gently working them like she was kneading bread. Lovely had nice long pink nipples that were extremely hard. Candace started massaging her hand and each finger individually, at the same time she sucked on Lovely's nipples. The sensation of having her hands above her head being massaged and having her nipples sucked caused an orgasm that left Lovely a little light headed. Then Candace went down on her again, first eating her hungrily, then slowly and tenderly until another orgasm covered her lips. She moved down the front of Lovely's thighs, her calves, her foot, and toes. Then she continued to bring Lovely pleasure with her fingers. Candace had delicate, slender fingers and she slowly increased the amount of fingers. Lovely was damn near in a stupor by now and so wet, juice dripped from inside her. Candace continued until she made Lovely's body convulse like a seizure victim. Her gasp was loud and sounded pained. Candace's hand was soaked before she eased her finger completely out of Lovely.

They now lay beside each other, and Lovely's speech resembled a drunk's, she was so spent. Candace questioned her some more about her and Big Dre's fight, trying to keep her awake. She told her Dre accused her of not being a virgin when they got together.

"You was, wasn't you?" Candace asked.

Lovely in her weakened and sensitive state, for the first time told somebody about Rick's rapes and other abuses she had suffered. That night they cried together, but Candace still couldn't let this opportunity pass.

Everyone is more susceptible to suggestion, more agreeable,

more willing to please in the after glow of sexual fulfillment. Lovely Sinclair was no different. She cuddled up next to Candace and listened to her devise a plan to get revenge on both Big Dre and Rapist Rick. After all the pleasure Candace gave her, in contrast to all the pain and suffering she had endured at the hands of men, she could do nothing but agree. Lovely was eventually allowed to sleep, thoroughly exhausted and satiated, her body collapsed into a deep slumber. Candace soon dozed off herself, confident that Lovely was now under control and her plans were on their way.

15

He Raped Me

Rick's other self had done it—that's what he kept trying to convince himself of. He looked down at his hands with a dumb, confused look on his face.

"How did this happen? How did this happen? How did this happen again?" he asked no one in particular. All he could remember is fucking her doggy-style, the car windows fogging, she acting like it hurt—fake little whore, like Lovely. He remembered fucking her harder and harder, his hands on her shoulders, on her breasts, around her neck. Now she was dead. "What did you do?" he asked the fourteen-year-old corpse.

Rick's vaguely remembered two other girls that did something wrong, and they too had ended up dead somehow. He looked down at the body not knowing for sure if he was sad or happy. All these little fast-ass sluts ain't shit he said to himself, just little dick teasers like Lovely. He hadn't seen Lovely in more than a year, ever since she had acted like she didn't want him and stabbed him with scissors. It was no wonder she wanted to be an actress. Her worn-out mother Delores had told him all about it.

He had been thinking, Lovely should be a good actress, she been acting like she don't want me to fuck her as long as I've known her.

Now he had to figure out what to do with the body. He dumped the first two girls' bodies on Niskey Lake Road in southwest Atlanta. He now wondered if their naked, pretty bodies had been found, because he hadn't seen anything in the news about it.

He stripped the young girl of all her clothes and jewelry. Looking down on her body now, he noticed she didn't look as much like Lovely as he originally thought. He decided to use another famous location from the Atlanta Child Murders. He picked Redwine Road in East Point. It, like Niskey Lake wasn't too far from his home, but far enough to escape suspicion. Plus he wasn't really worried: over 110 murders had shared a similar geographic and/or social connection, but police had been so inadequate that only twenty-nine names made their Atlanta Child list. Connections were ignored in over sixty similar cases and at least twenty more were ignored after Wayne Williams arrest. Wayne Williams had only been convicted of two murders. Rick was sure that if someone could get away with about 110 murders, he could definitely get away with three little murders.

Delores no longer harbored thoughts of a better relationship with Rick. In the last year or so, she's seen his decline from a moody individual to a downright mean and sadistic asshole that relished any opportunity to fuck her up. She hated his guts, but was in mortal fear of leaving him. Her only hopes were that he would get hit by a truck and die or get tired of her and just leave. Everyday she prayed for that truck, because he was having too much fun whooping her ass to leave on his own.

Now she realized that Lovely hated and feared Rick too, but she still thought that was all. She and Lovely had been meeting up at the mall, the movies, and restaurants. Anywhere but the house she shared with Rick. Lovely refused to come back there even for visits.

She suspected that Rick was involved in some sick and depraved activities at night. He was always out to the middle of the night, always broke and taking her money, and would take very long showers when he came in. she also noticed that he had thrown away some of his late night clothing. Whatever he was doing it got him off her back, from upside her head, from between her thighs and mouth.

She was even starting to have a life outside of Rick, which made her happy. To her surprise, her boss had turned out to be quite inventive and entertaining in bed. He was starting to get his halitosis under control and was even going to a gym. He still had a long way to go before he would even be considered average looking, but his kindness, generosity, and bedroom antics were making up for that. Of course, she was loving the yellow corvette that had cost her nothing. All their activities had to take place during work hours. She did a lot of overtime and had taken a few ass-whippings from Rick because of it, but now that he used up her money, overtime was okay.

She often dreamed of a better life with a man that really loved and appreciated her and would continue to long after the pussy stop being new. She wanted a better house, a better relationship with her daughter, and a safe and stable home life. None of this would be possible as long as Rick was around.

THE FIRST PART of Candace's plan seemed easy enough, even though Lovely was unsure if she could be a part of the second.

Tonight's scheme would take all of Lovely's charm and a lot of her acting ability. She made sure Dre was coming over that night, then got everything prepared. They hadn't spent any time together since he slapped her four days ago. Her face was still slightly bruised, which she hid with make-up. He had tried to call and talk to her over the last three days, but she told him she wanted to be left alone for a while to think. Today when he called she told him to come by later.

Dre spent a small part of the day looking for the perfect gift for Lovely. He eventually settled on a new, green Coach bag and matching emerald and diamond necklace and ankle bracelet. He didn't want to lose Lovely, he was still wide-open over her. She still had the prettiest face, the hottest body, and best pussy of all the girls he fucked with. Her pussy was so good, he would think of it when he was inside his other women. Even his new baby-mother that he moved into the house out in Gwinnett County couldn't hold a candle to Lovely, and she was fine as hell.

He had told Lovely before that her pussy felt like little velvet fingers were massaging his dick whenever he was inside of her, especially when she was on top. He definitely didn't want to lose her. He would have to control his temper better. He brought a bottle of Piper's Champagne and a large cherry cheesecake from Lovely's favorite restaurant and headed to the apartment intent on making up.

Lovely didn't want to look too obvious, so she had on a Hugo Boss T-shirt and a pair of shorts she knew showed off her curves well. She had made turkey wings, peas & rice, and broccoli with cheese. She hoped Candace's plan worked; it would eliminate a major problem in her life.

She was surprised Dre rung the bell downstairs instead of using his key. He was trying really hard to seem respectful. She buzzed him in and when she opened the apartment door he looked attractive in a Versace outfit she hadn't seen before. He also had a small department store bag in his hand that piqued her curiosity.

"Hi Lovely," he said bending down to kiss her on the cheek.

"Hi Dre. You looking good, new outfit?"

"Nah, I just never wore it before," he lied.

"I made some turkey wings if you're hungry."

After they ate, they went into the living room to talk. Dre sat on the sofa he had spent a small fortune on. He appraised the whole room quickly, adding up how much he had spent to please Lovely. His appraisal did not escape Lovely, she knew he was thinking about the cost to remodel the apartment to Lovely's approval. She sat in a loveseat across from him under the lamp so he could get a good look at what he bought her. Knowing full well he would feel she was worth it.

"We need to talk, I'm really sorry about what happened that night," he said in his most sincere voice.

"Are you?" she asked.

"Yes, I know you're faithful, and I should of never got jealous over that guy in your acting class."

"Dre, you really hurt me. I never would have thought that you would hit me," her voice cracked and tears slid down on cue. He got up and went and sat on the floor next to Lovely's leg, rubbing it to comfort her.

He said, "I'm sorry baby. It will never happen again. I love you, Lovely."

His submissive actions were totally unrehearsed.

"You scared me Dre. I don't know if I can trust you. You reminded me of my stepfather," she said as tears slid from her eyes.

"What you mean?"

"My stepfather use to beat on me a lot, that's why I haven't been over there in almost two years."

Even though he himself had just recently hit her, his overly possessive mind couldn't fathom someone else hitting her.

"Why didn't you tell me? " he asked soothingly.

"I guess I was embarrassed. He always threatened to kill me and my mom if I say something. He constantly beats my mom and when I call he says he don't give a fuck about my boyfriend, when he catches me it's all over for me," she choked up like the memory of it all was killing her.

The part about not giving a fuck about her boyfriend was suggested by Candace.

"He said that, huh?" Dre said nodding his head, murder in his eyes.

"There's one more thing I have to tell you Dre," the tears started flowing now and Dre stood up and hugged her.

"What is it? You can tell me."

"You swear, you ain't gonna be mad at me," she pleaded.

"I swear I won't," watching his young girl cry like this was tearing up his nose-open ass.

"Dre, I never told anybody this before," she paused for a long time to give her words more drama. Even though she seriously hated Rick for everything she had endured, she had learned to deal with it emotionally.

"Dre, he been raping me since I was twelve-years-old," she turned her head acting too embarrassed to look at him.

The tears flowed hard now, some were for effect, but a lot were born from her inner pain.

"He *what*? Oh my God! Damn Lovely, I'm sorry about all that."

He held her tighter, kissing her forehead, "I'm sorry you had to go through all of that baby, but I promise you he will never touch you or your mother again."

Lovely held Dre tighter and cried onto his expensive shirt.

Dre was more upset than he could remember. He took Lovely's violation as a personal affront to him. He was determined to pay Rick back for stealing his girl's virginity. Lovely could feel that the first part of Candace's plan was working out perfectly.

That night they had a gentle lovemaking session, which involved mostly Dre trying to pleasure Lovely. After he went to sleep she got dressed and went to his car in the garage. She checked his car registration and his insurance and found his home address. Then she hit pay dirt: a letter from a veterinarian about a sick kitten. It was addressed to a home in Gwinnett County. She then rushed to a drugstore that stayed open late to get Dre's keys duplicated. On the way back home she stopped at a store and brought some ice cream. She was prepared to lie and say she had an ice cream craving and took his car 'cause hers had been acting up lately. Her well-prepared lie was unnecessary, Dre was still asleep when she returned and she got undressed and slid in bed beside him like nothing happened. Then she remembered the ice cream and got up to throw it down the garbage chute. There was no reason to arouse his suspicion. She couldn't wait to tell Candace everything went as planned.

She had one thought before going to sleep that made her laugh. Oh, his soft ass has a cat at his secret home in Gwinnett, huh? The new bag and jewelry he had given her right before their lovemaking did very little to lessen the anger towards him.

16

I'm All Tied Up

Rick wasn't hard to follow. His battered, burgundy Thunderbird with the busted exhaust pipe and tattered cloth roof left a distinct trail. This was too personal a job not to get his own hands dirty, so Dre and Gator followed Rick in an Aerovan. That Friday morning, they followed him to his job on Industrial Boulevard. After work they figured he would make a few stops before heading home with his pay. They hoped he would go to the Shaker Booty Club, but no such luck. He stopped at the liquor store near the Cambellton Plaza. They parked where they could observe his actions.

"It looks like he's cashing his check, Gator said.

"Yeah, now seems like as good a time as any," Dre replied.

"It's a lot of cars coming in and out of here," Gator surveyed the area.

"But look at them. They not paying anything or anyone any attention. They are focused on buying they liquor."

"Okay, I'll try and holler at him when he gets out," Gator checked his equipment before exiting the van.

Rick left the store upset with his small amount of pay. His cheap, piece-of-shit bosses had docked his pay because he came in late twice this week. He smiled thinking of the two nights he had stayed up late fucking young girls, which made him late the next morning. Good for those two, they shouldn't have done wrong and caused their own deaths. He was still smiling when a stranger walked up to him.

"Hey buddy could I interest you in a top of the line stereo system for real cheap?"

"No!" he answered too soon.

Rick thought about it and how he could probably buy it and resell it to those idiots at his job. If he hurried he could probably go back there now and sell it to one of the bosses that liked to work late.

The man had turned and started walking away, so Rick hollered to him, "Hey buddy tell me some more about that stereo system." The man came back all smiles and salesmanship. "Well it's a complete home stereo system with professional speakers. It's made by Aiwa, and cost at least $1,800 in the store, but I'll sell it to you for $500."

Rick thought it over and decided he could get at least $1,200 for it from one of his dumb-ass bosses. They was always buying stupid shit.

"Listen man, I'm fucked up. Motherfuckers already garnished my check for child support," Rick lied.

So all I have is three hundred and fifty dollars.

"My nigga, I'ma a work with you because the bastards use to garnish my check too," Gator lied back.

"Come with me to my van and I'll show it to you. You can even listen to it," Gator led him through the parking lot where Dre sat waiting in the van.

The van was blue and white, clean, but not new. There was no tint on the windows and as soon as Dre saw them coming he slid open the side panel. As Rick got closer he saw that a very expensive stereo system and speakers were already set up in back. He got happy, knowing he was gonna get paid. Shit, I get at least fifteen hundred for that. Rick thought.

"How it sound?" Rick asked Dre.

"Turn it up and check it out for yourself," Dre replied.

The system was connected to some kind of generator. Rick reached inside the van and turned the system up a little, not wanting to attract other possible buyers who could out bid him. At that exact moment Gator slid a blackjack out of his back pocket. When Rick stood fully erect, Gator smacked him in the back of the head, rendering him unconscious. Gator then pushed Rick into the van and slid the door close. Gator walked back to the driver side and got in while Dre kept a look out for any unwanted attention. Nobody seemed to have noticed anything peculiar and they drove away, leaving Rick's burgundy eyesore in the parking lot.

Dre wanted to torture Rick, but more rational thoughts prevailed.

"Let's just get this over with nice and clean. Remember we have to concentrate on getting G-Man and his people. Plus, we might need to use this van again." Gator stressed to Dre.

"Yeah you right. I don't have time to torture the motherfucking pervert because I gotta go secure this package my uncle sent."

"What you want me to do with him?" Gator asked.

"Put him out of his misery, but don't dump the body til I get back."

"Yeah alright. Beep me when you ready," Gator was relieved that Dre took his advice.

"Drop me off at the next block, and I'll catch you later." Dre said as he took another look at Rick, who was out cold.

THE NEXT MORNING four young boys were walking through the

woods near Stanton Road and discovered Rick's body. He was tied to a tree and naked. A pink ribbon was tied around his wrist and his dick dangled from the other end of the ribbon. The pink ribbon was meant to be a message, but the kids couldn't figure it out and decided to get their asses out the woods. Two of the boys led other neighbors back to view their discovery; most of whom were the early morning hustlers. Like typical ghetto dwellers, they told their neighbors before they told the cops. Rick had a full audience now, a couple of ballers even recognized him.

"Yo, ain't that the man married to that real light skin lady with the super bad daughter?"

"Yeah, that's him, they live in that little house up the street. Shit, he must've really pissed someone off to get his dick cut off."

Eventually someone had enough sense to go call the police. Rick's days of raping and murdering young girls had come to a humiliating end.

THE BODIES WERE piling up and the stench of it all was angering the hell out of Detectives Hutchins and Greenlee.

"What the hell is wrong with these animals? First we find the young girls dead, and now there's a dead nig—, dead man naked and tied to a tree," Detective Hutchins had almost said nigger, but he caught himself because he knew niggers, even the different ones like Greenlee, were super sensitive.

"Listen, I don't think getting murdered makes those people animals, and we have to be overlooking some kind of connection. Why would someone choose the same spots as the Atlanta Missing and Murdered to dump those girls bodies?" Detective Greenlee's patience with Hutchins' racist comments was wearing thin.

"Maybe that sick bastard, Wayne Williams, had a partner, and now his partner has started back up," Hutchins added.

"Maybe he was never guilty in the first place and was just a convenient scapegoat," Greenlee retaliated.

"Bullshit, that crazy nigger did it. They had proof he did it," Hutchins answered.

Detective Hutchins and Greenlee were about to square off when the Captain called them.

"Greenlee, Hutchins, get y'all's asses in here," he hollered from his open doorway.

"Oh shit. What done crawled up his ass?" Hutchins murmured under his breath.

"Let's go face the music," Greenlee replied, their earlier tension now broken.

They arrived in the Captain's office and Greenlee started to take a seat.

"Don't sit down. Y'all are not gonna be here long. I want y'all in the streets solving these goddamn murders!"

"What the fuck y'all been doing all this time—playing paddycake, paddycake, baker's man?"

They both found that funny, but neither detective dared to laugh.

"Captain, we…"

"Shut up Hutchins. I don't wanna hear shit. Just get your ass out there and find out who cut that poor man's dick off and left him dead on that tree."

"Okay Captain," they both tried to say.

"Now, motherfuckers, now," the captain screamed.

They both left the Captain's office laughing.

"The Captain's gonna have a nervous breakdown soon," Hutchins told Greenlee between laughs.

"Yeah, I guess we better go pound the pavement for some clues," Greenlee replied.

"Shit, not before we go get some breakfast. IHOP good with you?"

"Sure," Greenlee replied, their fragile camaraderie back in place.

17

Freedom for Joy

Lovely sat at Candace's kitchen table reading the newspaper. "Oh shit, look, here it goes."

"What?" Candace asked.

"About Rick."

"Let me see. Let me see," Candace said as she snatched the newspaper from Lovely.

She skimmed through the article. "Damn this article is so small and they barely mention any of the details, just that he was found dead in the woods near Stanton Road."

"Yeah," Lovely said, "I wonder why they didn't write more about it?"

"The police probably asked them not to. Maybe they don't want people to panic. You know they found some young girls dead on Niskey Lake Road and Redwine Road, don't you?" Candace asked.

"No I didn't hear anything about that."

"Yeah, somebody killed three teenage girls and dumped their bodies on those streets a couple of weeks ago. The newspaper article was real small too."

"Ain't those the two streets that guy Wayne Williams was supposed to have left some people at?" Lovely asked.

"You mean the Ku Klux Klan, yeah that's the same streets. I think the police are trying to keep things quiet to not panic people."

"Yeah probably." Lovely didn't want to discuss the Atlanta Missing and Murdered. She remembered how frightened everyone had been when it was happening. She was around six-years-old when it started.

"See I told you it would work. You got that dumb ass Dre to get rid of Rick for you, and now your mother don't have to worry about his retarded ass no more."

"Yeah, I guess," Lovely answered half-heartedly.

"What you mean you guess? Our plan is working out perfectly."

"Your plan," Lovely whispered.

Candace ignored her. She only needed Lovely to go with the plans, not go with them enthusiastically.

Lovely had a movie audition for a small part as a young southern belle that would be filming in Savannah. The audition was being held at an auditorium in downtown Atlanta. Navigating her way through downtown traffic, lovely's thoughts traveled to Rick. She thought of all the years of suffering and violations she had endured and she knew she was glad Candace's plan had worked. Getting Dre riled up so he would do away with Rick worked as easy as Candace said it would.

When Lovely got to the auditorium she was surprised by the turnout. Beautiful women and girls of various shapes, heights, and complexions stood in a block long line waiting for auditions to start. Competition was thick, but she was full of confidence. Her acting coach, Madame Denwa, had spent extra time with her getting her ready.

"Lovely, you have a natural acting ability, but you must stayed focused," Madame Denwa told her. "You must stay in the character, and lose all association to Lovely while in role. No thoughts, concerns, or feelings should appear that aren't your character's," she continued.

"I know Madame Denwa."

"You don't know and that's what's wrong with you young ladies. You think you know. And to make it big in this business you will have to move out of Atlanta go to New York or California, and there you can perfect your art and be seen by the right people."

"I'm thinking about it, Madame."

"Don't think-do. Acting is an adventure, and you must be willing to take chances," Madame Denwa explained passionately.

Now Lovely waited in line about to put all of Madame Denwa's teaching and lectures to practice. Two hours and twenty minutes later Lovely had her big chance.

"Now Ms. Sinclair, in this scene it's 1940 and you are in the Deep South and the Sheriff is looking for your brother for a crime. Okay," a suntanned surfer looking guy told her.

"Yes, I got it," Lovely replied.

"Quiet everyone. Okay, one, two, three—action!"

"Sheriff sir, I swear I haven't seen Buster all week. I think he done gone down to Atlanta with them there McDaniel twins to do some catfish catching, but as soon as I sees him I'ma tell him the Sheriff be looking for him," Lovely expressed in perfect southern diction and mannerisms.

"Okay, cut!" surfer boy hollered.

A small but energetic round of applause praised Lovely and she blushed.

"Ms. Sinclair, that was excellent. Somebody will be calling you soon to let you know if you got the part."

Lovely left the audition in high spirits.

Lovely drove to her mother's house wondering how she had taken Rick's death. She knew her mother had loved Rick deeply at one time and suspected that she hadn't been too happy with him recently. She hoped her mother wasn't in too much pain. Death had a way of romanticizing the past. Everyone spoke well of a person at a funeral, even those that couldn't stand the person. *Damn*, speaking of funerals, *I hope she don't expect me to come to his. I hope I'm able to hide my happiness over his death when I'm with her.*

Lovely parked and headed towards the house. As she got closer, her old fears resurfaced and she stood glued to her mom's front lawn staring at her bedroom window.

Finally her mother came out. "Girl, what you doing standing out here? Come on in," she said ignorant as always to her daughter's suffering.

As soon as they got in the door they hugged. "How you doing Ma? You okay?"

"I'm fine. The police came around and asked some questions, but other than that nobody really seems to care. I hate to see anybody hurt, especially as cruelly as the neighborhood said Rick was found, but I really didn't love him anymore, " Delores said. Delores was glad his sadistic, brutal ass was dead and couldn't wait to see them throw the dirt on his ass, but she was too ashamed to tell Lovely any of that.

"Well now maybe you can find a man you really love." She saw a twinkle in her mother's eye "you sly dog, you got somebody in mind already, don't you?"

"Girl stop, my husband ain't even buried yet," but she blushed giving herself away.

"Who is it?" Lovely asked.

"I don't want to talk about it. Are you going to the funeral," she asked to change the subject.

"No!" Lovely answered.

"Why not? He was your stepfather."

"He wasn't nothing to me, and I don't like funerals."

Delores almost got a glimpsed of the horrors Lovely had suffered at the hands of her men, but the truth was too brutal and again she chose to ignore the signs.

They spent most of the day together and a sort of morbid bonding took place over Rick's dead body. Rick had left very little life insurance, so Lovely promised to give her mother $4,000 she had saved up. By the time Lovely left that evening, mother and daughter had enjoyed an easiness they hadn't experienced in years.

JOY COULDN'T WAIT to leave her filtered existence. The last twenty-one months she felt like a genie stuck in a dirty beer bottle. Being in and out of solitary confinement had turned her heart icy cold. Even now, eight days before her mandatory release on her eighteenth birthday, these warped-minded rednecks had her in the hole. They acted like nobody started fights but her. They all hated her—staff and her fellow inmates.

She refused to act like a passive pushover and allow the staff to treat her like a child or a private experiment. Joy refused their programs, refused their Ritalin, and refused to talk about her past, especially her mother's alcoholism and her brother's death.

Joy still hated ballers, even more so now that she witnessed the end results of their callous manipulations. So many young girls were in juvie for holding their *so-called* boyfriend's packages or guns and now those same boyfriends totally ignored them. Others were given packages to juggle on the corners, and the ballers would fuck them at will, fuck over their supposed pay, then when they got caught, said, "Fuck them."

They were victims and Joy made them feel good by being their friend, listening to their whining, being their protector, sharing some of her possessions, and sucking their young pussies. Many of them had never been shown any tenderness before and Joy manufactured it for their behalf. Joy had no interest in males at all. She got a chance to observe their behavior up close being around so many male guards and she despised them. To her they were all brutal dummies that thought with their penises, inferior to women in every aspect except brute force. All her short stays in general population involved her being with the prettiest girl and having to whip a bitch's ass over her.

Now the only *real* family she had was Lovely and Candace who loved like a sister and were true friends. She had actually developed some real feelings for Belinda, aka Pork and Beans. Whenever Joy was in population they shared a room. They stopped having sex and became each other's best friend. Joy messed with different girls sexually but everyone knew her and Belinda feelings ran deep and blood shed would follow any drama inflicted on Belinda. They talked openly about everything and shared whatever possessions they had. Of course, Joy had much more since Lovely and Candace had provided for her handsomely during her whole bid. Joy and Belinda even discussed getting an apartment together on the bricks. Belinda had maxed her juvenile life out four months earlier than Joy. Belinda had very little so Joy gave her $500 off her books to get herself situated out there. Saving money had been easy for Joy since she was hardly in population to spend all the money Candace and Lovely gave her. Since Belinda left, Joy never heard from her again, not even one letter. Her feelings were crushed. Joy thought they had really bonded and would be friends for life, but Belinda fooled her. After that Joy vowed to keep her feelings to herself. She had two proven friends: Lovely and Candace. Fuck everyone else – even her mother.

Joy still missed Calvin and never forgot her vow to make the ballers in Atlanta pay for his death. In her last letter Lovely said she had some info about Calvin, and would tell her when she came home. She hoped that Lovely had a clue about who killed Calvin so she could finally make pay with their own life.

18

It's a Party Y'all

"There go the birthday girl right there!" Lovely shouted, exiting the car.

" Joy, Joy, Joy, over here!" Candace also got out the car and they both ran towards Joy. When they hugged Joy they damn near knocked her down.

"Hey you heifers. Y'all gonna knock me down and get my outfit dirty." Joy replied all full of smiles, hugging her two best friends back.

"Come on let's get out of these white people's parking lot acting a fool," Candace told them and they walked towards Lovely's BMW.

"Damn girl, you doing it up. Candace told me you was driving a Beemer, but I didn't know it was some new million dollar shit," Joy's excitement bubbled over and it was infectious.

"It's just a little something, something, you know." Lovely was more confident then last time all three was together, Joy noticed.

"And where your ride at Candy? I know your ride sharp

too."

"I left it home girl, so we could pick you up in real style."

"Where to first?" Lovely asked.

"Let's go shopping," Candace said and handed Joy two thousand dollars." That's from me and Lovely."

"Wow I never had this much at one time before."

Joy gave Lovely and Candace hugs.

"Shit, we can do what we use to do and save this money."

"No boosting. We shopping with money today," Lovely said.

"Yeah that's right, plus we got bigger things planned," Candace said.

"What bigger things?" Joy asked.

"I'll tell you later. Now what store do you want to go to?" Candace asked.

"Anyone, but the last one," Joy said and all three laughed thinking about that bullshit store in the Omni Mall that had busted Joy and Candace.

"Let's go to the Lennox Mall, they have a lot of new stores," Lovely said headed in that direction.

They spent the day together shopping, laughing, eating and catching each other up on the last twenty-one months. They crashed three malls and some specialty shops, saw a Denzel Washington movie, and afterwards questioned Joy on her gender preference.

"Whew, I wonder how Denzel Washington is in bed? He always be making that look with his lips pushed out. I wonder if he's trying to tell his audience he love eating pussy. If so he could come eat some of this pussy anytime," Candace said. "What you think Lovely?" she continued.

"Yeah, he is handsome and can act his ass off, but that don't mean he can *really* eat some pussy," Lovely answered.

"What about you Joy, would you let him eat your pussy all

day and night?" Candace asked.

"Only if he paid me or was divorcing his wife for me."

"Why you wouldn't give him none for free?" Candace teased.

"A man can't get nothing from me for free but a foot up his ass."

Lovely and Candace busted out laughing, but Joy was dead serious.

"Love, what did you have to tell me about my brother?"

"I'll tell you later when we get back to Candace's house."

"I wanna know right now!"

"Later Joy I promise. Come on, let's go to this spa I know where they give you Swedish massages and manicures and pedicures. And right next door is a hell-a-fide hair salon."

"Okay, let's go!" Candace announced changing the mood back to celebration.

IT HAD BEEN TWO DAYS since Joy had been released and now she was enjoying herself at a party given by her two best friends. Candace's apartment was full of women and a select few lucky men. Most of the women were strippers that worked with Sylvia at Dante's Inferno. Ox was there with her cousin Tammy from Brooklyn who was a pretty hip-hop chick with enormous door-knocker earrings and a rough Brooklyn attitude. Most of the girls who had been present at Tangie's baby shower were there.

Candace watched Joy to see if she was having a good time. Most of Joy's time was spent bugging out with Lovely. They were drinking and off to themselves laughing about every damn thing. Candace noticed that Joy had her eyes on a particular stripper for most of the night. She was sure that Joy's preference was girls and nothing but girls.

Ox had provided some New York mix tapes and by midnight most of the guests were tipsy from champagne, hard liquor and beer. That's when the strippers started dancing outrageously. A strong sexual energy prevailed. Everyone was enjoying themselves immensely, especially Joy who was enjoying the company of a young red-bone, full in the pants and shirt, with eyes the color of jade and pouty lips.

"How you know you not into girls if you never tried," Joy said, licking her lips indicating her intentions.

"I just know, that's all," The red-bone said as her resistance to Joy's macking faded.

"Don't you like your whole body kissed? Your pussy sucked like a blow-pop? Your clit nibbled like a Ritz cracker, and your insides licked like a ice-cream cone?"

"Yeah I do."

"Well who you think is better at it? Some clumsy dumb man only interested in himself or a woman, like me who knows every spot, knows what we like, and knows how much we need?" With that Joy leaned in closer and ran her tongue gently across the young strippers mouth. Eventually she opened her mouth and Joy kissed her deeply, moving closer, reaching under her dress and feeling her wet lace panties.

"*Oohhh, Oohhh,*" The red-bone moaned as Joy expertly slid her finger around the panties and into her opening. Her pussy was wet, slightly sticky, wide-open and ready for play.

"Let's go upstairs where we can get some privacy," Joy invited.

"Okay, but just for a little while," she said following after Joy, her pussy almost wet enough to drip on the carpet.

Those still conscious enough to notice watched Joy and the object of a lot of people's desire head upstairs. There were a lot of amused smiles, like Candace's and Lovely's but mostly there were looks of envy.

Upstairs Joy knew what her target needed, and she deeply kissed her again while removing her clothes. How Joy fingered her so expertly while undressing her so smoothly the young stripper would never know. Her clothes hit the floor so swiftly she barely noticed them. Soon her breasts were teased, licked and sucked with the skill of a person who lived with breast twenty-four hours a day. Joy's finger on her G-spot was like a remote control; she was able to push her back onto the bed with the strength of just that finger. The transition was instantaneous, one-minute Joy's finger was driving her wild and the next Joy's mouth covered her pussy entirely, her tongue darting in and out, her upper lip working her clit. Then Joy moved her around so that her legs were spread apart, her pink pussy fully exposed, open, and enjoying the best head it ever experienced. Joy lifted red-bone up to her mouth, arms under her body, with her damn near upside down, Joy drunk greedily from her fountain. Afterwards they relaxed into a sixty-nine position with Joy on top still controlling the action. Joy came all over her mouth, smearing it all over with her wild waist motion. Joy then allowed the young stripper to experience for the first time the hand maneuver. Gently Joy had two, then four then five finger's inside red-bone's pussy. Joy then made her hand as small as possible and slid the whole thing inside her with some resistance, some force. Joy made a fist inside her and started fucking her from the inside out. The effect was some indescribable pleasure the stripper had never experienced before. Women locked up had time to experiment and young girls were the worst. By the time Joy was out of her, there was half-a-dozen orgasms worth of juice on her hand. They lay together intertwined and naked and fell asleep. Joy would never have to work that hard to convince red-bone, who was now wide open in a couple of ways.

19

Dre Day

Lovely waited until they were alone at Candace's apartment before telling Joy what she had learned from Dre.

"G-Man? Who the fuck is G-Man? I swear I'm gonna kill that motherfucker," Joy stomped back and forth across the room.

"G-Man is a baller who just started making a lot of noise out here. He owns a club called G-Spot near Greenbriar Mall."

"Well, where do he be at, 'cause I'ma kill his motherfucking ass."

"I don't know, he probably be at his club. Candace might have a plan to catch his ass, because her, Ox and Tammy been trying to follow him and Dre around the last couple of weeks," Lovely answered.

"I'ma see what she talking about, and if I don't agree with it then I'ma run-up in that club and kill his ass. Believe that!" Joy said.

Candace had been able to follow G-Man discreetly several times, but she was still unable to determine where his stash was kept. From what she saw, G-Man rarely got his hands dirty, and most of his travels involved chasing pussy not dollars and he loved his club. He was there most mornings accompanied by a bunch of soft-looking associates. If Candace would have had to guess, she would have said that the club was the location of most of his drug revenue.

Ox and Tammy had been following Dre around, and they all came to the same conclusion. The bulk of his money was kept at his house in Gwinnett County. The girl he kept there was usually home, with their child and no one else. Soon Candace had a plan devised for Dre, and G-Man would have to be dealt with later.

CONSCIOUSNESS ARRIVED SLOWLY. Dre tried to shake the fog from his brain but couldn't. His mouth was dry like cotton and his tongue felt too thick to call out to Lovely. He didn't feel the weight of Lovely's body next to his and wondered why. Dre was finally able to open his eyes and there stood Lovely. Or was that Lovely? Or was that other one Lovely? His vision was badly blurred, and it looked like three women stood in front of his bed. Maybe he was still dreaming. His vision improved slightly and he saw Lovely, and two other women. Distinct features were still unrecognizable, but he was able to focus on Lovely's incredible face and body. Maybe this was a nightmare, which would explain why it looked like the other two girls had a gun pointed at him. His young girl looked scared. She must *really* love me he thought. She all in my nightmares being worried about me. He tried to move but he felt so heavy. He struggled with all of his strength to lift his arm, but it immediately fell back to the bed feeling like lead instead of flesh and bones. The shapes moved closer. They were on the side of the bed now. *Shit, that's one hell of a scar heavy-weight has on her face*, he thought to himself.

The night before Lovely had poured him a large glass of orange/pineapple juice. Unbeknownst to Dre she had added a poison called VTX to his drink, which slowed down his heart, and made him lethargic and easy to control. Dre's mind was clearing up, but it would be hours before he could maneuver his body much.

"Lovely *what's* going on?" he managed to whisper.

"Just lay still you'll find out in a minute," Lovely responded. Despite his past actions Lovely felt a little sorry for him. Dre looked and sounded like a pitiful little boy.

Ox used the phone to sens a message to Candace's beeper.

Candace called back, "Everything cool?"

"Everything cool over here. What about you?"

"The cat is in the bag and totally cooperative, and the kitten is cute as hell."

"Yeah, yeah, stay on point. We will be over there in a little while," Ox responded.

After Ox hung up the phone she told Lovely and Tammy, "Come on let's get him dressed."

Ox decided they needed an additional insurance policy. She coded Candace again on her beeper.

"Put the cat on the phone and tell her what to say," Ox told Candace.

Ox then held the phone to Dre's ear.

He heard, "Dre help us, some girls have taken over our house."

Dre could barely speak and said, "Just do what they say. Everything is gonna be okay. Trust me." The phone was then snatched away by Ox.

"Dre, we are after your money. Don't do anything brave or stupid, and you, your cute child and your baby mother will live through this. I have someone at your house who will kill them in the most painful way if anything goes wrong. Do you understand? Nod your head if you do," Ox instructed.

Dre nodded his head like a robot, the fire draining from his face and eyes.

"One more question, and you better be truthful. Do you have money stashed at your house in Gwinnett County?" Ox asked.

Dre once again shook his head yes.

After they dressed Dre they walked him out of the apartment, down the elevator, and into the garage. Lovely helped Dre walk and Ox and Tammy had their guns tucked and walked behind them. The trip to the garage was uneventful; few tenants roamed the building that early on a Sunday morning. Lovely took the wheel of Dre's Benz with Tammy in the passenger seat and Dre lying down in back with Ox watching over him. The four headed to Gwinnett County to Dre's house and Dre's money.

Candace had a key, but it was no good, because Dre had installed an alarm system between the time Lovely made the duplicate and their arrival. Candace had to come up with a plan of entry, quick. They drove off to contemplate their obstacle.

"What we gonna do now, how we gonna get in?" Joy asked.

They sat in McDonalds parking lot eating egg McMuffins and drinking orange juice. The McDonalds was a considerable distance from the house. A Target department store was on the other side of the avenue.

"Well, what are we gonna do?" Joy asked again.

"I got it!" Candace announced, staring at Target.

Forty minutes later Candace stood at the door to Dre's house again. This time she was conservatively dressed in a formless skirt and a bland blouse. She wore heavy make-up and looked at least eight years older and had a clipboard in her hand.

Candace had to ring the bell three times before the door was answered. Freda wondered what the harmless looking woman at her front door wanted this early on a Sunday morning. She opened the large oak door but left the metal screen door closed.

"Yes, can I help you?" Freda answered the door in a pretty

nightgown.

"Good morning. I'm so sorry to bother you but I'm with the Census Bureau. I was supposed to ask you to answer some questions and sign a form on Friday, but I got sick before I could finish my route. If I don't have this done by tomorrow I will be fired. Could you please answer my questions now?" Nothing but passivity and servitude registered on Candace's face. Had Freda asked to see the form, Candace's ploy would have been revealed, but she didn't. It was too early for this bullshit Freda thought, but she didn't want the woman to lose her job. She knew a lot of woman who struggled to get money.

"Sure come on in, I'll answer your questions," Freda said while opening the screen door.

Candace wasted no time. As soon as she stepped into the house she smacked the shit out of Freda with the clipboard. She was dazed off her feet, blood flowing from her nose and mouth. Joy came to the door as soon as she saw Candace disappear inside. They commandeered the house with military efficiency. Checking all the rooms, they secured Freda to a kitchen chair. They were in the dining room, and they sat the baby in a bassinet on the table. He was a good baby, who didn't cry or make any noise. Freda remained in her seat with a small shirt stuffed in her mouth until Candace put her on the phone with Dre.

When Dre, Lovely, Tammy and Ox got to the house, everyone headed into the dining room. Dre was still under the influence of the VTX, but when he saw his son and baby mother a lot of fire returned to his eyes. He reached out for them suddenly and received a smack across the back of his head with Ox's automatic for his effort.

Freda was gagged and muffled out "Dre."

He was drugged and muffled out "Freda."

Then he looked lovingly at his son in the middle of the table. The son reached for him and Lovely felt as if she would be sick.

Ox sternly poked Dre in the back with the gun.

"Sit down," her gun directed him to one of the dining room chairs directly across from Freda.

"Dre tell us where the money is stashed and we will leave," Candace instructed. By now Dre was also tied to a chair.

"Upstairs in the bedroom closet in my safe," he told them.

"What's the combination?" Candace asked.

She wrote down the numbers he gave her and left the room with Joy.

"Lovely why you do this?" Dre had a pleading voice.

Freda turned her head towards Lovely, recognition registering in her eyes. She must have heard of Lovely already.

"Just do what they say and everything will be okay, Lovely replied, believing it to be true. Ox shot her a hard glance. Candace had told her last night when they went over the plans, to not talk to him.

Candace returned downstairs with a duffle bag full of money. She mouthed "one-sixty-five," to Lovely, Ox and Tammy. Candace, Joy, and Ox had a little conference in the next room.

"He should have more money or some drugs stashed around here," Candace told them.

"How you know?" Ox asked.

"Because he sells plenty of keys and has been having his way for years now," Joy answered.

"Yeah, let's go press him some more," Candace said.

Candace immediately noticed a look of sympathy on Lovely's face and became concerned.

They didn't feel a need to gag Dre, because they figured his child and child's mother's safety would be enough to keep him quiet.

Joy approached him.

"We know you got some more shit stashed. Where is it?"

"That's it, I don't have nothing else."

Candace had already given Ox some instructions.

"That's bullshit. Where's the rest of the shit before we get ugly?" Joy threatened.

"That's it, I swear."

Candace gave Ox a slight nod.

Ox punched Freda squarely in the right eye, probably cracking her eye socket.

It swelled right up into a grotesque black and purple monstrosity.

"Stop. Stop please. I'm telling you I don't have anything else," Dre sounded sincere but Candace still didn't believe him.

Candace, Joy, and Ox stepped into the next room again, and this time Lovely followed. Tammy's gun was now the only thing keeping Dre in control. His fear and adrenaline was starting to overpower the VTX.

"He's bullshitting," Joy said.

"He should have some bricks around," Ox replied.

"Well, I believe him. He wouldn't lie with his woman and child in danger," Lovely said.

"Why wouldn't he lie? He been lying to your ass for years," Ox said to Lovely.

"*What*!? This is different," Lovely didn't want to argue.

"Chill I got a way to find out," Candace said.

Lovely looked at her with apprehension. Candace then whispered something to Ox.

They all returned to the dining room except Ox.

"I'ma ask you one more time: Where the rest of the shit at?" Joy asked.

"I'm telling y'all that's it. I'm waiting for a package to come from Miami. Most of my money went to that," Dre answered.

Just then Ox returned to the dining room with a microwave from the kitchen. She sat it on the table with the door and the controls facing Dre. Ox plugged it in and Candace set the timer for 30 minutes. Ox and Tammy now stood directly behind Dre with guns at the ready.

"You got 30 minutes to think about it," Candace told him.

She then scooped the baby up and tossed him into the microwave, closing the door and pressing start.

Dre leaped to his feet, Ox smacked him with the gun again, but he kept moving towards his son. Joy had a .38 revolver, pulled the hammer back and sat the barrel on Freda's forehead. Freda cried through the shirt stuffed into her mouth.

"I'll tell you! I'll tell you! Stop, stop!" Dre screamed.

Candace pressed stop. The timer read 29:57. She opened the door of the microwave and took the cute little boy out. He looked okay He was still breathing, still handsome, still quiet, but maybe a tad bit darker —who could tell?

Dre told them about a couple of floorboards that could be pulled up in the corner of the basement. Ox and Joy went to retrieve the hidden coke, while Candace and Tammy babysat Dre and Freda who were both frightened and horrified. Freda's eyes blamed Dre and Lovely for her and her son's predicament. Hatred, anger, and rage flooded Dre's eyes, leaving little room for tears. Candace looked at Lovely and she had a few tears in her eyes as well.

Damn she soft, Candace thought. After fifteen minutes, Ox and Joy returned upstairs with twenty-two kilograms of Miami's best cocaine.

Candace then told Tammy and Lovely to go wait in the car. Once they left Candace looked around the house and made sure everything looked like normal suburbia. She then went and wiped off the outside door, the handle, the doorbell and the inside of the door. Candace had instructed everyone to wear gloves inside the home, but she hadn't worn any when she first encountered Freda. Satisfied, she returned to the dining room.

Candace looked at Dre's hate-filled eyes, and at Freda's horror-filled eyes, then turned and shot Dre in the head. Freda started screaming as blood trickled down from the gaping hole in his head. Candace slowly approached Freda who tried to jump up and run although she was still tied to the chair. Candace forced the gun into Freda's hand and pulled the trigger, the bullet blew out the right side of Freda's brain. The baby boy quietly looked on. Candace looked at him, still quiet and thought, he hasn't made a sound all morning, maybe he's retarded or something.

Joy and Ox removed the ropes from around Dre and Freda. Candace let the gun fall naturally from Freda's hand to make it appear as if she had shot herself after killing Dre. Candace put a bowl of cereal in front of Dre. Their plan was that the scene would look like Dre had beat up Freda, hence her black eye. And then Freda shot him in the forehead while he enjoyed his cereal. Then she killed herself, sparing their son. Of course, the microwave was returned to the kitchen.

Candace looked outside before exiting the house. There didn't seem to be any unwanted attention. They all drove off. Candace rode back with Lovely and Tammy. Each car took separate routes, checking constantly to make sure they weren't followed and went to Candace's apartment.

"We never said anything about shooting them," Lovely said.

"We had to or Dre would have killed all of us, and his girlfriend would have told on us," Candace answered.

"What about the baby? Y'all didn't do nothing to him did y'all?" Lovely sounded like she would start crying any minute.

"Of course not, he's okay we left him sitting in his chair smiling."

"I'm not doing anything else—I *swear*," Lovely said before getting quiet.

Whatever, Candace said to herself.

There was no more conversation during the ride.

20

So Much Blow

For the first time in her life, Lovely laid in bed missing a man. It had been so easy to forget the good things about Dre. She now remembered their first meeting and his corny line. She remembered his not forgetting her birthday and the expensive bracelet, he gave her that she still treasured. How could she forget that he had provided her safe haven from Rick. When she was with him she felt so safe, and when he looked at her she felt special.

She no longer felt special. Now Lovely felt like a common thief, a murderer, and a person capable of orphaning a little kid. For three days she saw Freda's accusatory eyes, the hurt and anger in Dre's eyes and their son reaching out for his father. Since that day, she threw herself into her dancing and acting classes, but she lived in a constant state of self-loathing.

She had avoided Joy and Candace and couldn't stand Ox and her slimy cousin. She sensed they were worried about her or that she would do something stupid to hurt them. They didn't have to worry because she loved Joy and Candace. She just hated what they had helped her to become. The three of them were getting together tonight at Candace's house. It would be their first bit of quality time since Dre and Freda's demise.

More and more, Madame Denwa's suggestion that Lovely leave Atlanta for New York or California was looking better. Lovely knew she would have to move soon. Not only was the rent of the apartment she shared with Dre above her means, but she didn't want to be forever reminded of the man she helped kill.

Lovely stretched, yawned and looked at the clock radio. "Woo, I got to get up. If I'm late Madame Denwa will holla' all day." Today she and Madame Denwa went through her lines for her movie role. The role was so small that it was only three lines, but Madame Denwa often said "There are no small parts just small performances. Any amount of time in front of the camera was a chance to shine!"

At Candace's place the excitement was feverish.

"How much can we get for the keys?" Ox asked Candace for the sixtieth time in the past three days.

"Chill out. My aunt in Philly is supposed to call me back today," Candace told Ox again.

"I told you I can get them sold in Brooklyn," Ox suggested.

"My aunt will come through and nobody will fuck with her," Candace stated firmly. She was not about to trust Ox with twenty-two kilos of coke up in New York.

"Is we gonna have to take them to her?" Joy asked.

"Yeah, probably," Candace answered.

"Instead of all the unnecessary bull shit, why not get rid of them around here?" Ox asked.

"Because we don't want to attract attention, maybe?" Joy answered sarcastically for Candace. Every so often Ox's cousin would look up from the TV to check the action in the dining area, especially when Candace, Joy, and Ox got loud. It was obvious she wasn't a team player, and that she was there looking out for her and Ox's best interest.

They had the $165,000, but had decided to sell the keys before breaking the money down. Candace had already started to distrust Ox's judgment and loyalty. Candace hoped that if everything was split up at the same time Ox and her creepy cousin would disappear and go back to Brooklyn or something. Candace also wanted to make sure nobody started spending lots of money all of a sudden, drawing unwanted attention.

Their dining room discussion had broken up. Joy went upstairs to change clothes, Candace was searching the fridge for something to cook later and Ox was watching videos. When the phone rang everybody except for Ox's creepy cousin, rushed to the dining room. On the third ring Candace answered it. It was her aunt.

"Hello? Yeah that sounds good... okay give me two days." Candace hung up and they returned to the dining room.

"What she say? What she say?" How much can we get for 'em?" Ox exploded.

"She said she had a buyer that would take all twenty two of 'em at ten a piece," Candace answered.

"*Damn*! That's low," Joy replied, having learned a lot about the coke game and prices listening to talk around Juvenile.

"Shit, that's good," Ox quickly added.

Ox wanted the deal completed as soon as possible. If the opportunity arose she and her cousin might take the whole thing.

"The price is pretty good since we getting rid of all of them at one time, and my aunt is gonna make sure everything is straight."

Candace's aunt was actually getting twelve a piece for each key, so yeah for $44,000 she would make sure everything was straight up.

"I told her we should be in Philly ready to make the deal by

Friday," Candace told the women.

"Ox, you Joy and me will go up to Philly for the transaction and your cousin can stay here with Lovely 'til we get back," Candace continued.

"Cool," Joy replied.

"Yeah, that sound good," Ox answered satisfied. She had no intention of letting Candace and Joy make the transaction alone. It was bad enough that Candace had stashed the $165,000 and didn't tell anyone where it was.

"How we getting there?" Joy asked.

"I'll tell y'all later. I have to check out a few things first." Candace said with a dismissive tone.

Joy didn't mind Candace's tone. She trusted Candace's judgment and liked her making the decisions. Plus Joy had other things on her mind. She wanted to go freak off with the stripper from the party before she had to be to work. Ox didn't like Candace's tone of voice, but she tolerated it since all this had been Candace's plan and she and her cousin were about to be paid.

AT FIRST STAN WAS ECSTATIC when he found out Dre was dead. It had taken him a lot longer to get rid of a key of coke then he originally thought, especially without attracting G-Man's attention. Then he thought maybe G-Man killed Dre and found out Stan's crossing him. Stan was worried sick, scared to leave the house and barely able to maintain his fledgling coke business.

G-Man stood in the middle of his club admiring his creation. The G-Spot was now Atlanta's number one hot spot and every weekend the crowd grew, along with G-Man's popularity. He admired his appearance in the wall mirror. "Wow, a nigga is looking good. They can't fuck with me," he whispered to himself.

It was amazing what money did for one's appearance. Maybe

it was his imported Italian linen that made his average looks more handsome, or it could have been the confidence he exuded. He didn't care one way or another; his paper was stacking up and the women were now fucking him out of both pants leg.

He was in a very good mood. One of his most hated competitors was dead and he didn't have to get his hands dirty. He knew it would have been just a matter of time before he and Dre engaged in all out war. That's why his security had been so tight. Now G-Man could relax and enjoy the fruits of his labor.

Now was the time to start expanding. He could start supplying weight near Stanton Road and other areas Dre had on lock. He would have to get a couple more safes up in here to hold his dough. He kept his club proceeds and his drug proceeds in a large cast-iron safe in his office. No one would try and rob him around a crowd of people and he was never alone at the club. And the police wouldn't dare run-up in here; everything was totally legit about the club, and the lawyers he had would leave bruises on their asses if they fucked with him. All and all G-Man was living it up with few worries.

21

Close Down Shop

Gator was summoned home by Dre's uncle Ranell, in Miami. Dre's uncle did not like Gator, never had and that's why Gator was scared to return to Miami. While Dre laid up trying to get rid of the extra crispy look it was Gator who held everything intact. Did the uncle appreciate that Gator kept money flowing? No. The arrogant motherfucker always talked to him like he was a peon. He would question him repeatedly about Dre's ass getting burned like he had something to do with it. He had even cut their supply in half like he didn't trust him, petty motherfucker. After sending for Dre's body, the uncle had asked for an accounting of what was left. Gator tried to gather up debts from the streets, but it was hard. He had searched a couple of places he thought would hold cash or coke. He had located $119,000 and eleven keys, but he told Ranell he found $59,000 and five kilos. Now Ranell wanted to see Gator in Miami, hopefully to supply him with more coke and new terms since Gator was now the boss in Georgia. But for now he exited Miami International Airport with trepidation.

A familiar face walked up to him and said, "Gator, my nigga, what's up?"

Recognition was slow on Gator's part, "I'm cool what's up with you?"

"I'm just living the good life dog. Ranell told me you was coming in and suggested I give you a ride."

That's right, he was Spanky from Liberty City. They used to play football against each other in high school, and now he was working for Ranell.

"Thanks man. I could use the ride. You know how these cabs act," Gator replied.

"Yeah, they just want the white fares," Spanky answered.

"Let's be out," Spanky, said, leading him to a car parked nearby.

Gator noticed he was riding good in a brand new Cadillac Eldorado. Not expecting to be in Miami long, Gator had traveled light. He tossed his carry-on bag in the backseat.

"Ranell want you to shoot past his restaurant and holla at him before you get settled," Spanky told him.

Gator knew there was no use refusing, that's what Spanky was there for. Gator would have been no match for his six-feet-three inch, 275 pounds, ex-defensive lineman's girth. They both rode in silence thinking about the opportunities for wealth Ranell could offer them.

Ranell's restaurant was located along the stretch of highway between Miami and Key West. The restaurant also featured a disco that specialized in Jazz. The whole ambience was one of laid-back opulence. The restaurant was accessible by ocean. Speedboats and small yacht owners were regular patrons. Ranell's club was the best spot for food, partying, and rubbing elbows with the wealthy in the southern tip of Miami. When they got to the restaurant it was fairly empty. A black 600 Mercedes Benz that Gator assumed correctly belonged to

Ranell, was in the parking lot. The absence of activity should have been a harbinger of danger. Another large man that looked of African and Grizzly Bear descent stood out in the parking lot. No gun was visible but Gator didn't fool himself. He knew he was having this meeting with Ranell whether he wanted to or not. He no longer cared about more coke or more equal terms, he just wanted to wake up in the morning.

Ranell sat alone feasting on scrambled eggs and large lobster tails. He washed it down with champagne and orange juice. Gator took the seat across from him. "How you doing Mr. Ranell?" he said, a little fawning seemed like a good idea.

"Would you like something to eat?" Ranell replied.

There was no way Gator's stomach could handle a meal right now, so he declined. "No thank you."

"So out of fifty joints all you could find was $59,000 and five of 'em huh?" Ranell said, getting straight to the point.

Gator now wished he turned in the whole 119 thousand and eleven bricks but it was too late to be honest.

"That's all I could find. The rest must have been at his house with him," Gator lied.

"First you let my nephew get burned up, now you let him get murdered, huh?"

"I didn't let!" Gator caught himself and lowered his voice, "I didn't let those things happen. I often told Dre he should use more security around himself."

"But you never did find out who set him on fire, did you?" Ranell asked in his normally calm tone of voice, while still eating his breakfast.

"I tried, but there were so many other hustlers we had beef with I just wasn't sure. We did go to war with that other crew out of Miami though. I swear I'm gonna find out. I got all our people in the streets trying to find out now," Gator replied, becoming more confident he would see another day.

"Well I have decided to shut the Georgia operation down," Ranell said calmly.

Just then Spanky and the Grizzly Bear appeared alongside Gator's chair. For guys the size of mountains they moved quietly. Gator should have been thinking escape instead of how silently they appeared. But it was too late now. They snatched him up from his chair.

"Hold up, hold up. Ranell, what's going on? What I do?"

"You heard me. I'm closing Georgia. Your services are no longer needed."

Ranell got up from his table, leaving Gator and the two monsters together.

Gator was dragged towards the docks where he noticed a filthy, mid-sized fishing boat, which would be his final transportation. Gator looked back hoping to get in one more plea, but all he saw was the back of Ranell's cream-colored shorts and shirt heading towards the parking lot.

"Wait. Wait, Ranell. Please give me one more chance," Gator sobbed as he was half dragged-half carried to the boat.

Another man greeted them with a blackjack that he proceeded to beat Gator with. He fell on the deck, which smelled like death. The smell of blood and guts from thousands of captured fish helped keep the captured Gator from losing consciousness. Gator had no sense of time and he lost count of the blows. Without warning the blows stopped. Maybe his assailants arms had grown tired. Gator lay there whimpering like a broken dog, maimed and immobile but still conscious, unfortunately. This was one time when awareness wasn't a good thing. Gator felt his body being wrapped in chains. He wanted to fight, he wanted to kick and scream, but his will to survive had been lost somewhere among those blows. Now he wished for a quick death, with no more pain. Please, God, no more pain.

It had been over thirty minutes since Gator watched any

hope of reprieve walk out that restaurant door wearing beige linen. The crew found the spot they were looking for and Gator was hoisted overboard, fully enveloped in heavy chains with a couple of fifty pound weight plates to help insure his body never resurfaced. Gator barely heard the splash or registered the wetness, he wanted to pass into death peacefully, but his body's natural responses fought for air. All he wanted to do was die without any more pain, but again his God was a merciless God. His body was attacked by the tiny and the large occupants of the Atlantic Ocean. The pain was unbearable and Gator cursed his creator, cursed Ranell, cursed Dre, and even cursed Aquaman and his vicious ocean friends. Before Gator reached the bottom, the relief he sought finally came, no more life. Now the Atlanta portion of Ranell's drug empire was officially closed. Big Dre and Gator were no more.

AT THE DINNER the night before they left for Philly, Candace and Joy questioned Lovely.

"You didn't tell anyone anything did you?" Joy had asked.

"Of course not; I'm not stupid," Lovely answered, slightly pissed.

"Are you okay? We haven't seen you lately." Candace asked with a little more tact.

"I'm fine. I've been busy rehearsing for the movie role. That's all,"

Lovely said as she tried to ease any concerns.

Candace thought. *Shit it's only three lines. How much practice you need?* But she said nothing. "Well we missed you," Joy said and gave Lovely a real big hug that Candace soon joined.

During and after dinner Candace and Joy discussed how much stuff they could do with the loot. Lovely acted like she was excited about the money, even though more and more she just wanted to leave Georgia, money or no money.

The following evening, Joy, Candace and Ox were on their way to Philly, and Lovely was stuck there with the creepy cousin, Tammy. They had eaten pizza and were now watching the movie 91◁2 weeks, which Lovely found more than a little silly. She couldn't see how a woman could let a man treat her like that, especially a weird one like Mickey Rourke. Tammy seemed to like it and it kept her quiet, so Lovely was pleased with the outcome.

It was after midnight when the movie ended, and Lovely headed upstairs to sleep in Candace's bed. Tammy made herself comfortable on the sofa in front of the TV. Lovely craved sleep and climbed into a pretty nightgown and within minutes entered a sound sleep.

It was late that night when the increase of weight in the bed interrupted Lovely's sleep. She wasn't fully awake, and Lovely lay on her side and the first thought was of Candace and how they shared this bed many times. Maybe Candace had returned already. Then when an arm circled her and a body pressed against hers, she detected a scent that was not Candace's. She jumped out of the bed.

She saw her intruder. "What the fuck is you doing?"

"I was uncomfortable on the sofa," Tammy replied.

"I don't give a fuck, go in the other room."

"Damn, calm down bitch. I thought you was with it," Tammy replied.

"Who the fuck is you calling bitch, 'ho, and with what?" Lovely answered in a fighting stance.

"I already know that you *like* girls."

"What...I don't like your trifling ass. Now get the fuck out of here," Lovely was not playing.

"Fuck you, bitch!"

"No. Fuck you, bitch!" Lovely answered back.

The cousin got up and walked past Lovely. She tried to look

mean but the truth was that Lovely's fierce change in character had her a little intimidated. *Maybe I underestimated her,* Tammy thought.

After she left the room Lovely locked the bedroom door behind her. Lovely tried to go back to sleep but thoughts of that weird bitch trying to have sex with her made her flesh crawl. It took a long time for sleep to return, but before it did, Lovely decided she would definitely get away from Georgia and these people. She would miss Candace and especially Joy, but she couldn't live like this, live like them. She hated leaving her mother, especially while she was getting used to being on her own again. This was the first time in Lovely's life that she saw her mother acting independently and not completely relying on a man, and she was real proud of her. Lovely decided as soon as Candace and Joy got back she would see if Madame Denwa would help her get started in California.

22

Carry and Cash

The Amtrak train rolled along smoothly. The night trip from Atlanta to Philadelphia was very popular and Candace, Joy, and Ox shared a crowded train. Instead of a room they slept in their seats and kept a cautious eye on their luggage. Riding Amtrack was second nature for Ox; it was her normal means of travel between Brooklyn and Atlanta. Candace was as cool as a cucumber, showing no apprehension about traveling with twenty-two keys of coke. Joy was extremely nervous. Even though no law enforcement was around, the uniformed stewards working the trains spooked her. They left Atlanta at 7:10 P.M. and expected to arrive in Philly at 10:45 A.M. the next day.

They arrived at 30th Street Station on time. Being back in Philly gave Candace a charge. Ox had been here before and wasn't impressed. 30th Street Station was small compared to Grand Central Terminal in New York. Joy had never been out of Georgia and was thoroughly impressed. She especially like the Philly girls' fly hair styles and different style of clothing. Joy and Ox visited McDonalds, while Candace called her aunt.

Candace's aunt had the customer on ice, and he was on standby ready to move when the aunt gave the word. They agreed to meet in the food court of the Galleria Mall. Candace figured the mall would be quiet enough at that time of day for them to conduct their business, but far too busy for anyone to try anything slimy.

The cab ride from 30th street to the Galleria Mall took less than ten minutes. Candace decided to place the coke in a locker inside the Greyhound bus terminal, which was around the corner from The Galleria. Ox was left at the station to watch the coke while Candace and Joy went to make the deal. The locker key was in Candace's possession.

They sat at a hamburger joint in the downstairs food court after a lot of walking around. Candace was almost done with her curly fries when her aunt and a large man sporting a thick beard approached. Joy and Candace remained seated while the aunt and her companion joined them.

"Hi" is all Joy managed between bites of food.

"This the guy?" Candace asked her aunt.

"Yeah, this is a friend of mine. He's cool," the aunt replied.

Candace now turned her attention to the man. He was obviously Muslim, because he sported a large Sunna. Most the Muslims in Philly followed the Sunna, which followed the examples of the Prophet Muhammed, which included not cutting the beard

"How you doing? I'm Candace," she introduced herself.

"I'm doing fine Candace, I'm Hev. You ready to do this?"

"Yes, I am. I would like to go take a quick look at the cash in the girl's bathroom, over there, and if everything is cool, I'll go get the stuff and you could go take a quick look. After we are both satisfied we'll make the switch right here." Candace explained.

"That sounds good, here you go," he said and pushed the

shopping bag he had been carrying towards her with his foot. A Hugo Boss sweatshirts sat on top, concealing the stacks of money underneath.

Candace walked to the girl's restroom, found an empty stall, and checked the money. It was official. She returned to the table and slid the bag back to him.

"Everything looks good. I'm gonna leave my friend here 'til I get back with the merchandise. It shouldn't take more than ten minutes, okay." Candace asked Hev and her aunt Sharon.

"Sure," he answered. The aunt nodded her head affirmatively. Joy showed none of her nervousness she exhibited on the train, and she just continued eating.

Candace returned with the merchandise and Ox and then Hev left to look at the bricks. He was real pleased and he let Candace know that when he returned.

The exchange was made and, nobody in the mall seemed any wiser to what was happening. Candace, Joy, and Ox left first, exiting the mall immediately. They caught a cab on Market Street and headed down Delaware Avenue.

On Delaware Avenue, they ate at a Fridays then went and watched a movie. They had time to kill until their train for Atlanta at 3:20 P.M. They made it back to 30th Street Station at 3:05, purchased their tickets, and boarded the train. They were on their way back to Atlanta with $220,000. Today had been a good day!

"OKAY CUT!" the director hollered.

"Ms. Sinclair, can I speak to you for one minute?"

"Yes Mr. Flowers. Is everything alright?"

"I just wanted to tell you that you are doing an excellent job and there may be another role for you after this one," the director told her.

"For real!" Lovely couldn't hide her enthusiasm.

"Yes. A director friend of mine is looking for a young talented actress for a starring role in a small movie."

"A *starring* role?"

"Yes, Lovely, a starring role. So just keep up the good work," he said, then walked off.

"Oh shit, wait 'til I tell Madame Denwa that I might get a starring role," Lovely spoke out loud even though nobody was around to hear her.

Lovely's role had been expanded, and what had started as one scene with three lines was now five additional scenes. The camera loved her.

She wondered who this director was. She tried to guess what kind of role she would be asked to play. Maybe the cold, uncaring lawyer, or the studious teacher, or the sensitive nurse. Most likely a slutty street girl or the heart of gold street 'ho with the abusive pimp. Roles for black women, even those as light-skinned as her, were very limited. Lovely knew an actresses chances were limited, but she would make it. She rushed off to tell Madame Denwa.

23

Westside

Detectives Hutchins and Greenlee had received their first break in the murder of the teenage girls. Forensic had left a message that they had something.

"We got a match!" the petite, mousy looking forensic technician announced.

"What you have?" Detective Hutchins asked impatiently.

"The man who was found dead and bound to a tree with his...penis cut off.

"Yeah, yeah, what you got?" Hutchins asked again.

"There's a genetic match between the dead man and pubic hairs found on all three of our dead teenage victims," the technician proclaimed.

"Are you sure?" Detective Greenlee finally spoke up.

"It's a 99.9 percent probability that he had sex with these girls just prior to their death," the mousy forensic, proclaimed, obviously proud of her find.

"Good. Now we can close those cases. I knew that piece of human garbage probably deserved to have his dick cut off,"

Hutchins said with venom in his voice.

THAT NIGHT DELORES laid in bed with her boss. He was now thirty-seven pounds lighter, sported a very good toupee, and with regular teeth cleaning his breath had become bearable. Delores was a lot happier now with Rick gone. Delores' yellow Corvette was parked in his garage. He was head over heels in love with Delores and wanted her to move in with him. She told him she wasn't ready for that yet, even though she spent most nights there.

Delores was laying in his arms when the news anchor announced, "A man found dead and tied to a tree last week and identified as Rick Benton was positively connected to the three murdered teenage girls found in the last two months on Redwine Road and Niskey Lake Road. Both were locations used by Wayne Williams in the Atlanta Missing and Murder cases. Forensic experts have proven that Rick Benton had sex with the very young girls just prior to their deaths and was probably responsible for their demise."

The news anchor was being irresponsible by calling Rick the probable murderer without the police's say so, but it made for a more sensational story and she was ambitious.

Delores watched the news with rapt attention until she became nauseous. She then bolted to the bathroom and vomited their earlier Chinese dinner into the toilet. Delores sat there bent over the toilet emptying her stomach and crying. She couldn't believe that she and Lovely had been living with a monster all these years.

"CANDACE, LOVELY, COME HERE quick!" Joy yelled to the two girls, "They talking about Rick on the TV—listen," Joy commanded.

"...had sex with the very young girls just prior to their

deaths and was probably responsible for their demise," is what they heard.

"I knew something was wrong with that bastard," Joy said.

"What we miss?" Candace asked.

Joy looked at Lovely and she stood there stunned, looking like someone had punched her in the solar plexus and knocked the wind out of her.

"Here take a seat," Joy said as she helped her sit down.

"Are you alright?" Candace asked.

Lovely nodded, but she didn't look alright.

"That sick, disgusting, fucking pervert. That's good someone cut his dick off, and I hope he was still alive when they did," Candace said with a hate-filled voice. Candace kneeled down and hugged Lovely. Joy quickly joined the hug.

"Are you alright, Love?" Candace was the only person alive that knew of Lovely's nightmare.

"Are you gonna be okay? Do you want something?" Joy didn't know but always suspected that Rick was mentally fucked up and a lot of horrors took place in that house.

"I'm okay. I just need to call my mother."

The phone rang and rang. Nobody was home, and Lovely didn't know her mother's boyfriend's number. Later that night while Lovely slept Candace told Joy about Rick raping Lovely.

Lovely hadn't gotten a chance to tell Candace and Joy she was leaving Atlanta yet. As soon as they had gotten back from Philly things had moved pretty fast. Candace retrieved the $165,000 from behind the screen at the bottom of the refrigerator. The money was split equally among all five of them. They each received $77,000 dollars, and Ox and her cousin announced they were heading back to Brooklyn much to everyone's relief. Candace and Joy had been talking so much about what to do with their money, Lovely hadn't gotten a chance to tell them she was going to California. Now Lovely knew she had to leave soon. She would invite her mother to come too. She probably needed a change of scenery. Maybe if I had said something or done more, those girls wouldn't be dead, Lovely, thought. For now she just enjoyed the comfort of her friends and appreciated the fact that Rick's reign of terror had come to an end.

The next morning Lovely awakened with a throbbing headache. She had nightmares about the horrible atrocities inflicted on her mind and body by men, especially Rick. She took some Tylenol and journeyed downstairs.

"Hey Love, is you feeling better?" Candace was the first to greet her.

"Besides this headache, I'm fine." Lovely said. Wondered if Candace told Joy about their sex, she doubted it.

"Love, is you gonna open a business up with us?" Joy asked.

Now was as good a time to tell them as any, "I'm thinking about moving to California," Lovely answered.

"Oh shit, the girl done got some money and trying to go Hollywood on a bitch," Joy said jokingly.

"I'm serious. I want to go to California so I can pursue my acting. Madame Denwa said…"

"That *bitch* don't know nothing," Joy interrupted, scared to lose her best friend.

" Joy to get noticed I need to be in either New York or California. Plus I got too many bad memories here," Lovely insisted.

"But…I thought all three of us was gonna open a business together." Joy was near tears and she didn't want her only real family to go away,

"Come on Joy. We can't stop Lovely from being a *big* movie star. Plus, I really wanted to go back to Philly and open up a business, Candace added in.

"What! Now you wanna leave too? That's fucked up," a couple of tears did fall, but Joy dried them up real fast.

"Hold up. Hold up. Y'all gonna help me get that fucking G-Man. Y'all promised y'all would help me kill that motherfucker for killing my brother," Joy said, suddenly serious.

"We still gonna help you, right Lovely?" Candace said as she turned in Lovely's direction.

Lovely did not want to have anything to do with more murders, but felt she had no choice.

"Yeah," is all Lovely said and not convincingly.

Joy was obviously upset and left the house. She needed to walk and think. On Washington Road she found a phone booth and called the young stripper. The stripper came and picked her up. Joy felt abandoned by Lovely and Candace and needed to reaffirm her worth in the pleasure she gave someone else's body.

24

Kryptonite

They came up with a plan. Lovely would have to draw the target out, isolate him from everyone else, and they could make their move. In order for Lovely to get near G-Man they needed to go to the G-Spot.

The G-Spot was an orgy of lights, mirrors, and loud music. The gyrating bodies added to the ambiance, which was that of a modern day Sodom and Gomorrah. Nothing was taboo at the G-Spot: alcohol was the appetizer, drugs were the main course, and sex was the dessert. Cocaine was being consumed all over the club. Women in various states of undress were being seduced, groped, and were having their morals corrupted. Sex appealing to a wide variety of appetites was commonplace in the corners, in the bathroom, and in the lounge area. G-Man ruled over this depraved atmosphere proudly, like a new age Caesar.

Lovely, Candace and Joy had never been to the G-Spot, Their entrance was simple but effective. Lovely looked magnificent. She wore a gold Versace dress that looked like a thin layer of honey poured over her ample body. The dress shimmered, slithered and sparkled, drawing everyone's attention. Lovely's hips swayed like the sails on ship, her ass bounced smoothly like ocean waves, and her full breasts and semi-erect nipples dazzled all on-lookers. G-Man's lustful drooling was a very undesirable sight, but nobody noticed. All eyes were on Lovely, especially G-Man's. Her beauty had intensified with maturity and her innocence had blossomed into a strong sexual aura. Lovely rendered men and woman powerless, the way kryptonite did Superman.

The three women stood at the bar as a steady stream of men, wallets in hand came offering to pay for their drinks. After about twenty minutes of standing at the bar watching the spectacle that had become Atlanta's hottest nightclub, a bouncer approached.

"Hello ladies. Is everything to your satisfaction?" he asked.

"Yes, everything is fine," Candace replied.

"Good. Would you ladies like some more drinks, or have any special requests for the D.J.?"

Joy was tempted to take him up on his offers, but Lovely immediately answered, "We're fine thank you."

"Okay then. The owner of this club sent me over here to ask if you ladies could join him at his private table in the V.I.P. area. He said he would like to get to know you." It was an open invitation, but his attention was directed towards Lovely. They looked towards the V.I.P. area and saw G-Man standing at a table alone, smiling in their direction. From the distance he looked real handsome and cultured, all covered in ghetto wealth.

"Tell him thank you, and we will join him soon as we finish our drinks," Candace replied. Lovely and Joy looked in G-Man's direction, checking out the rest of the V.I.P. area.

"Okay, well you ladies enjoy yourselves, and I'll tell him what you said."

As soon as the bouncer left, Lovely's uncertainty kicked in. "Now what?" Lovely asked.

"In a little while we'll go over there, and you wrap that nigga around your finger. That's what," Candace answered.

"Yeah once you get his nose wide open, we get him away from all this security and do his ass in," Joy added.

"I hope I don't have to sleep with him."

"If that's what it takes, that's what it takes. Come on, Love, you know we need you to get close to this bastard. Do it for Calvin."

Joy's pep talk worked.

"Okay, Joy, I already said I would do it. Is y'all ready?"

"Not yet. Let him wait a little longer," Candace replied.

Damn, I got to have that bad motherfucker right there," G-Man told his most trusted bouncer and part-time bodyguard.

"She is the finest woman I ever seen." The bouncer didn't want to say too much and risk G-Man's anger. G-Man was known to flip on a person with very little provocation, especially over women. But G-Man wasn't even listening. His mind and his eyes were transfixed on Lovely. G-Man was ready to beg, pay or take what he wanted. There was no way that he wasn't getting some of that fine, tender meat. If she could fuck that bitch-ass nigga Dre, there was no way G-Man wasn't getting a piece. One way or another, G-Man had decided he was going to fuck the baddest young girl in Atlanta: Lovely Sinclair.

"Hi ladies, welcome to my club. Everyone calls me G-Man. Have a seat and join me."

"Sure my name is Candace."

"How you doing? My name is Joy."

"Hello G-Man. I'm Lovely."

Each of the ladies gave G-Man a light handshake before taking a seat. Upon closer inspection, G-Man wasn't that handsome, but his confidence and his tailored Italian suit gave him some appeal.

"Don't you ladies go to Therell?'

"We did, but we're graduated now," Lovely answered.

"I went to Lakeshore," Candace added.

"I be seeing y'all around but I never really got a chance to meet y'all. I'm glad you decided to check my club out. How you like it?"

At that moment, a platter of jumbo shrimp was placed before each person and champagne was poured. The gigantic bottle was left chilling in a bucket of ice and the waiters disappeared as quietly as they had suddenly appeared.

"I took the liberty of ordering y'all some of our shrimps and champagne. It's delicious, go ahead and try it," G-Man offered with a dazzling charming smile. Joy tore into the shrimp with zeal, Candace ate slower but enthusiastically. The shrimp was very good. Lovely ate very conservatively, taking small bites, careful not to drip any of the butter sauce on her clothing. Her full pouty lips and wide mouth, set off by those enchanting eyes, further inflamed G-Man' desire to have her.

"I hear they just opened a new ride at Six Flags. Would you ladies like to come with me there tomorrow?"

"Me and Joy have to go shopping tomorrow, but maybe Lovely is interested," Candace replied.

Lovely knew that was her cue and she followed up, even though she didn't want to be alone with this so-called G-Man." I have a small part in a movie and have to be at rehearsal early in the morning, but I'm free after twelve o'clock," Lovely submitted.

"That's cool. You want me to pick you up somewhere?" G-Man offered.

"How about I meet you here tomorrow at 12:30," Lovely suggested.

"That's excellent. I'll be waiting," G-Man said, smiling. They talked for a little while longer and parted company. Candace and Joy were real pleased with the way things had worked out and told Lovely lead him on for a little while.

THE NEXT MORNING after rehearsals Lovely met the director that was interested in casting her for his next movie. He was an older black man that she judged to be around forty years old. He looked very academic. He wore spectacles that gave you the impression that he was a knower of all things. He looked very capable of doing anything effectively and Lovely looked forward to acting under his guidance.

His voice was a smooth baritone when he introduced himself.

"Hello Ms. Sinclair, I'm Travis Hopkins, and this is one of the major investors in the film I'm directing called *All About Eve*.

"Hello, Ms. Sinclair. I'm Quentin Taylor, and I think you are an excellent actress," the man, who had the most beautiful eyes she had ever seen, said.

"The role for Eve, who starts off painfully shy and overlooked by everyone. Then her sister comes down from New York to live with her, givers her a makeover and a boost of confidence, and suddenly all the men are crazy about Eve. We think you would be perfect for the role. Are you interested?" the director asked.

"Yes I am. The part sounds very interesting," Lovely answered excitedly.

"Good, very good. We start rehearsals and filming in two weeks here in Atlanta. I will get a script to you in a few days. It was real pleasure meeting you, and I look forward to working with you," the director said.

"Thank you for giving me the opportunity," Lovely replied.

"Ms. Sinclair, it has been an immense pleasure as well," the investor said, extending his hand. They shook hands and again Lovely looked into his smoldering, smoky brown eyes. Their hands held on to one another a second or two longer than necessary. Lovely felt a surge of energy from him and recognized that this was no average man, there was something extraordinary about him. While their hands parted company, his fingers stroked her palm. The two men ventured off with Lovely looking after them excited to be a starring role. *My luck is finally changing for the better.* Then she remembered the rest of her day. "Shit I got to go meet this fucking murderer, G-Man," she said under her breath. She checked her watch and knew that she would be late meeting him, but she also knew he would wait for her.

LOVELY'S TRIP TO SIX FLAGS turned out a lot better than expected. G-Man's company was surprisingly pleasant. She still had reservations when she parked her BMW at G-Spot and rode with him in his new Benz. They left his entourage behind, but she couldn't help but notice them piled up in the club's doorway staring after them. Maybe they couldn't believe she was going out with someone as crude as G-Man.

One of the cutest things to happen was when G-Man repeatedly tried to win her a large Pink Panther at the Ring Toss and couldn't. When he thought she had looked away he bribed the operator to let him win and sure enough, she had a big fuzzy Pink Panther stuffed animal. They enjoyed a bunch of rides except the roller coaster, which scared the shit out of her. He also got a big kick out of the water slide that wet her clothes and messed up her hair. G-Man was a complete gentleman the whole time and even stayed under control when a group of guys kept following them. She had no idea that he had told them, "I don't know if y'all know who I am, but my name is G-Man and if y'all don't stop following us and annoying the shit out of me, I will track each one of y'all down later and kill you in the most painful way I can think of."

The high school guys were shocked and frightened by G-Man's death threat and made themselves very scarce, very quick. Lovely was thoroughly impressed that whatever he told the group made them stop pestering her.

Even though he was good company, Lovely felt no sexual attraction towards him, not even in the Haunted House. She held him tight out of fright, but still didn't feel any romantic chemistry. Lovely was aware that G-Man's reaction was much different. He felt something was there, that he was closer to the drawers and possibly being her man. He even asked, "Lovely do you think one day me and you will be a couple?"

Her job was to lead him on, so she replied, "I don't know—maybe."

After Six Flags they went to Ponderosa and had something to eat. Driving back to Candace's apartment from G-Spot, Lovely felt a little regret over what she was doing. G-Man turned out to be an okay guy. It was hard to believe that he was the one that killed Calvin and his friend Quick. After she helped Joy get her revenge, there would be nothing to keep her in Georgia except her role in *All About Eve.* The investor with the smoky brown eyes did pique her curiosity also.

25

Lovely Attention

Lovely aced her last scene in one take. The director was pleased as was Lovely and her co-star. It was a make out scene and her co-star acted like he didn't hear the director holler "Cut!" Lovely had to pull away from him.

After being congratulated by the cast and thanked by the director for a job well done, Lovely noticed Quentin Taylor watching her. Even from a distance their eyes found one another. For a few minutes she was oblivious to the celebration over the completion of filming. Her mind and eyes feasted on Quentin Taylor. He was about five-feet-ten with the muscular definition and posture of a seasoned athlete. His smile revealed perfect pearly white teeth, and his eyes twinkled, hinting at a bit of mischievousness and mystery. His goatee accentuated his milk chocolate complexion and wavy hair.

On her way to the dressing room Quentin approached her.

"You were breath-taking out there. When the world discovers you, another star will be born," he complimented her.

Lovely blushed, something she hardly did, "Thank you," she

replied.

"The director asked me to give you this script and honestly, I was looking for an excuse to see you again.

"Thank you. I *can't* wait to read it," she answered shyly.

She felt inadequate in this man's powerful aura. She straightened herself out, making sure she wasn't slouching, flattened her clothes out and ran her fingers through her hair. For some reason his approval was important to Lovely.

"I saw what they were trying to pass off as food on the set. If you would allow me I would like to take you to a delicious vegetarian restaurant," he told Lovely, flashing his thousand-watt smile.

"That sounds really nice but I promised the cast I would stop by a little party they're having to celebrate wrapping the film," she told him.

"How about I accompany you there, and we go talk afterwards?"

"Okay. Just let me go get out of these clothes, and we can go."

"Fine. I'll be out here talking to some of these cameramen. We may be able to use them on *All About Eve.*

Lovely rushed to change, clutching her first script as a lead actress. They spent about forty-five minutes with the cast and silently took leave, both anxious to be alone with each other. They ordered a chef salad, vegetarian lasagna, and raspberry tea. Alone in a corner, Quentin Taylor's smile and energy was even more mesmerizing. Even the baritone in his voice was hypnotic. He told Lovely how his family had gotten rich in Louisiana real estate, and how he had graduated from LSU with a degree in business management. He said his family was looking to diversify their assets by investing in music and movies. Lovely told him how she was planning on going to California to concentrate on her acting career.

Long after their meal was completed, they continued talking. The restaurant was semi-empty and Quentin requested some music be played.

"Let's dance," he suggested.

"You serious?"

"Yes, come on," he said as he grabbed her hand and led the way to an open area.

They started dancing to some oldies but goodies like Peaches and Herb's *Reunited, then Turn Off the Lights* by Teddy Pendergrass By the time they played Rolls Royce, *This Ring*, Lovely was totally comfortable in Quentin's arms, enjoying the heaviness of his manhood pressed up against her and the way he nibbled on her neck and ears. So it was music to Lovely's ear when he whispered, "I hope I can change your mind about going to California, I want you here with me." Lovely didn't reply, she just held him closer and smiled on the inside.

They finally left the dance floor. Quentin needed a break before he got blue balls, and Lovely wanted to give her panties a chance to dry. Neither was ready to consummate their attraction, but they wanted the courtship to continue. After leaving the club, Lovely dropped her car off at Candace's and rode with Quentin to Buckhead where they went to a car show. Lovely saw a lot of exotic cars she had never seen before. Quentin arranged to purchase a brand new black Lotus. Lovely was thoroughly impressed, especially since it had been the car she had told him she was unfamiliar with but thought was the prettiest. Quentin Taylor had done everything right, and Lovely was feeling him to the tenth power.

She told him, "Quentin I really, really enjoyed myself today and would like to see you again, but I have to get home."

"No problem, I apologize for keeping you out so long. I just enjoyed your company so much, that I lost track of time."

"It's okay. It's just that I told my girlfriends I would hang out with them tonight."

"Come—let me get you home. Can we get together in a couple of days, say Monday around five o'clock?" he asked.

"Sure I'll give you my phone number and beeper number when we get in the car."

He gave her a light kiss at the door of Candace's apartment. Lovely watched him stride back to his car. He walked with so much style. Lovely was infatuated, but she put that in the back of her mind to get ready to go meet G-Man at the G-Spot. He probably just wanted to show her off to his friends. Lovely hoped Candace and Joy came up with a way to get rid of his ass for good before he started pressuring her for some pussy.

AT 10:15 G-MAN LOOKED AROUND the club for Lovely, "Where is this bitch at?" he said to his favorite bouncer. "Watch, in a little while, I'll have her fine ass trained just like any other bitch," G-Man continued ranting.

"I know you will boss," the bouncer said, but he didn't believe it.

It was another twenty-seven minutes before she arrived—G-Man kept count. She wore a backless cream-colored dress that looked contoured to fit her. She looked in his direction and gave him a smile, but continued to walk the floor before coming over. Jealously he thought, *that little bitch is trying to show her ass off to everybody first*. She finally approached. "Hi G. Sorry I'm late."

"Hi Lovely. You are looking lovely today."

G-Man laughed at his own corny joke, and the bouncer felt obliged to join in. Lovely just stood there and gave a half-hearted smile. She had heard *all* the corny jokes about her name.

Lovely really wasn't feeling G-Man, especially after such an exciting day with Quentin. She stayed a couple of hours, most of the time being G-Man's trophy in his own V.I.P. area. He made a point of calling over a bunch of men for greetings who all gawked at Lovely like she was out of place being with G-Man. She also felt out of place. After a bottle of champagne, G-Man started begging her to go home with him, "Come on, we don't have to do nothing. I just want to lie near you tonight, that's all."

"Not tonight. I told my mom I was coming there tonight so we can go visit my grandmother together,' she lied.

"I can drop you off early."

"Next time, I promise, but I can't tonight," Lovely insisted.

Lovely waited a respectable amount of time and made her exit.

"I'm leaving G. I'll call you tomorrow, okay?"

"Let me drive you."

"No that's alright. Stay and take care of your club." No way was she letting his drunk ass drive her anywhere.

"Okay, give me a kiss," he said, grabbing her around the waist.

She gave him a kiss on the mouth and fought the urge to gag when his saliva-drenched tongue probed her mouth.

When she left, lustful carnivorous looks followed her to the door. On her way to the car, Lovely was accosted by two men in the parking lot.

"So a nigga have to have money to get in those drawers, huh."

"Yeah, if I was selling poison to the whole city could I then get some pussy?" the other one asked.

"Fuck you lames. Get away from me," she told the strangers.

"Fuck you bitch, you ain't…" he was unable to finish.

G-Man's favorite bouncer hit him in the solar plexus, cutting off his last statement. The other guy he pushed forcefully in the chest.

"You want some too?" he asked him.

"Nah man, I don't want no problems," he told the giant.

"Are you okay?" the bouncer asked Lovely.

"Yes, thank you very much," Lovely answered and gave him a reassuring smile. Lovely got in her car, glad to escape the clutched of G-Man, G-Spot, and those clowns in the parking lot. She headed to Candace's apartment, her regular resting place since Dre's murder.

26

Missing Pieces

"Captain, Captain, I think we found a connection."

The two burly detectives rushed into the Captain's office. Their presence instantly made the room seem miniscule.

"Calm down and tell me what you two are so excited about," the Captain commanded.

"Well I think we found a connection between the Miami drug dealer found killed in his home with his girlfriend, the man found dead with his dick cut off and him tied to a tree, that same Miami drug dealer being set on fire in his car on Campbellton Road, and the three people that was killed a couple of years ago in that dope house in Kings Ridge Apartment," Detective Hutchins told him.

"Okay, now that you two geniuses have my attention, why don't you explain your findings? This should be good," the Captain said with a smile.

They both sat "Explain it to him partner," Hutchins said giving Greenlee the opportunity since it was Greenlee who made the connection at first.

"Well Captain, an anonymous male caller with an obvious grudge against an up-and-coming Atlanta drug dealer that goes by the name of G-Man has been calling and providing pieces to the puzzle," Greenlee continued.

"It seems that our Miami drug dealer had gotten upset when G-Man set up shop in his area and ordered the house in Kings Ridge burned down, resulting in the three homicides. In retaliation, the Miami dealer known as Big Dre was attacked by G-Man with a Molotov cocktail on Cambellton Road. A Molotov cocktail was also used in King Ridge," Greenlee paused for greater effect.

"Now the story really gets interesting. Big Dre soon started dating a young woman named Lovely Sinclair. She is also the stepdaughter of the man who was found tied to the tree, who killed the three teenage girls we were investigating."

"This is interesting," the Captain spoke up.

"I told you," Hutchins added in.

"So we been watching and our Atlanta dealer G-Man has opened a nightclub called G-Spot."

"I've seen it. He is coming up," the Captain commented.

"Yes," Greenlee continued. "So we're watching G-Man and guess who pops up? Lovely Sinclair."

"Captain we want to bring this Lovely Sinclair in for questioning," said Greenlee.

"Are you crazy? With that little bit of circumstantial bullshit so the news people can get wind that we are harassing a young girl about a possible one, two, three, four, five, six, seven, eight, nine bodies," he had to count them up, on his fingers. "They would cut the department's nuts off during prime time if you did such a thing. Just continue watching G-Man and dig up some more info on this Lovely Sinclair person," the Captain instructed.

Detectives Greenlee and Hutchins left the Captain's office a little disappointed by his reaction. They were even more determined to put the pieces together and find out Lovely's Sinclair involvement, if any, and bring down Mr. G-Man.

It was unfortunate for the two detectives that one of the calls that came in from Stan had been taken by a deficient policeman. The policeman failed to connect him to the detectives. Placed on hold Stan never got the chance to tell that it was G-Man who killed Calvin and Quick. Had the detectives had that piece of the puzzle they may have connected Lovely to Joy and their plan to get rid of G-Man. But like in most police work, it was the missing clues that made all the difference.

The phone calls to the police had been just another attempt by Stan to rid himself of G-Man. G-Man was still fucking his baby-mother and there was nothing he could do about it. He also feared that G-Man knew that Stan was hustling for himself, as unsuccessful as it was. Stan's lack of real street cred had foot soldiers running off with packages like it was the baton in the four-by-four meters relays. Good thing Big Dre had taken a big sleep 'cause Stan definitely would have been in arrears. Most of the proceeds from that kilo had been spent or fucked over, plus avoiding G-Man kept Stan from developing his full potential as a baller. Stan hoped G-Man's days on the streets were numbered.

LOVELY HAD BEEN STRINGING G-Man along for three weeks, and he was becoming very impatient. Lovely feared that she would soon need a bodyguard to keep him out the pussy. Last time they were together they saw a movie and he had tried to force the issue then.

He even had the nerve to say, "Come on give me some head, ain't nobody looking."

"What! I don't do that G-Man. Plus I ain't no 'ho. I don't just have sex with anybody," she replied.

"Shit, you had sex with that Miami nigga, Dre, and I know you gave *him* head."

"It was almost a year before I gave him some pussy and I *never* gave him head," she lied.

"Yeah, whatever," he said, very irate.

Lovely realized that the statement about Dre waiting a whole year could possibly turn G-Man off or provoke him to do something crazy. So when G-Man slid his hand up her thigh, she allowed him to clumsily finger her as a consolation prize. She should have known better than to wear a short skirt anyway.

At the same time Lovely was stringing G-Man along, she was falling in love with Quentin Taylor. To Candace and Joy's objection, Lovely lied to G-Man that she and her mother were going away for the weekend. Her real plan was to spend the weekend with Quentin Taylor at his cabin on Lake Lanier.

Quentin's cabin was enormous and filled with all the amenities like a hot tub, water beds, big-screen TV, state of the art sound system, bearskin rug, fully stocked fridge and a wet bar. That first night they went sightseeing in his Bronco. They found a nice restaurant and had shrimp, lobster tails, and virgin daiquiris. Lovely only ate fish when she was with Quentin. She was glad he at least still ate fish. After dinner they went to a club and danced for a few songs. But mostly he stood behind her, embracing her while they watched the other dancers.

"Baby, you feel so good in my arms."

"You have such nice arms," Lovely replied.

"I could hold you a lifetime and not get tired."

"I might just let you do that," she sincerely answered.

"Lovely, I don't want you to feel pressured into doing anything this weekend. I plan on being with you a very long time, and it's your heart I want—not just your body."

"Thank you," she said and turned towards him and kissed him passionately. She loved the fact that after three weeks he hadn't pressured her to have sex. She was about ready to give him her heart and body completely. Lovely was falling deeply in love for the first time and he seemed to be falling just as hard.

That night they laid on the bearskin rug in pajamas, eating ice cream from the same bowl, as they watched the movie *Mahogany* on the VCR and discussed their goals. Lovely discussed her desire to act and Quentin said he eventually wanted to not just represent his family in investing and movies, but also to produce and direct his own projects. They talked into the wee hours of the night, dozed off in each other's arms and awakened and retired to separate bedrooms for another sexless night.

They awoke after noon the next day and decided to go horseback riding. After horseback riding they played a couple in volleyball and won, then they decided to take a wilderness hike. After a while Lovely said her feet was bothering her and she wanted to return to the cabin. Quentin carried her more than a quarter mile, only needing to put her down once on the way back.

Once inside the cabin, Quentin made cheese omelettes and fresh squeezed orange juice. They took separate showers and met up in the hot tub. Lovely was a knockout in her two-piece, Donna Karan swimsuit, and Quentin was chiseled in his Ralph Lauren shorts. The water was very calming, and they held hands under the water, content to just be with each other. Lovely decided to climb into Quentin's lap, facing him and kissing his mouth, his neck, his ears, then his mouth, neck and chest. She felt herself being lifted when his manhood became stiff and this excited her even more. He slid the bottom of her bikini to the side and slid two long manicured fingers inside her. She pulled his shorts halfway down and started stroking his penis with her hand. Then she removed his fingers and pushed her wonderfully wet pussy onto his dick and started riding him with soft, sensual, smooth strokes. He was the biggest she had ever experienced and every centimeter of her pussy felt filled. He wasn't impatient. He glided into her down strokes like it was choreographed dance. Her insides pulled him like a vacuum, and their bodies ceased being two as they created one rapture-filled rhythm. They silently rode their wave until they both exploded with orgasmic release.

At that moment they both said, "I love you," with labored breathing into each other's ear.

Still inside her, he picked her up and carried her into the bedroom, laid her on the bed, and unfastened her top and took her bikini bottom off. Then with powerful thrusts he made love to her. After they both came, he pulled himself out of her and they laid above the sheets, her head resting on his chest, in love.

"*Wow*!" she said and meant it.

"Lovely, I'm in love with you and I want you to be my woman."

"I love you too, and I want to be."

"So what about your plans to move to California?"

"I don't know Quentin. I have to finish your movie. We'll see."

He ended their conversation by opening her legs and using his mouth to make love to her body again.

They spent the next day in the cabin in various positions. All day they alternated between sex, talk, eating, sleeping and falling deeper in love. Sunday night on the way home, Lovely held his right hand while he drove with his left. They did very little talking, and instead listened to his mix tape of old and new slow jams. Most of the love songs seem to be speaking for her heart and she enjoyed the high being in love gave her. Quentin Taylor was now her man.

27

I Shot The Sheriff

Lovely returned to Atlanta feeling good from her head to her toes. Even though no music was on she pranced around the apartment singing "I Shot the Sheriff," like she had been handsomely fucked by Jacque St. John of Jamaica himself from Eddie Murphy's *Raw* jokes.

"Look at that heifer, all full of cum and loving it," Joy whispered lightheartedly to Candace.

"She smiling like she had some Superman dick," Candace whispered back.

They knew Lovely was dying to tell them about her weekend so they fucked with her by not asking, even though the suspense was killing their nosey asses.

"Okay, okay you silly bitch. Come tell us about your weekend," Candace broke down first.

Lovely galloped over to where Joy and Candace were sitting, smiling from ear to ear.

"Ahhh girl, Lake Lanier was beautiful. The trees were…"

Candace cut her off, "You know we don't give a fuck about

no scenery. How much fucking did y'all do?" she asked affectionately.

Joy really wasn't interested in dick or it's adventures, but she was pleased that Lovely seemed so happy and if this Quentin could do that, he got four stars in her book.

"You is so nasty," Lovely told Candace. "The first night he showed me around. It was pretty and we went to a restaurant and then to a club. Then back to the cabin, which was plush with waterbeds, hot tub, big screen TV, and the works."

"Yeah what happened at the cabin, *freak*?" Candace asked playfully.

We stayed up real late talking and watching movies. We even roasted some marshmallows over the fireplace. We slept in separate rooms that night and didn't do anything."

"Of course y'all didn't, acting like damn girl scouts and roasting marshmallows,"

Candace said, pretending to be disgusted.

"Ha, ha, ha, ha," Joy laughed.

"Be quiet or I ain't gonna tell y'all what happened." Lovely knew threats of the guillotine couldn't keep her from telling what happened.

"The next day we went horseback riding, demolished a couple in volleyball, and went hiking. When my feet started hurting, my man carried me back to the cabin without getting tired," she bragged.

Candace and Joy noticed her use of the words, *my man* and gave each other a smirk.

"Lovely could you stop dragging this story out all day? I do have some where to be," Joy teased.

"A'ight damn. We did it in his hot tub and he has a big juicy dick and knows how to use it. His body is cut up like a bad bag of dope, muscles everywhere. And as good as the dick was, his pussy eating was better."

"Oh shit, so the brother was like Aqua-man all under water breathing and eating the coochie?" Candace asked.

"No stupid, he carried me to the waterbed, and we didn't leave the bed until the next day."

Lovely eyes glowed when she talked about Quentin. Then she started again, "That's why I shot the sheriff, but I did not shoot the deputy." All three of them broke out laughing.

QUENTIN TAYLOR DID NOT COME to Atlanta to fall in love. He was no more able to control his feelings than he was able to control the changing of the seasons or the Earth's rotation around the Sun. He was there to handle family business, but Lovely was making it hard to stay focused. Quentin was used to the affection of women, especially in Atlanta. Actually, the whole of Georgia was a smorgasbord of beauties with bodacious bodies and giving natures. Quentin had sampled plenty and had remained unattached and eventually unaffected by Georgia's peaches up to now.

Quentin entered the office plaza on Peachtree Street and headed to the third floor via elevator.

"Hello. Is Ms. Cableton in?" Quentin asked the receptionist.

"Yes sir. Can I tell her your name?" the receptionist asked.

"Yes. I'm Quentin Taylor."

"One minute, sir." Tracey, the receptionist, called Janet Cableton's office.

"Ms. Cableton, there is a man by the name of Quentin Taylor to see you."

"I'll be right out, thank you," Ms. Cableton replied.

"She'll be right out," Tracey instructed Quentin.

"Thank you," he said as he continued looking at a map of Atlanta that covered the entire wall.

Tracey Blair stared at Quentin wondering what his dick would taste like. She wondered how thick and long his dick was. Neither she nor any of her girlfriends from Stone Mountain had been with a black man, but they all heard the rumors of black men and their extra large dicks. Tracey's panties had become wet and now she moved her leg back and forth under her desk trying to create friction for an orgasm.

Quentin noticed the blond-haired, breasty receptionist's look of lust but ignored her. At another time he might have hammered her little pink twat for her, but that was before Lovely. Now Lovely had his dick's full attention.

"Hello Mr. Taylor. I have been expecting you," Ms. Cableton offered her hand.

"Hello Ms. Cableton."

"Please, call me Janet."

"Okay Janet." Quentin wasn't surprised to see another blond woman with big breasts, but Janet was a lot better looking than Tracey.

"Would you like to go out and look at those properties?" Janet asked.

"Yes, I would," Quentin replied.

Quentin and Janet drove around Atlanta for three hours looking at properties. A lot of flirting took place inside Quentin's new Lotus, mostly initiated by Janet.

"So Quentin, are you married?" Janet asked.

"No I'm single," he replied.

"A handsome man like you is going to 'cause quite a commotion in our city," Janet gave him a smile that invited him to her drawers.

"Maybe, but right now I'm just focused on business," Quentin replied while thinking of Lovely.

"That's a great attitude," Janet said disappointedly.

They had looked at thirteen houses and Quentin told Janet his investment group was interested in purchasing eight of them.

After house shopping Quentin called the director of *All About Eve*.

"Travis my man, how you doing?" Quentin asked.

"I'm okay Quentin, just very busy that's all."

"I kinda figured that. So when do you expect the actors' rehearsals and filming to start?" Quentin asked.

"We should be ready to start rehearsals in about a month. Right now the stages are being built and costumes being picked," Travis replied.

"That sounds good. Give me a call if you need anything," Quentin instructed.

"Sure. Thanks a lot friend," Travis told him.

"No problem. I'll talk to you soon," Quentin said before hanging up.

After his phone call, Quentin headed over to a travel agency. He hoped Lovely would be willing go on a trip with him. Back at his apartment, Quentin stripped down for a much needed shower and a nap.

Ring, ring

Very few people had his number.

"Hello?" Quentin answered.

"How are things going?" his caller asked.

"Things are going as planned," Quentin immediately recognized the voice.

"What going on with the film?" the caller asked.

"Rehearsals and filming start in about a month," Quentin answered.

"Will everything be taken care of then?"

"Yes, sir," Quentin answered.

"Alright. Call me if anything goes wrong." The caller hung up, not even waiting for Quentin's reply.

After his shower Quentin fell right to sleep. He still hadn't fully recovered from all the energy he exerted over the weekend at Lake Lanier making love to Lovely. Damn that young girl got some *good* pussy, Quentin thought before falling asleep.

28

Front and Back

Lovely was anxious to conclude her business with G-Man. She was sickened by the abundance of death surrounding her lately, and Candace and Joy's callous attitudes towards it. Lovely really regretted setting Dre up. Lovely wasn't a churchgoer or strong believer in the Word, but she was pretty certain that being involved in the death of an innocent woman and orphaning a young child reserved her a seat in hell.

"Lovely, why you so quiet up there? What you thinking about?" Joy asked.

"You mean who is she thinking about, don't you Joy?" Candace asked.

"I wasn't thinking about Quentin. I was wondering what my moms is up to that's all. Y'all don't mind if I stop by there first, do you?" Lovely asked.

"Nah, go ahead. G-Man can wait. If he knew what we had planned for him, he wouldn't be in hurry either," Candace said.

"I might as well check up on my moms too while we here," Joy said with little enthusiasm.

When they pulled up in front of Lovely's old house of horrors, she experienced the same feeling of trepidation she used to experience when Rick was alive. Even with Rick dead, and the house remodeled and repainted to reflect a happier Delores, Lovely hated the house. The sight of it brought back such horrible memories, and her mother's convenient blindness to her torture. But that was another time. Now Lovely and her mother were on good terms.

Lovely parked her BMW and told Joy and Candace she would be right back. Lovely ran up the walkway and used her key to let herself in the house.

"Ma, Ma, you home?" Lovely hollered out. Lovely never went past the living room when her mother wasn't there if she could help it. No one answered Lovely's hollering. She must be with her boyfriend, I hope she's happy, Lovely thought to herself. Lovely returned to her car.

"Let's go. She wasn't there," Lovely told Joy and Candace.

Joy had never been so embarrassed by the squalid conditions she once called home. Now that Joy had seen better pastures, her former residence was a shameful sight. Joy definitely wasn't inviting Lovely and Candace inside. There was no telling what kind of deplorable shape her mother was in.

"I'll be right back," Joy told Lovely and Candace as soon as the car parked. Joy was a lot less anxious to see her mother than Lovely was. Joy's steps were much slower. The raggedy project apartment was looking worse than last time Joy had been there, something that seemed like an impossibility at the time.

Joy opened the door with her key and saw the living room's occupants immediately; Joy's mother was bent over with her ass facing the door. Her filthy blue jeans were around her ankles Her mother was shirtless and her ribs showed through her skin. Her dirty bra was more beige than white. In front of her mother was some young boy around nineteen that Joy recognized as one of the neighborhood drug dealers. The dealer was having his dick sucked by Joy's mother while another young boy fucked her from behind. This sight confirmed Joy's suspicion that her mother graduated to crack. It looked like her mother had found an easy way to pay for her habit. Another miserable soul had fallen prey to crack and was trading her dignity for it. Joy was appalled by the sight and just stood there, door halfway open and her hand still on the doorknob. Joy hated the sight, but couldn't look away until the guy enjoying the blowjob smiled at her.

She closed the door, doubtful that her mother even noticed that she had witnessed her degradation. Joy walked back to the car stunned, fighting back tears. She forced herself to regain composure by the time she rejoined Lovely and Candace.

" Joy, you alright?" Lovely asked.

"Yeah. I'm cool. My mother wasn't home. The apartment just made me think of Calvin that's all." Joy replied.

"Yeah. I really miss him too," Lovely said, reaching back to touch Joy's hand.

"That's why we need to take care of that piece of shit G-Man," Candace added in.

"Yeah, you right," Joy said.

"Yeah," Lovely said.

They continued their drive to The Greenbriar Mall in silence, listening to Keith Sweat on the radio.

That Sunday night, Lovely, Candace and Joy decided to stay in the house together.

"We need to decide what we gonna do about G-Man, because I'm getting tired of him. He wants me to spend the night with him," Lovely told Candace and Joy.

"Do we know where he keeps his money?" Candace asked.

"It still looks like he keeps most of his money in a big safe at his club," Lovely answered.

"We got money. I just want to make sure he suffer for killing my brother," Joy said.

"I just want to get this over with," Lovely said. *The only man I want to be spending the night with is Quentin*, Lovely was thinking.

"Shit, we only have about seventy-five grand a piece. We need to get some more. It's not gonna last," Candace said sternly. *I love you Joy*, Candace thought to herself, *but I'm not killing nobody for free*.

Something on TV caught Candace's attention. "Oh shit turn that up," Candace said. Joy grabbed the remote and turned up the volume. *America's Most Wanted* was profiling Pistol and Jay.

"Pat Johnson aka Pistol and Joe Mackey aka Jay are being sought for allegedly arranging the murder of two rival drug dealers operating in Atlanta." The show went on to re-enact the alleged events of the violent night in 1989. The actors portraying Pistol and Jay were seen giving orders to two other men. Then the two men who received their orders from Pistol and Jay pulled alongside a car and opened fire with a machine gun.

"Damn they is on their ass," Joy said.

"Yeah, it's just a matter of time before they get caught. That's the number one snitch show in the world," Candace said.

"That actor they had playing Pistol was fine. Maybe if Pistol looked that good I would have gave him some," Lovely said.

"Shit! Your legs were clamped tighter than an ant's ass," Joy joked.

"Yeah, that was way before you became the slut that you are now," Candace teased.

"Fuck y'all," Lovely replied laughing and throwing pillows off the sofa at Candace and Joy.

Candace and Joy jumped on Lovely and all three girls wrestled on the floor, laughing their asses off the whole time. They finally settled down and resumed their earlier conversation.

"Lovely what day is the club empty?" Candace asked.

"Monday," Lovely answered.

"Well do you think you can get him over my mother's house alone?" Candace asked.

"For some pussy he'd meet me *anywhere*." Lovely said.

"Why you have a plan?" Joy asked.

"Yeah, but it has to be tomorrow night," Candace replied. "My mom will be back soon."

"Let me call him and see if I can get him to come over tomorrow," Lovely told them.

Persuading G-Man to come over for dinner and possible sleepover had been a piece of cake. Lovely told G-Man it was her grandmother's house and she was out of town.

"He sounded real eager to get with me tomorrow. I told him to pick me up over here at seven o'clock and we would drive over there for dinner and romance," Lovely told Candace and Joy.

"That's good. We have a whole lot to do before then. Come on you lazy 'hoes. Let's get dressed." Candace threw a pillow at Lovely and one at Joy before running upstairs. All three of them had been lounging around the apartment in their panties and bra.

"Put some jeans and sneakers on, we might have to get dirty" Candace told Lovely and Joy. Lovely stole a look at Candace while her back was turned. Lovely admired Candace's take charge attitude. Lovely and Candace stopped their occasional sexual activities together ever since Joy came home from Juvenile. Now Candace, Lovely and Joy were all like sisters.

"Are you going to tell us what the plan is?" Joy asked Candace.

"I'll tell y'all when we get to my mother's house. Now come on y'all get dressed," Candace said. *Finally my brother's death will be avenged*, Joy thought. "I love you Calvin," Joy said under her breath, looking upward hoping Calvin heard her.

"What you say?" Lovely asked.

"Nothing. Let's go," Joy answered.

This time all three girls rode in Candace's Camry to her mother's house in Marietta.

29

Revenge is Sweet

Brown and green leaves crunched underneath Lovely's Nike Air Max sneakers. Lovely couldn't believe Candace's greed and Joy's revenge had brought her to this.

"I'm telling you, this is a stupid ass idea," Lovely said.

"Lovely, trust me. This is the best way," Candace said.

"I agree," Joy added.

"What about your mother? This may be dangerous for her," Lovely told Candace.

"Nobody is gonna come out here. I'm not even sure this part of the lot is hers," Candace replied.

"Whatever. Let's just hurry up then," Lovely was clearly upset.

Joy was impressed with the vastness of the area. Candace's mom must have plenty dough. All Lovely could think about was how out of control things had become. *Damn, I can't wait to get out this state, and I have to get away from Candace and Joy before they get me fucked up*, Lovely was thinking while angrily stomping along.

"Are there any animals out here?" Lovely asked.

"No!" Candace answered.

"How you know?" Lovely asked disbelievingly.

"Because I've been back here a few time, that's how I know," Candace answered, voice full of attitude.

"Come on Lovely. You said you would help me," Joy said.

"Let's just hurry up and find a spot. My name ain't Grizzly Adams," Lovely replied, frustrated and angry.

Nothing much else was said. They found a suitable spot and headed back to the house. Lovely, Candace, and Joy had a lot of hard work to do the next day so they spent the night at Candace's mom house.

Lovely arrived at Candace's apartment ten minutes before G-Man was supposed to pick her up. Lovely had become more comfortable with her beauty and body. At nearly eighteen it seemed like she had been a woman for years. Lovely knew she looked and smelled good. She had on Obsession perfume and was deliciously covered by a Norma Kamali blue dress that made her body talk nothing but seduction. This was G-Man's night: a dinner of steak, potatoes and shrimps awaited him. When the time was right Lovely was gonna surrender her body to G-Man's advances. Lovely sat in the living room until she heard G-Man's Benz pull up. She joined him in his car and they headed to Marietta.

Things were going as planned and G-Man and Lovely were alone. "You got all dressed up for me and everything, huh? You must have really missed me," G-Man said, smiling bashfully.

"Of course I did. I like spending time with you." Lovely said and patted G-Man on his thigh. G-Man blushed a little. Lovely's tease game had improved a lot in the last year or so.

"I was starting to think you was playing games when I didn't hear from you in a while," G-Man still couldn't believe he would be getting in those drawers tonight. He had already decided that if she fronted, he would put his force game down.

"Nah, baby, it wasn't nothing like that. My aunt in Florida got sick, and we went down there that's why we have the house to ourselves tonight," Lovely lied.

"What did you cook?" G-Man asked.

"I'm not telling you; it's a surprise, Lovely teased.

"Oh boy! I hope it don't *kill* me," G-Man told her.

"I *might* if you insult my cooking," Lovely sounded serious.

G-Man looked at Lovely, Lovely looked at G-Man and they both started laughing. Lovely and G-Man enjoyed a nice exchange the whole twenty minutes it took to get to the house.

Dinner was superb and Lovely even surprised herself. They talked some more, mostly about future plans.

"So you really want to be an actress, huh?" G-Man was impressed.

They sat in Sylvia's expensive living room listening to Luther Vandross and talking.

"So where do you see yourself five years from now?" Lovely asked.

"I'm gonna have the most successful night clubs in South Carolina, Tennessee, Mississippi, Louisiana, Alabama, and Florida," G-Man said, confidently.

G-Man sounded so sure of himself. Lovely couldn't help but admire his drive. Lovely had downed a few wine coolers, and G-Man had finished a few beers. Luther had changed to Babyface, then to the Isley Brothers. The atmosphere was charged with a built-up sexual energy. G-Man leaned over and kissed Lovely, and she kissed him back with open willingness.

G-Man lay on top of Lovely and grinded into the softness between her thighs. Lovely could feel G-Man's erect penis trying to push through her dress, through her panties and into her tenderness. He now had his hands between her thighs trying to work his way into her moistness. Lovely stopped his progress.

"Come on, let's go upstairs," Lovely told him.

"Okay," he stood up trying to cover his erection with his shirt.

Lovely straightened out her dress, stood up and ran her fingers through her hair to make it look orderly once again. Lovely led G-Man upstairs to Sylvia's bedroom. Once in the room, Lovely undressed as she faced G-Man whose eyes damn near bulged out of his head. Lovely peeled her dress, bra, and panties off and placed them in a lounge chair that occupied a corner of the room. G-Man undressed himself and placed his clothes on the same chair. Lovely walked over, kissed G-Man on the mouth and then climbed into the bed.

G-Man was on top of Lovely pumping away and she was making all the appropriate noises. Her body was in rhythm with his and it was everything G-Man had thought it was. Lovely was getting loud now.

"Yes! Yes! Yeah baby keep going. That feels *so* good," she said loudly.

"I want you to be my girl forever," G-Man said while ramming away.

"Yes, baby, I'm your girl forever. Don't stop baby, harder, harder!" Lovely yelled.

Just then G-Man heard a creaking noise behind him and tried to ignore it. The pussy was too good to be distracted now. Then he heard another creaking noise too loud to ignore. It originated from somewhere in the room. G-Man looked over his shoulder and saw Candace and Joy exiting a closet.

"Oh shit, what the fuck you..." G-Man jumped out the pussy landing on his feet and turned to meet Candace's and Joy's advance head on. Something was in their hands, but he didn't know what. He charged Candace and punched her in the forehead sending her flying into the lounge chair. He was too late for Joy, though. He felt a sharp, stabbing pain and a thunderous twitch that pushed him back. He tried to advance again, but was forced back again with an even bigger jolt of pain. Then another jolt. He felt himself losing consciousness. Joy hit him again with a jolt of electricity from the stun gun and G-Man was out like a light laying there naked on the floor.

"Candace, you okay?" Lovely stood over Candace, still naked.

"Yeah I'm okay. He hits like a bitch," Candace said. She looked at Joy and Joy looked at G-Man's knocked out ass and all three girls started laughing.

"Oh girl, you was liking that," Candace teased.

"I was faking," Lovely countered.

"It sounded like you was liking it to me," Joy added.

"*Whatever*. Let's get him downstairs before he wakes up," Lovely said.

Lovely got dressed in a pair of jeans, a sweatshirt, and sneakers. Joy was pretty strong from lots of push-ups in Juvenile, so she grabbed his feet and Candace and Lovely each grabbed an arm. They carried G-Man down into the basement and used bicycle chains to fasten him to a stripping pole Sylvia had installed in her basement. G-Man was naked and secured around his legs and with his hands behind his back.

"Here Lovely, plug this in," Candace said.

"Let me wake him up," Joy said.

"Where are those gloves?" Lovely asked.

"On the bar," Candace replied.

Lovely put the industrial strength gloves on. She was still leery of Candace's latest idea.

"Cover the tips with the sponges. Wet them first," Candace told Lovely.

"Is he gonna be able to handle more so soon?" Lovely asked.

"What difference do it make?" Joy asked.

"It makes a big difference. We want the money first," Candace said firmly.

"Wake up motherfucker," Joy slapped G-Man with all her might.

G-Man failed to regain consciousness.

"Maybe he's dead already," Lovely said.

"Let me see," Candace stepped on the stage that held the pole, approached G-Man, and kicked him in his nuts.

G-Man let out a guttural groan that sounded more like a wounded animal than a human.

"See, he's not dead at all," Candace said.

"Wake your bitch ass up," Joy continued smacking and punching G-Man in the face.

"What, what?" G-Man finally awoke, unsure of his location and circumstances. After a few seconds of gathering his senses, G-Man asked, "What the fuck is going on? Let me go."

"We will let you go after you tell us how to get the money from your club," Candace said.

"Bitch please. I ain't giving y'all shit. Lovely, I can't believe you tried some bullshit like this," G-Man said while struggling against his chains. Joy punched G-Man in the mouth, splitting his lip and causing his mouth to bleed.

"You low-life motherfucker. You killed my brother," Joy said while continuing to beat G-Man.

"Wait, wait I don't know your brother. I never killed nobody," G-Man pleaded.

"Yes you did motherfucker, and I'm gonna make you pay," Joy said, beating him more.

"Look, we don't have all day. If you want to live then you will give us that money," Candace said.

"Just tell us how to get the money, and we will leave you here until the owner of the house comes back and we leave town. We know you killed her brother, Calvin. This is your payback," Lovely said, wanting this over with as soon as possible.

"Please Lovely don't do this. I care about you," G-Man said

between tears.

"Fuck that. Lovely hand me those cables and gloves," Candace said.

Candace put the gloves on and touched the two cable ends together, which caused a great spark.

"You still ain't gonna tell us?" Candace touched G-Man with the sponged tips of the battery charger.

G-Man screamed at the top of his lungs as the electricity savagely surged through his body. Candace stopped momentarily.

"Are you ready to tell us?" Candace asked.

"I don't have…" G-Man tried to say more, but the next electricity surge froze his voice. G-Man's body shook uncontrollably in response to the electricity. He started peeing, and Candace jumped out of the way just in time, but a little got on Joy's sneakers.

Joy started punching him again. "You bastard—why did you kill my brother?"

"You gonna tell us how to get the money, or you want more electricity?" Candace asked after G-Man came back to consciousness.

"I'll tell you. I'll tell you" he managed to whisper.

Lovely stood to the side, sickened by all the violence.

G-Man told them which key on his ring opened the club, what the code was to turn off the alarm, and the safe combination.

It had already been decided that Lovely would go retrieve the money from the club. Lovely scrubbed herself clean of makeup and placed her hair inside a baseball cap. They hoped from a distance that no one would notice it was Lovely, and that they may even think it was G-Man. Lovely drove G-Man's Benz to the club. It was dark, traffic was low, and Lovely didn't think she attracted any attention. G-Man hadn't lied, everything went smooth and sixty-five minutes after she left, Lovely came back with a gym back full of money.

While Lovely was gone, Candace and Joy kept watch over G-Man. Joy continued beating on G-Man, crying as she did. "Why you kill my brother?" she continued to ask.

G-Man realized his continued denial pissed Joy off more, so he stopped answering. He refused to admit he killed her brother, Calvin. Joy beat on G-Man until she tired herself out.

"Let me shock his ass some more," Joy told Candace.

"Nah he probably will die if we hit him with more electricity," Candace answered.

"So, we gonna kill him anyway," Joy said.

"Yeah, but let's wait 'til Lovely get back. Let's make sure the numbers he gave was right and she didn't run into any problems," Candace convinced Joy.

When Candace and Joy saw the heavy gym bag they both broke into Kool-Aid smiles.

"Did you have any problems?" Candace asked.

"Not one. Everything went smooth," Lovely replied.

"We can get rid of him now?" Joy asked.

"Yeah shock him some more 'til he passes out," Candace instructed Joy.

"My pleasure," Joy said smiling.

"Yeah, I know," Candace smiled back.

After they were sure that G-Man was unconscious, the part that Lovely really hated started. Candace took the chains off.

"Now we have to drag him to the spot," Candace instructed.

"Are you sure nobody can see us? Shouldn't we cover his body?" Joy asked.

"Nobody lives close enough to see but we can cover him with a blanket just to be safe," Candace said and ran and found one.

"He's still alive. Shouldn't we make sure he's dead first?"

Lovely asked.

"Nah, that's good. I hope he comes to later and has to suffer even more," Joy said, smiling with malice.

"Okay, let's get this over with," Lovely said.

They resumed their prior positions. Joy grabbed G-Man by his ankles, and Candace and Lovely had an arm apiece. Out the back door and through the woods they headed with G-Man's naked body partially covered by a large pink and blue floral pattern blanket.

"I hear animals out here," Lovely claimed.

"There you go, Miss Bionic Ears," Candace said. She was getting tired of Lovely's frightened nature.

"For real. It do sound like I hear something," Lovely insisted.

"Would you two shut up and carry. This piece of shit is getting heavy," Joy ordered.

They carried the body to the far end of the woods, as far away from the house as possible. About thirty feet away from the designate spot G-Man started to stir.

"Hurry up, he's starting to move!" Joy said.

G-Man came around a couple of seconds too late.

"Where…?" G-Man wanted to say more but they tossed his body into a five feet deep grave, which they had dug early that morning.

"Y'all bitches let me out of here," G-Man tried to get his footing. He'd fallen onto his back into the grave and felt as if most of his body was broken and battered. I got to get out of here G-Man thought right before dirt fell onto his face. Using every inch of his strength he got to his feet and tried to claw his way out. The soil around him gave way and he couldn't get a grip. His feet slipped again and again and more dirt fell on top of his head. No way. I can't let no bitches bury me alive—I'm G-Man, he told himself but the dirt didn't know that. His grave was filling up and his chances of survival slimmed down. With the last of his strength and resolve, G-Man leaped up and Joy caught his unfortunate ass with the stun gun, this time in his neck. G-Man fell back into his eternal home, barely alive, and just laid there while being covered with dirt.

After the grave was completely filled, Candace, Lovely, and Joy packed the dirt down as hard as they could. They jumped up and down on it until it was nearly flat. Then they smoothed the footprints away and walked off carrying the blanket back with them. Lovely was smart enough to know it was probably impossible, but she felt she could hear G-Man screaming her name from his grave. Joy was satisfied and felt she had finally kept her last promise to her brother—to avenge his death. Candace smiled inwardly, anxious to see how much money they had from G-Man's club.

They counted $275,000 and felt rich. With what they took from Big Dre, each girl now had about $170,000 apiece. They cleaned the house up and drove back to College Park. Before going to the apartment for some much needed rest they found a quiet empty parking lot and burned G-Man's clothes and the blanket. Then they tossed his jewelry in a dumpster and left his Benz in a parking lot with the keys in the ignition and the inside was wiped clean. After they were satisfied they had rid themselves of G-Man and his belongings, Lovely, Candace and Joy went back to the apartment in Candlewood feeling good about a job well done.

30

America's Most

Pistol had the presence of mind to watch *America's Most Wanted* every week to see if he and Jay were featured. Pistol had already been sporting a full beard, dark shades, and a baseball cap pulled all the way down on his head. Pistol doubted that anyone in Jamaica, Queens would recognize him as the man profiled on *America's Most Wanted*. Pistol believed in being safe not sorry so he and Jay were relocating immediately.

Jay on the other hand, was sure someone would recognize him and call the Feds. Jay couldn't grow a full beard to disguise himself and only sported stubble. He also wore shades and a baseball cap, but was sure his short height and stocky build would give him away. Even the actor portraying him on America's Most Wanted was too much of a look-a-like for his comfort.

Pistol and Jay relocated to Newark, New Jersey and were trying to keep a low profile. After becoming accustomed to the fast pace of New York, Jay started getting restless. "Yo dawg, how long do you think it will be before we can leave the country?" Jay asked.

"Now that we been on T.V., it will be best if we chill for another week or so. Let things die down a little. I should have our fake birth certificates, driver's licenses and passports this week for sure," Pistol replied.

"I'm bored. Let's go do something. Let's go shoot some ball or find some freaks," Jay said.

"Naw, we need to chill. Once we get out the country with our loot we can live like Kings. But for now we need to keep low," Pistol explained.

"Yeah you right," Jay admitted as he got up and went into the kitchen to fix himself some breakfast.

"Yo dawg we out of orange juice and a few other things. I'm fixin' to go to the store and get a few things. You want something?" Jay asked.

"Naw, just be careful," Pistol warned.

Their Ford Taurus was the perfect car. It was a boring blue with the legal amount of tint and no attention grabbing extras. The grocery store around the corner carried all the necessary goods, but Jay wanted a change of scenery and drove an extra five blocks so he could shop at a large market with a more colorful selection of goods and customers.

Damn, I'm so bored that going to the grocery store is now an adventure, Jay thought, looking around the store. It was a dry, hot summer and many women found comfort leisurely cruising the well air-conditioned aisles. Jay saw himself in the overhead mirror and decided that his Fila shorts and shirt hid his developing gut very well. When Jay stopped checking himself out in the mirror and returned his focus to the food aisle he realized a woman was watching him watch himself in the mirror. Jay was a little embarrassed, but the mocha-colored sister with long braids and half-filled grocery cart gave him a beautiful smile. Jay relaxed and returned her smile.

"Don't worry about it, I can't go past a mirror without

checking myself out neither," she said.

"Yeah. Well I'm not that bad, I just wanted to make sure my clothes were fitting right," Jay told her while straightening his shirt.

"Baby, your clothes is looking real good on you," she gave Jay a real friendly smile this time.

Jay now approached, "You looking pretty good in your clothes too," Jay's eyes toured her body brazenly.

"Thank you. My name is India. What's yours?"

"My name is Mark," Jay answered.

She surveyed his shopping cart noticing three containers of orange juice, two large boxes of cereal and a gallon of milk.

"All that cereal means you must not do a lot of cooking," India said.

"Nah I can't cook at *all*. Can you?"

"Of course, don't I look like I eat a lot?"

India said turning around giving Jay a better view of her robust ass and athletic large thighs.

"Yes, baby you are thick and beautiful – just the way I like it. So when you gonna cook for me?" Jay asked.

"If you want, you can come over for breakfast now." Her smile invited him to more than just breakfast.

"I am hungry!" Jay said in a way that suggested food wasn't all his appetite needed.

They paid for their purchases and Jay drove India two blocks to her apartment. In the kitchen, India prepared French toast. Jay stood behind her grinding into her ample ass the whole time. Jay dipped the hot French toast in a saucer filled with syrup and ate while India cooked. He remained behind her, his erection growing into the soft fold of her white shorts. Jay reached around and into her shirt fondling her already erect nipples. Jay removed her shirt and started rubbing syrup onto her breasts. India turned around so Jay could get a mouthful, grabbing his dick and balls.

"Come on Mark, let's go in the bedroom." Jay followed closely behind, hands still fondling.

Jay first explosion was almost immediate but he settled into a groove and was on a down stroke when he heard, "You *stinking* bitch!"

Jay whipped his head around, caught totally off-guard but not unprepared.

"You stinking bitch, I'ma kill you," a very angry man about six-feet-one said and left like he was retrieving an object of mass destruction. Getting dressed was not an option and getting to his jockey strap that held a holster containing a black 38 automatic was Jay's only objective. India had become speechless when just a minute ago she was making all kinds of noise. The angry fellow returned with an aluminum baseball bat ready to play Sammy Sosa upside India and Jay's head.

"I'ma kill y'all," angry said, advancing into the room.

"Bitch ass nigga put that bat down before I blow a hole in your chest bigger than first base," Jay said, standing there nude and menacing.

"*Please* don't shoot him. Brian please put the bat down baby," India whispered.

Oh now the bitch speaks. I should shoot both of they asses, Jay thought.

Brian still hadn't dropped the bat and Jay's patience was non-existent.

"Pow!" a shot reverberated in the sex scented room. The bat fell, and so did Brian.

"Shit! *My* leg!"

India tried to leap off the bed and run to Brian's aid.

"Get your ass back on that bed bitch," Jay told her.

"You. Get your bitch ass over here!" Jay told Brian.

"I can't. My leg hurt." Brian whined.

"Get your bitch ass on the bed before your head hurt." Jay

looked ready to fire again. Jay grabbed his clothes and got dressed standing in the doorway, still holding the gun in one hand. Brian and India hugged.

"Y'all miserable motherfuckers look like y'all deserve each other so I'm gonna let y'all live. But if y'all call the police, I'll come back and murder shit," Jay admonished.

India's house was a few feet apart from her neighbors and Jay thought the shot would go unnoticed. He under estimated the keen hearing of the retired schoolteacher, Miss Crablock, who saw India come home with a man other than her husband and was now paying close attention to the house. Miss Crablock couldn't help but smile when she saw Brian return home early from work. After the shot Crablock called the police, but they were their usual slow selves. When Crablock saw Jay drive off she called in the color, make, and license plate of his Ford Taurus. Jay was arrested a block away from the house he shared with Pistol.

It is taking too long just to go to the store, Pistol started thinking. Damn, something must have happened, Pistol decided. Grabbing up his meager possessions and a duffel bag filled with drug earnings, Pistol made a quick exit. Pistol waved down a cab, took it to the train station, and caught a train to Trenton. Pistol couldn't take chances; if Jay was alright then he would beep him on his skypager. If Jay had been apprehended, there was nothing Pistol could do but save his own ass.

Six days in Trenton and Pistol hadn't heard from Jay so he prepared for his exodus alone.

"Beep, beep, beep, beep, beep," Pistol picked the normally quiet pager off of the cheap blanket the hotel provided. It was a number he had been anxiously awaiting.

"You got those things for me?" Pistol asked the person on the other end. "Good, good. Meet me at Penn Station at six o'clock today," Pistol told him and hung up.

Pistol spotted Benny and indicated with his eyes that they go into a donut shop.

"Let me see the papers," Pistol instructed.

Pistol reviewed the documents.

"This is good. Here's your money," Pistol handed Benny ten thousand dollars for the fake birth certificate, drivers license, and passport.

After Benny left, Pistol boarded an Amtrak train for Texas. His paranoia kept him awake the first five hours, but the solitude of his tiny cabin and the steady hum of the train eventually lulled Pistol to sleep.

Once Pistol got to Houston, Texas he sought out a less formal car lot. There he purchased a red Jeep without showing any identification. Pistol then drove to Brownsville, Texas and crossed the border into Mexico without any hassle. A month into his stay in Mexico, where he had been sharing a house with a beautiful and very quiet young Mexican woman, Pistol found what he was looking for.

"Doc, I need this to be private as possible," Pistol said.

"No problem. For $20,000 I will perform the operation by myself, at my house and no one will ever know about it," the doctor promised.

"Okay, that's perfect," Pistol replied.

"So you come to my house tomorrow night at ten o'clock and by next morning you will be perfect."

"I'll be there Doc," Pistol said.

While Jay lay in a cell twisting and turning while he contemplated a bleak future, Pistol was securing his.

"Doc, you're sure nobody knows about this correct?" Pistol had to be certain.

"I assure you señor, no one knows but me." The doctor was anxious to earn Pistol's $20,000. Pistol hated the idea of being under general anesthesia, but wasn't fool enough to think he could undergo hours of surgery without being knocked out. The doctor applied the gas and Pistol cruised into unconsciousness thinking of Georgia, the origin of all these problems.

Pistol woke up at 7:38 the next morning with a throbbing headache. He reached up to his face, and it was completely bandaged.

"Doctor."

"Good morning Mister Smith. Your operation went very, very well. You wouldn't even recognize yourself," the doctor assured him.

"How long do I have to wear these bandages?" Pistol had now walked over to the mirror in the corner of the doctor's makeshift operating room.

"You can remove the bandages in ten days. There will still be some swelling, but in a month you should be perfect," the doctor said smiling anticipating his money. Pistol surveyed the room. For an operating room in a modest home in the middle of nowhere it was well equipped. Pistol reached in his pocket and handed the doctor the money. The doctor took the money gleefully. Pistol was more weak than he had anticipated so his first plan of action had to be abandoned.

The doctor stood there counting the hundred dollar bills while Pistol toured the room. When the doctor looked up Pistol was walking up on him. Assuming that the rich American wished to say his goodbyes, the doctor switched the money from his right hand to his left hand preparing for a handshake. Pistol's right hand was raised but it wasn't empty. The scalpel sliced through the air, barely seen before the doctor was holding his throat, trying to keep himself from bleeding to death. The doctor reached for Pistol, more in search of aid than retaliation. Pistol stepped aside and the doctor fell face down, his blood defiling an otherwise spotless room. Pistol watched him die, then searched the house with surgical gloves on to make sure no pictures or information about him had been retained by the doctor. When he was satisfied, he went out into the hot oasis of southern Mexico and hopped into his Jeep.

Pistol couldn't let the only person who knew what he looked like both before and after his plastic surgery live. With his old face having appeared across millions of T.V. screens, Pistol needed a new one. He drove to the home he had rented in Belize earlier, just for this purpose. He would stay in this house fully stocked with all his necessities for a month and a half. The plastic surgery was a complete success, and Pistol left Belize for parts unknown.

31

I'm Back

The streets were talking, but no one could say what happened to G-Man.

"I think he was playing games with somebody money and they iced him. Probably the Columbians," Fred, a loquacious drug dealer said.

"I believe the Feds were on him so he disappeared with his millions," Tommy said.

They stood around the Martin Luther King Boulevard selling drugs, smoking weed and, making lewd remarks.

"Big butt, big butt, come here and let me get a ride on that yellow bus," Fred hollered to a teenage girl in yellow shorts.

"Damn shawty, let me make a sandwich with all that meat," Tommy told a young lady in red daisy dukes that were so short that they revealed cheeks a shade lighter than her tanned legs.

"Nah, y'all don't know what y'all talking about. Stan had G-Man plucked and gonna take over his operation," Skeeter announced like it was a certainty.

"Hell nah, Stan is soft. Stan is not cut like that," Flip added in.

"I'm telling y'all it had something to do with that bad young girl, Lovely. I bet she had a man that did G-Man in before he could get the drawers," Hickeyman announced.

"Five-O, Five-O," someone hollered, alerting the area to the arrival of the police. The corner cleared out. Dealers scattered like gazelles when the lions came. The girl in the red daisy dukes saw someone throw down their weed bags and picked them up. She placed them in her purse for later. Today she would get her boyfriend high. She loved when he fucked her weeded up.

STAN WAS IN HEAVEN. He hadn't gotten rid of G-Man, but he was loving the rumors that he did. His drug business had experienced a resurgence in the last three weeks. He now gave out packages and got all his money back. People now thought he would be their next big money maker, and they flocked to him with more money making opportunities. Best of all, the women were showing him a lot more respect and attention, especially his son's mother.

"Stan can we do something together today?" Sherrie asked.

"Not today, I'm busy. I did have fun last night though," Stan told her.

Damn, the sex been unbelievable since G-Man disappeared. Maybe she's scared I might kill her too, Stan was thinking.

"Okay, I love you. Will I see you tonight?" she asked.

"I don't know. Stop bothering me," Stan said enjoying his new dominant role.

"Okay baby. I'm a go fix you some breakfast."

"Yeah, go do that and wake my son up so I can play with him before I go."

"Stan can you leave me a few dollars so I can buy groceries and me and little Stanley a couple of outfits."

"I'll see. Now go fix my breakfast."

Sherrie had never been this docile towards Stan.

"That's right you cheating bitch, I'm the man now. Go fix my breakfast." He didn't say it loud enough for her to hear. Stan was still soft inside and didn't want to push his luck.

Stan was working hard to change his old image and foster the newfound belief in his gangsterism. If the streets wanted to believe that he was a cunning individual then Stan would help them. Stan made another bold move by purchasing a Kawasaki Ninja motorcycle for the summer. He no longer made phone calls to the police, and he had found another coke connection.

"Ju was a friend of G-Man, and now Ju want to buy some car parts too?" the coke connect inquired.

"Yes, I want to come get my car parts from you," Stan told him.

"Okay, Ju come down. G-Man was good friend and customer. Ju friend of his, Ju friend of mine," Juan said in his thick accent.

Stan would be going down to Pensecola, Florida to buy two kilos from G-Man's old connect, Juan.

Stan looked down at his right calf, the burn had started to heal, leaving a darker pigmentation. In the three weeks since purchasing the motorcycle Stan had become a much better rider. He no longer accidentally touched the exhaust pipe with his calf.

Stan was on I-95 riding behind a stolen red camaro driven by sixteen and seventeen-year-old brothers.

"Robert, go ahead and light that weed up."

"Yeah," Dexter said, digging in his pocket for the joint.

The stolen car started to fill with the strong aroma of southern marijuana.

A car with four Spellman college women bored and on school vacation spotted Stan in the next lane looking good on his motorcycle. Windows down already in their old Toyota, they started flirting.

"Hi sexy."

"You sure got some nice legs," another female hollered.

"Can I ride with you?" another yelled while the car tried to keep pace with the Ninja. This was the kind of attention Stan was starting to experience all over town, and it nourished his growing ego. Stan just smiled in their direction. At that same moment Robert dropped the joint in his lap, and it burned a hole through his cheap cotton shorts. Robert stomped on the brakes.

"Whoa. What the fuck is you doing?" Dexter asked.

"The reefer damn near burned my dick," Robert answered.

Stan only turned his head momentarily, but that was enough. Stan's motorcycle crashed into the back of the Camaro, sending his body flying through the air like a ball shot out a cannon. He wore his protective helmet, but that didn't keep his neck from snapping like a twig in a windstorm.

The girls saw the accident in their rear view mirror and kept it moving not wanting to spoil their day being bothered with police and ambulances. The brothers saw Stan lying three feet in front of their car, his head twisted an unnatural angle.

"Man let's get the fuck out of here," Dexter said panic stricken.

Robert didn't even bother to answer, he just drove around Stan. They drove on hoping the hoodrats they were going to meet had some more weed.

Stan died on I-95 that day in the sweltering heat of Atlanta. He never really got a chance to enjoy the fruits of his slimy ways and the street's false rumors. Before he was buried four days later, another up and coming drug dealer was the focal point of the street's attention.

SYLVIA HAD RETURNED from her shopping trip. She had purchased two Brazilian women with wicked bodies and angelic faces. Sylvia picked up two Norwegian blondes six feet tall, with hard chiseled bodies and a little mean streak that would be perfect for their dominatrix roles. She also found two Asian women with so many skills at sexual manipulations that they could start their own sex college. These six women were cheap and very subservient to Sylvia who had rescued them from a mundane existence that almost guaranteed a lifetime of poverty. Sylvia was determined to have the best escort service in the south. In each location after she found the perfect young lady, she made arrangements with a local lawyer to handle paperwork and send the ladies to America. She spent yesterday going back and forth to the airport to pick the girls up. Right now all six ladies were roaming around the large house, awed by it's opulence. All the ladies knew a little English, had cute accents, gregarious personalities and were already bonding. They were now part of a sisterhood: Sylvia's sisterhood of sex.

Sylvia went around surveying her home. *I'm glad that girl, didn't destroy my house*, Sylvia thought about her daughter Candace.

"Ladies come down to the basement so we can have our first meeting," Sylvia told the exotic mix of sexual delights. After everyone was seated comfortably and looking up at Sylvia with rapt attention, she gave them their most important talk.

"Ladies, look around you. These are your new sisters and business partners." Each girl looked to one another with friendly, sincere smiles.

"Me? I'm like your surrogate mother and C.E.O. of our business." Sylvia looked around and received all knowing and agreeing nods. Sylvia noticed Mae Wong was already becoming the leader of the six women and Sylvia liked that. Mae was twenty-three-years-old and had been the mistress of a rich businessman since she was fourteen-years-old until he was murdered in a teahouse in downtown Hong Kong. Mae had been more desperate than any of them to come to America and work for Sylvia.

Mae would make an excellent second in command. Sylvia continued her speech, " We will provide professional entertainment and conduct ourselves in a business like manner at all times. All proceeds will be returned to the company and you will receive twenty-five percent of each transaction and all your expenses will be taken care of by me." She paused for emphasis. "If I find out you are not conducting yourself professionally or you are a thief, I will return you home immediately. Back to your old existence," Sylvia saw the fear in their eyes when she threatened to send them back home.

"Ladies this will be your home. All work will be conducted in first-class hotels. I will provide cars for your transportation. Can any of you drive?" Sylvia asked. Mae and the two Norwegians were the only ones who raised their hands.

"Good. I'll get you three driver's licenses and get you an instructor to adjust you to driving in the U.S. You other girls will be driven by those three. Now you beautiful women go clean yourselves up, and I will take y'all on a shopping spree." Sylvia concluded her meeting. The women ran off gleefully to get ready. Mae hung back.

"Mae, I'm gonna need you to watch them and help them along, okay?" Sylvia asked.

"Yes, Ms. Sylvia. I won't let you down," Mae said sincerely, relishing her important role.

"Now go, get ready. I'm gonna buy all of y'all beautiful clothes."

"Yes, ma'am," Mae replied and hurried off to join her sisters.

Sylvia went outside to check her garden while the women were getting ready. Everything was going as planned, and Sylvia didn't have a worry in the world. She would never know G-Man was buried in her woods.

32

Looking for Me

"Captain, remember we told you how all those murders were somehow connected to Lovely Sinclair?" Detective Hutchins asked.

"Yes. I also remember she was a teenager with no record, and you had no solid evidence against her," the captain answered annoyed.

"Remember we told you she was now seeing another drug dealer connected to this whole blood fest named G-Man?" Greenlee asked.

"Yes, I remember that too."

"Well now, he has disappeared. His car found stripped and abandoned, but he hasn't turned up," Detective Greenlee spoke up.

"Well do you now have any hard evidence?"

"She was seeing him," Hutchins said.

"We still don't have any hard evidence, but we wanted to bring her in for questioning," Greenlee continued.

"Okay, but not as suspect. Just go nice and ask her if she

knows anything about her boyfriend's disappearance,"

"Can't" Hutchins said.

"What you mean can't?"

"Now we can't find her," Greenlee said.

"Then get the hell out my office, and go find her."

"Okay," Greenlee said.

"Can I have that Danish?" Hutchins asked.

"Get the hell out my office now."

Detectives Hutching and Greenlee left the office laughing. They had saw the food stains on the Captain's shirt and ugly tie. Now they would tear the streets up looking for Lovely Sinclair.

LOVELY WAS IN THE BATHROOM taking a shit before Quentin got back. She had been staying with Quentin in his condo for two weeks and still hadn't taken a shit around him. It was still too early in the falling in love stage. Lovely still felt she had to be 100 percent perfect around him. It had been the best two weeks of her young life. His intellect, sensitivity, love for her, and excellent lovemaking skills had captured Lovely's heart completely. He even talked about them sharing a home in California after filming of the movie was completed. Quentin said it was just a matter of time before his family business made it out west, and Lovely was perfect reason to go now.

Lovely hadn't spent much time with Candace and Joy since G-Man's death. Last night Joy had called her sounding panicky about an emergency she didn't want to discuss over the phone. All three girls were getting together today at Candace's apartment. Lovely hoped they weren't going to try and convince her to come with them again. They had decided against Philly and were now moving to Richmond, Virginia to open a clothing store. Filming for her starring role movie was to begin next month and soon as she was finished, Lovely was moving to California. If everything worked out right, Quentin Taylor would be coming with her. Lovely cleaned the condo and went over Candace's.

As soon as Lovely entered the apartment, the excitement erupted.

"Girl, the police was over here looking for you," Joy shrieked, worried.

"They probably just want to ask you some questions about your step-father," Candace said, trying to convey calmness.

"Girl it was two big detectives, and they looked serious. What we gonna do?" Joy asked.

Lovely was unable to speak. She just sat down on the sofa mortified. All of Lovely's fears washed over her like a flood.

"Fuck them. If they had anything, they would have came with an arrest warrant for Lovely and at least would have wanted to talk to us too," Candace said.

Candace seemed completely unfazed, but she couldn't wait to get the fuck out of Georgia.

"What should I do?" Lovely finally spoke.

"You need to get out of Georgia and come to Virginia with us." Joy gave her a predictable suggestion.

"She's right. You should avoid them until you know what they want. If it's serious they will go to your mother's house with a warrant." Candace sounded certain of police procedure.

"Well I'm not turning myself in to answer no questions, but I'm not leaving either. I have a movie to make next month."

"There will be other movie roles. You should come with us to Virginia for a little while," Candace suggested.

"Yeah," Joy agreed.

Lovely just sat there thinking for while, worry clouding her hazel eyes.

"I'm not leaving. I'm gonna stay over Quentin's make my movie, then move to California," Lovely decided she wouldn't let her dreams be derailed over this.

QUENTIN HAD DELAYED inviting Lovely on the romantic trip to Barbados. He had been enjoying her stay over his house and they had gotten so close. If they were going they would have to go soon because filming on *All About Eve* was going to start soon. It would be impossible to get Lovely on a trip then. He had rented an ocean front property for their trip. He would ask her tonight while they enjoyed dinner together.

"Oh baby, you cooked?" Lovely was thoroughly surprised.

"Yes. You been cooking me such delicious meals lately, I wanted to treat you," Quentin said.

He opened a pot lid and an aroma of spices filled the kitchen.

"*Uhm*, it smells good. What is it?" Lovely said.

"Seafood Jambalaya. Now why don't you go get comfortable while I finish this up."

"Okay," Lovely said and trotted upstairs to take a shower and get into some of her Victoria's Secret attire. My baby is so sweet, making me dinner, Lovely thought on her way downstairs. Quentin must have used the shower downstairs, because now he was in a silk lounging robe lighting candles around the table.

He saw Lovely and smiled, "Wow you look great."

"You do too," Lovely said giving him a hug and kiss. Then they sat down to devour Quentin's delicious creation.

Quentin had gotten up to retrieve another wine cooler from the kitchen while Lovely remained in the dining room. He came back with her cooler and some brochures.

"What's this?" Lovely asked.

"I want you to come with me to Barbados for some fun and romance."

"I would love to, but what about my movie?" Lovely asked.

"The trip lasts two weeks and they won't need you for another three weeks—I checked," Quentin gave her the megawatt smile.

"I love you!" Lovely gave him a big hug and kiss.

Quentin had been kneeling down besides Lovely's chair. He picked her up and carried her upstairs to their bedroom. They made slow, gentle love before they fell asleep holding each other.

LOVELY HAD BEEN SPENDING a lot of her free time with Madame Denwa to sharpen her skills. After three hours of personal instruction, Lovely was pleased with herself.

"Lovely you have really gotten better these last couple of months. You now know how to tap into your own emotional well and bring that to your character," Madame Denwa said giving Lovely a rare compliment.

"Thank you Madame."

"Lovely, there is really nothing else. Now you must move on."

"What do you mean?" Lovely had grown attached to Madame Denwa's eccentric ways.

"I mean after you finish filming your movie, it's time for you to go to California. I have spoken to some people out there about you. The best acting coach out there wants you to join his class, and I arranged for you to meet with one of Hollywood's most influential agents," Madame Denwa told Lovely.

"Thank you, thank you!" Lovely hugged Madame Denwa.

She let Lovely hug her for a few seconds then said, "Enough, enough, enough. Now let me see you go over that scene again."

Lovely practiced her range of emotions and subtle gestures needed to give a captivating performance for another hour and a half, then went to meet her mother.

Lovely sat at a window seat watching the parking lot, like a fugitive on the run. She finally relaxed a little when she saw her mother's yellow Corvette pull into the parking lot. Delores was beautiful in her business suit skirt set. Delores had a youthful buoyancy Lovely hadn't seen in years.

"Hi mom."

"Hi my talented daughter. How's filming going?"

"We don't start filming until next month," Lovely told her mother while they embraced.

"Ma, you look great!"

"Well, I've been going to the gym lately," Delores answered as she twirled, giving Lovely a better view.

"*Oooh wee*, Ma, you got it going on!" Lovely said.

"You so silly. Come on let's order. I'm on my lunch break," Delores led them to a back table.

Lovely was unfamiliar with this Italian restaurant. As they waited for their chicken parmesean and spaghetti, Lovely opened the conversation.

"Ma, have any police been by the house?"

"Why would police be coming to the house?" Delores said alarmed.

"This guy I was dating is missing, and they probably wanted to ask me some questions," Lovely told her.

"Baby you really need to leave those street guys alone before they get you in trouble,"

Delores warned her daughter.

If she only knew, Lovely thought but instead she said, "I am. My new friend is very legit."

"I haven't been home in two weeks. I have been staying over Burt's house and haven't seen any police," Delores said, still sounding worried.

"It's nothing important. I'm not in any trouble. They just wanted to ask me a few questions. They came by Candace's apartment."

Their conversation paused when their food arrived.

"So Ma, are you serious about Burt?"

"Yes, and he asked me to marry him."

"For real? Are you gonna marry him?" Lovely perked up.

"No. I'm not ready to remarry, but I like him a lot and he treats me really good."

"That's great. I'm happy for you," Lovely said between bites.

"Ma, my friend, Quentin, and I are going on a two week trip to Barbados."

"Is this Quentin a nice guy?" Delores asked.

"Yes he is. He works for his family in film and real estate, and he has a college degree."

"Well baby, enjoy yourself. Be careful, and I want to meet this Quentin soon," Delores said.

"You will," Lovely said, glad she got her mother's approval.

"I love you baby. Please be careful," Delores said after their meal.

"I will Ma. I promise, and I love you too," Lovely said as she gave her mother a big hug and kiss on her cheek.

Lovely watched her mother pull off in her Corvette. Lovely was happier than she had been in a long time and glad to see her mother was too.

33

Welcome Back

The day before leaving for their trip Quentin spoiled Lovely.

"Quentin I don't need anything else. Let's go home," Lovely pleaded.

"What about some more bathing suits?"

"No, I have six new ones now. Thank you, sweetheart. I want to go to bed," Lovely gave him that seductive look that always got him revved-up.

They had four large shopping bags. Three of the bags were filled with new purchases for Lovely and Quentin's bag had a few more things for Lovely. They spent the day together, holding hands and making an enormous amount of purchases for their trip to Barbados. In one store Lovely and Quentin had even snuck a quickie inside the ladies' dressing room. With Quentin, Lovely was experiencing orgasms from penetration and starting to love sex.

Quentin dropped Lovely off at the condo promising to hurry back. He rushed off to meet Janet Cableton who had some more interesting properties to show him. The family business was thriving in Georgia, and everyone back home was pleased with Quentin. It was Quentin's family who encouraged him to take his well-earned vacation.

BARBADOS WAS BREATHTAKING. Lovely and Quentin arrived on the island in the early evening and were greeted by an azure sky. This had been Lovely's first flight, and she was a little nervous, but Quentin cuddled with her in their first class seats. The beautiful exotic scenery was enough to alleviate her nervousness. By the time the plane eased onto the runway, Lovely was her usual vigorous self.

Baby, it's so pretty. Thank you," Lovely said.

"Yes, it's lovely like you," Quentin replied.

Lovely gave him a big kiss. That was one of the few plays on her name that she liked. Inside the airport everyone moved at a leisurely pace. Most of the people looked so peaceful and Lovely took Quentin's hand, suddenly overwhelmed with romance.

"Welcome to Barbados. It would be my pleasure to drive you anywhere you need to go." The cab driver's melodious accent sounded good accompanied by his friendly smile. Lovely and Quentin watched the gorgeous landscape with wide-eyed excitement on their way to their love nest, which turned out to be a two-bedroom beachfront abode with all the amenities including a fully-stocked refrigerator, sauna, wet bar and entertainment center. With lush greenery, white sands, clear blue waters and a star-filled sky awaiting them, Lovely and Quentin didn't remain inside long.

"I'll race you," Lovely took off running barefoot and beautiful in a long linen skirt and cut off shirt.

"Wait up, you cheater," Quentin said. It didn't take him long with his athletic strides to catch up.

Lovely felt him approaching and curved left toward the

ocean. Warm and refreshing water washed over Lovely's feet and splashed her thighs. Quentin caught up, grabbed her by the waist and lifted her up carrying her deeper into the water.

"I won!" Lovely hollered.

"No you *didn't*," Quentin laughed.

They fell together in the water, which was up to their chests now. Quentin turned Lovely towards him, and they immediately melted into a lover's embrace. Their kisses were hotter than the 80-degree weather.

"I love you *so* much, Quentin!"

"And I love you even more, Miss Lovely Sinclair."

They kissed some more while the waves splashed them, unable to dissipate their passion.

At a small café near their beachfront dwelling, they enjoyed a Caribbean treat of conch fricassee, fresh salad, and a sherbet made with delicious fruit from the island. Holding hands, Lovely and Quentin walked back to their love nest. In a large canopy bed surrounded by a mosquito net, Lovely experienced the most intense, meaningful, love-filled orgasm of her young life. That night Lovely finally passed out while cumming, her pussy being feasted on by Quentin and her brain unable to stop her from repeatedly saying "I love you. I love you. I love you."

They spent their first week snorkeling, horseback riding, jet skiing, exploring the terrain, and lounging on the beach. Most of their days were spent enjoying all of Barbados and most of their nights were spent enjoying each other.

As their trip to paradise drew to an end, their passion took on more of an urgency. Less time was spent around others. Lovely and Quentin wanted all of their last utopian hours spent unbridled and uninterrupted.

Their last night together in Barbados took on a sad tender quality as if Quentin and Lovely knew it would be a very long time before they could spend time together like this again.

Lovely lay under the mosquito net, completely naked as Quentin fed her shrimp. Afterwards Lovely clipped her man's fingernails and toenails.

"Baby, I'm not ready to leave yet. I love it here," Lovely sighed.

"I know but this won't be our last trip. There are plenty of other exotic places for us to visit," Quentin assured her.

"Yeah but it will never be as special as our first time together out the country," Lovely said, as she laid in his arms.

"You're right. This trip was unbelievable. You were unbelievable," Quentin gave Lovely a long kiss.

"I love you Quentin. I have never loved anyone like I love you," Lovely said when their kiss ended.

"I have *never* loved anyone the way I love you either, Miss Lovely Sinclair."

They broke into big smiles, soon overcome by an intense need to make love again.

Quentin wanted to make the trip home as memorable as the rest of their time together and arranged the use of a boat for their return. Quentin surprised Lovely when he showed her the boat.

"Wow, that's a big boat. You sure you can drive that?" Lovely asked.

"Yes, I can drive it," Quentin answered laughing.

"Why you laughing?" Lovely asked.

"Cause baby you drive cars. We gonna sail this."

"Aw shit, I hope this isn't about to turn into another Gilligan trip," Lovely teased.

"Damn, you calling me another Gilligan?" Quentin pretended to be insulted.

"Well yeah! But you are a lot sexier," Lovely joked.

"Come on. Let me show you around," Quentin said as he led Lovely onto their new means of transportation.

The fifty-foot sailboat was in excellent condition. It also had a large diesel engine in case wind conditions weren't satisfactory. Quentin showed her the galley, the head and the sleeping quarters. The boat was small but posh, and Lovely seemed pleased.

Quentin had decided to take a leisurely cruise around the eastern Caribbean, then north through the Atlantic. His boating experience was good enough to get them to their destination, and Lovely would make a great first mate.

"Okay, raise the sails," he ordered Lovely, jokingly.

"Aye, aye captain," she replied with her most official-looking salute.

"You so silly," Quentin said before they started hugging and kissing.

Their first full day at sea they woke up to find a group of flying fish alongside their boat. The silvery incandescence of these wing-finned creatures shined like jewels as they gave a synchronized show. The school of fish would leap out the water and gracefully sail through the air in a flawless unison. Lovely and Quentin enjoyed the show until the fish decided there was somewhere else they had to be.

For any other two people the cramped quarters may have been unpleasant but for Lovely and Quentin it was intoxicating. They made love on deck day and night while the boat cruised. The couple acted like newlyweds on their honeymoon.

The S.S. Lovefest, which Quentin had aptly started calling their little love boat, made several stops along the way. They made short stops at Saint Lucia, Martinique. Virgin Islands, and the Bahamas before reaching U.S. shores.

Quentin Taylor had been neglecting the family business, but he phoned an important associate from the boat. Quentin told the associate that he would be arriving back from his vacation.

When the S.S. Lovefest pulled up to dock three men awaited. Sun tanned and holding hands, Lovely and Quentin exited the boat.

"Hello, you must be Lovely Sinclair," a tall well-dressed man said.

"Yes I am. How are you?" she answered.

"I'm feeling a lot better now. I've been waiting to meet you."

The men ignored Quentin for the time being and focused on Lovely. Lovely stood there holding Quentin's hand, used to the undivided attention of men.

"My name is Ranell. It's my understanding that you and my nephew Andre were seeing each other?" the well-dressed man asked.

"Yes, "Lovely answered nervously and stopped holding Quentin's hand.

"Why don't you introduce yourself, Quentin," Ranell said.

"Hello Lovely Sinclair. My real name is Dreyfuss Sparks. Big Dre was my cousin, and this is my uncle Ranell.

"Take her men," Ranell ordered his two goons.

"Wait, wait I don't understand?" Lovely looked towards Quentin who had turned into Dreyfuss for some sort of an explanation . . . for some assistance . . . for some help.

"Please mister, you have everything wrong. There's some kind of mistake," she pleaded with Ranell.

He walked up closer to her, and slapped her so hard, her head tried to detach itself. She entered unconsciousness immediately.

"You did good nephew," Ranell seemed pleased.

"Thank you," Little Dre replied.

The two of them walked off together towards Ranell's Benz in the parking lot of his Key West restaurant. Lovely was left in the ruthless care of Ranell's two goons.

"Let's hurry up and do what we have to do, because all this temptation is killing me," the most stocky goon said.

"Well forget about it. I'm not dying because your dick got hard," the smarter goon replied.

"Yeah, you right. Ranell would kill us if we disobeyed his

orders. But tell the truth, wouldn't you like to fuck her?" the stocky goon Buck, asked.

Buck carried Lovely from the boat towards an isolated barn under the control of Ranell's organization.

The stench of what smelled like a hundred dead carcasses aroused Lovely. Buck was reaching the deep pit as Lovely started to come awake.

"Otis, she's waking up!"

"Well hurry up throw her in before she's all the way awake. She don't want to be awake for this. Trust me," Otis replied.

"Yeah, you right" Buck said and tossed Lovely into the animal pit.

Lovely could feel her body being hurled through the air. She smelled the overbearing stench, heard loud grunts and snorts, but had no idea where she was. Something broke her fall. She landed on something slick and mobile with a loud thump. She rolled off and tried to get to her feet and immediately she felt a frenzy close in on her. She screamed, as she felt her body being gnawed and her flesh being torn apart. Her limbs were being devoured by near starving beasts with insatiable savage appetites. The screams, the stench, the sight of twenty wild, blood thirsty hogs ripping the flesh from Lovely's bones, ravishing her once beautiful body became too much for Ranell's goons to stand.

"Damn, that was the worst thing I ever seen," Buck said.

"Yeah, that was fucked up. I wonder what she did to deserve that," Otis replied almost saddened to tears.

Lovely died among her own tears and screams as the meal of a pack of ravenous wild hogs that left nothing but clean white bones when they were done. Lovely's murder took place in an isolated barn in the backwoods of Florida.

34

The Jungle

The death of Lovely Sinclair satisfied Uncle Ranell's need to punish those he thought wronged him or his family. Not long after Little Dre's release from incarceration, he was sent to Georgia. Dre's assignment was to find out if Lovely was possibly involved in his cousin's death. After more deaths and talk surrounded Lovely, it was impossible for Little Dre to tell his Uncle that Lovely was completely innocent. Dreyfuss knew, his Uncle had other ears and eyes in Georgia.

Falling in love had never been part of the plan, but had happened. Dreyfuss Sparks known to Lovely as Quentin Taylor, had fallen in love with Lovely Sinclair. Dreyfuss tried to fight it, but he couldn't. He tried to find proof of her innocence, but he couldn't. He tried to delay her death as long as possible, but he couldn't.

The Sparks family were multi-millionaires and Dreyfuss was the controller of their Georgia interests. They owned millions of dollars worth of Georgia property, were still in the film business, and had one of the largest cocaine distributions in the south.

THE BENZ RIDE WAS fairly quiet. Dreyfuss tried not to let it show, but his betrayal of Lovely had him hating his lifestyle. Ranell was thinking about Lovely also. *Man I could have enjoyed that body for at least one night before the hogs got her.* Ranell knew Little Dre had fallen in love and that he had tried desperately to delay delivering Lovely to her death. Ranell couldn't allow weakness in his organization and Little Dre had proven his worthiness by putting the family interests above his heart and his dick. That's why Ranell put Lovely to her death so soon after arriving; he didn't want her tempting anyone else, including himself. Little Dre was turning out to be a better businessman than his cousin Big Dre had been. Now that Dreyfuss had proven his complete loyalty, it was time to learn more about the family business.

"Are you hungry?" Ranell asked.

"No, I'm good," Dreyfuss answered.

"You look a little thin. You know your mom will try and fatten you up." Ranell tried to lighten his nephew's mood.

"Yeah, she's not gonna know what to do when I tell her I no longer eat meat."

"I bet you ate that girl. She was really beautiful," Ranell tested his nephew's reaction.

"Yes, she was beautiful and tasty, but she had to go." Dreyfuss hid his resentment well.

"That's right! Family first." Ranell was satisfied.

The Benz cruised along while both family member's minds were preoccupied. Dreyfuss' mind replayed the memories of his and Lovely's two weeks paradise. Uncle Ranell thought about his new venture, an unprecedented move for a black southern drug dealer.

Ranell drove down a seldom-used road until they came to a private airstrip. Two new Cessna airplanes sat on the runway.

"Are we going somewhere?" Dreyfuss asked.

"Yes. I want to show you another part of our operation," Ranell replied.

Two men heard the disturbed gravel and exited the larger of the two planes.

"Hello Mister Ranell," his security man said.

"Excellent day for flying, Ranell," the pilot said.

"Hello fellows. Ready for a trip?" Ranell asked.

"Yes."

"Yes."

"This is my nephew Dreyfuss. He will be flying with us."

The two men quickly moved forward and shook Little Dre's hand.

All four men entered the private plane. Inside the plane had been redecorated to better accommodate Ranell. Comfortable leather furniture was inside, a music system, TV's, and food and beverages could be prepared in a small makeshift kitchen.

Little Dre had endured a very stressful day and was exhausted. He fell asleep in a comfortable leather recliner. Little Dre awakened while the plane was landing. It looked like they had landed in the middle of a rainforest.

"Where are we?" Dreyfuss asked.

"We are in Peru," Ranell answered.

All four men exited the plane. The pilot now possessed a M-16 and stayed back to watch the airplane. Dreyfuss and his uncle both picked up automatics from a cache of guns on the plane. Their security also carried a M-16, and the three men started walking on a manmade path through the woods and away from the airport.

After a short walk, Little Dre, Ranell, and the security man approached a large brick structure, which looked out of place in the middle of the lush forest.

"This is a new addition to our operation. No longer will we be dependent on others for our product. Now we are manufacturers," Uncle Ranell proudly told Dreyfuss.

Inside the building there was a large assembly line. The building was sectioned off in three parts, full of small men and women of Indian descent. With a minimal amount of clothes and surgical masks, they prepared the family's cash product: cocaine. One tier of the factory was being used to convert coca leaves to a thick, wet paste. Then another one-third was converting the paste into a powder and the last one-third was weighing and packaging the raw powder.

A tall Peruvian man accompanied by two guards approached Ranell.

"Hello Sir. How are you today?" the tall Peruvian said

"I'm fine Manuel. How are things going?" Ranell asked.

"Very good sir. Everyone is working very hard sir."

"Good, carry on Manuel."

Manuel went back to watching the workers and supervising the coke production.

Ranell gave Dreyfuss a tour around the factory. Little Dre was thoroughly impressed. "We own 400 acres here. We grow our own leaves and process our own cocaine. We can produce over a thousand kilos of pure cocaine a month. We have a total of 163 workers. Manuel runs the whole factory in our absence. I have hired thirty ex-military men for security, and I have men fly down from Florida to supervise the shipping of the coke to the U.S." Ranell explained.

"What about the Peruvian government? Or competition?" Dreyfuss asked.

"Well the local officials are paid well and the people that count in the capital are also on our payroll. And our old suppliers, the Cali cartel, have given me their blessings in exchange for us sharing our resources in the U.S. like safe routes, money launderers, and distributors beyond our thousand a month capacity," Ranell told his nephew while they walked around.

Most of the workers were shirtless, including the women. A few of the women worked with babies in their arms. The babies also wore surgical masks. Good thing the place was well vented, a modern electric ventilation system removed the coke-saturated air through the roof and kept the factory full of clean air. The factory also had a top balcony that completely covered the whole factory area. On the balcony were thirty guards with an assortment of machine guns. Ten guards patrolled the place when the workers went home for the day. Each section of coke production was worked by thirty men and women. The workers seemed oblivious to Ranell's and Little Dre's presence as they walked around. "These are great workers. They do their job, mind their business, and very few speak English. Most Peruvians speak Spanish and something called Quechua. They treat Manuel like he's God, and they think of me as an even bigger God. I pay them hundred American dollars a week, and they love their job. Nowhere else in this poor county could they make anywhere near that," Ranell continued.

"Uncle, you are doing really big things," Dreyfuss said.

"We are doing big things nephew. You proved today that you are ready to run more of the family business." Ranell gave him a pat on his back.

"Thank you uncle. You won't be sorry," Little Dre smiled for the first time since Lovely's murder.

"I know. Now let's get out of here before the mosquitoes eat us alive."

The pilot had refueled the airplane and twenty-five minutes after the tour, Ranell, Little Dre, the pilot had the security man were on their way back to Florida.

The Sparks family business was definitely expanding, and Little Dre would soon be at the helm. Dreyfuss Sparks was happy with the idea of their family now becoming manufacturers of cocaine, but he still wished he hadn't delivered Lovely to his uncle for such a brutal death.

Three days after Lovely's murder, Little Dre walked around the condo, painfully reminded of Lovely at every turn. Her perfume still scented the air, her clothes still lined his closets, and her favorite food mocked him whenever he opened the refrigerator. Everything about the condo now reflected Lovely's style, her flavor, her uniqueness. Everything from the towels in the bathroom, to the curtains covering the windows, and linen on what use to be their bed.

Little Dre's last few days in Florida were spent trying to forget Lovely. He knew he would never see her again and had to move on. Uncle Ranell tried to help him forget by dragging him to all the strip clubs. There was also a party thrown at Ranell's restaurant and disco. Key West was flooded with beautiful willing sun-tanned women from all four corners of the planet Earth, but Little Dre just wasn't ready.

"Dreyfus, what's wrong with you? You don't like parties no more?" Uncle Ranell asked.

"I'm good Uncle. I'm just a little tired right now," he replied.

Little Dre saw his uncle whisper something to two Cuban twins. The two unbelievably fine women approached in matching bathing suits that showed off very hairy, thick camel-toes. They spent half the night whispering decadent things into Little Dre's ears, trying their hardest to entice him into a freaky threesome. They even told him they had a cousin as fine and as willing to fuck all his problems away as them. He declined, and the twins seemed flabbergasted that any red-blooded American could refuse their advances. They continued to keep him company and Dreyfuss couldn't stop himself from having a good time. They danced, and laughed a lot, but Dreyfuss never got a chance to sample their goods. He promised them a rain check on his next trip back home. He told them they would all get together next time, including their cousin.

The condo was becoming unbearable. He cleaned the condo of most of Lovely's things, changed the sheets, wash-cloths, and towels and threw away the contents of the refrigerator. Dreyfuss Sparks really had been in love with Lovely. Knowing he would never see her again made him want to cry, but he was too much of a gangster to do so, even alone. It was time to move on. Dreyfuss called Miss Cableton.

"Are you interested in dinner at my condo.?" He asked.

"Sure, I would love to have dinner with you" she answered very excitedly.

Dreyfuss promised himself he would get over Lovely Sinclair, starting that night.

35

Sunshine

It was like the sun had its own special glow here. The expensive stores that lined the streets beckoned like an invitation to social acceptance among the elite. People chased their dreams here, just to find that there was as much failure as sunshine. For this person, failure wasn't an option. The path here had been full of too much struggle, strife, and suffering to not succeed.

It seemed, all roads led to right here, right now. The sign above the door read All Star Film Company. Ushered into the main office, a thin-haired Jewish fellow with rosy cheeks and bright eyes greeted her.

"Good Morning. Welcome to my small but excellent company. I'm Mr. Rosenbaum."

"Good Morning Mr. Rosenbaum. I'm Tracy Stencil, and I would like to work in film."

"You came to the right place Tracy. You have great beauty and a star quality. That alone could get you far, but if you have talent, the sky is the limit."

"I can act Mr. Rosenbaum," she said very business-like."

"Good, very good. Come back here tomorrow at 9:00 A.M., and we will discuss the possibility of me hiring you.

"Thank you Mr. Rosenbaum, you won't be sorry."

"I know I won't, Miss Tracy."

They shook hands, and she left elated.

Now I have to find myself an apartment and something small to get around in, she thought to herself. She walked to the Mann Chinese Theater and looked at all the stars' names engraved in the sidewalk.

"One day that's gonna be me," she said out loud to no one in particular. People passed the beautiful young lady and gave her the once over and kept moving. They were use to seeing an exceptional array of drop-dead gorgeous women in this town. Most of them became hoes or waitresses, but Tracy Stencil was different. She had a head-turning aura, a unique beauty and a lot of talent. Plus money wasn't a problem. She came to California with a very big nest egg.

Her first purchase was a used Suzuki sidekick for a reasonable price. Then she visited a real estate agency. At her fourth one she found a studio apartment that was nicely furnished. She signed a one-year lease and gave the broker three months rent in advance. Tracy was now ready to work in movies.

While shopping at the mall Tracy saw a tanned woman purchasing wicker baskets. The woman reminded Tracy of another tanned woman she helped wrong a couple of weeks ago. It had been Quentin's idea after his revelation near the island of Saint Lucia.

About six miles from the shore of Saint Lucia after their love-making Quentin told her the truth.

"Baby I have to tell you something really serious," he looked her in the eyes.

"What is it?" she asked.

"First of all I lied. My name isn't Quentin Taylor; it's

Dreyfuss Sparks."

"Sparks?" She asked perplexed.

" Yes Sparks. I'm Big Dre's cousin from Florida."

Worry etched her beautiful features, but she said nothing.

"I was sent by my family to Georgia to oversee our business interest. They also wanted me to keep an eye on you."

"Why?" she asked innocently.

"Because they are convince that you had something to do with Andre's death.

"I didn't," she started to plead her case.

"It doesn't even matter. They are convinced, and I'm supposed to deliver you to your death," he said with complete seriousness.

Her eyes searched the cabin for something she could use as a weapon.

"I'm not gonna do anything to you baby. I love you," Dreyfuss told her.

"I love you too!" Lovely said, but her fear still hadn't subsided.

"I have a plan, but you have to do everything I tell you," he said.

"Okay," she replied, using this opportunity to get dressed.

They went above to deck and watched the birds soar over their anchored boat.

"I was in Saint Lucia a few weeks ago and found this very beautiful woman that speaks perfect English. She has a daughter and is desperate for cash, so I offered her $20,000 to help scam my uncle. I told her that I need her to pretend to be my girlfriend."

He paused to make sure she was getting all this.

"I told her that my uncle is rich and dying from cancer and if he believed I was soon getting married and planning a big family, he would leave me a big inheritance."

Dreyfuss' captive audience just stared at him.

"I told her if she sailed to Florida with me, answered yes that she use to date my cousin Andre, and told my uncle that her name is Lovely Sinclair, I would pay her $20,000 in advance. She agreed and will leave the money and her daughter with her mother while we travel," Dreyfuss concluded his narration.

"Oh shit,"Lovely said, finally understanding the plan.

"You gonna let that mother get killed?" Lovely said with indignation.

"Better her than you right?" Dreyfuss asked.

Lovely knew she should have said no, but self-preservation is a motherfucker.

"Now, if my uncle isn't totally convinced you are dead, he will probably kill me and your family members."

Lovely worried for her mom.

"So what do I have to do?" Lovely asked.

"I got one hundred thousand dollars for you and a new I.D. you have to take this money, change your name, and not contact your friends and family for at least a couple of years. My uncle has a lot of eyes and ears in Georgia. If he finds out you're alive he will hunt you down and kill you, probably after he kills your mom."

"Oh my god," Lovely had thought about her mother being a target, but hearing it out loud was worse.

Dreyfuss said nothing for a minute.

"What about us?" Lovely asked.

"There could never be no us again. It's far too dangerous, but I will always love you!"

"I will always love you too! Thank you," Lovely said. She had already put it in the back of her mind that she would be responsible for orphaning another child.

They hugged for a long time, and there were tears in Lovely's eyes and Dreyfuss was fighting back his own tears.

After they docked in Saint Lucia, Lovely was told to go to the airport, go back to the United States, and disappear. Her plane was taking off from the island around the time Dreyfuss and Gabriel, the woman who had been raised in the United States and spoke perfect English, left Saint Lucia. Lovely went to Georgia, picked up $180,000 from her stash spot in Candace's apartment. She then went past her mother's job and watched her from a cab outside. Lovely never went inside, and her mother never saw her.

Lovely sat there and cried a few minutes silently before saying, "To the airport."

"*Ow*," LOVELY GOT A BRAIN FREEZE from the slurpy she had purchased during her break from shopping.

The brain freeze broke her from her reverie and brought her back to the present and her new identity: Tracy Stencil.

Epilogue

After Lovely Sinclair's disappeared and clues were drying up fast, Detectives Greenlee and Hutchins were forced to put the string of unsolved homicide cases on the backburner. While she was not a suspect, Lovely was wanted for questioning and they hoped she could provide them with some answers. But they weren't allowed to wonder about Lovely for too long because they were in the midst of an explosion of criminal activity fueled by the drug trade.

Because Lovely had often talked of leaving Georgia, Candace and Joy assumed that her way of forgetting the violence they were involved in was to cut them out of her life. They were hurt at first, but they still loved her and hoped that she found happiness where she was. They were doing well in Virginia. Their clothing boutique was a big success as was their personal life. Joy was dating a gorgeous female attorney who adored her and could keep up with her in the bedroom. Candace was involved with a professional baseball player, who made sure she wanted for nothing.

Delores searched for her daughter to no avail and even filed a missing persons report. Something — maybe it was her mother's intuition—told her that her daughter was okay and wanted her to go on with her life. She is currently planning to marry her boss.

Dreyfuss "Little Dre" Sparks dreamt about Lovely each night and tried to forget her by day. The family business is still one of the most extensive and insidious criminal organizations in the Dirty South.

Tracy Stencil went on to great fame as an acclaimed independent film director. Although she was breathtakingly beautiful, she was more admired for her skill and talent and would go on to become one of the most powerful women in Hollywood. Her latest film about a young woman whose beauty affected all those around her and caused her great pain and loss until she used it to her advantage, was receiving a lot of Oscar buzz. It was called *A Lovely Murder Down South*.

TRU LIFE PUBLISHING

P.O. BOX 21224 Brooklyn, NY 11208

Shabazz, Rafael and Pat are true friends for life who spend years building a criminal organization, an East coast drug empire to rival any business corporation on Wall street. Now they've decided to walk away; retire with their riches and go legit.

Can three friends just walk away from the drug game?

Can money stained with blood ever be washed clean?

Who will pay for the innocent blood? Before it's all over one will be killed.

One will be sentenced to life without parole, and one would have saved himself by putting his best friend in prison for life.

maybe the only way to really play this game and win is never to play this game at all.

Blood Money is Paul Johnson's debut novel. It is a thrilling tale of the lies and the deceits of the drug game. Its politics and its power to corrupt. A must read diary of the way the drug game is played- and the way it plays you.

Paul Johnson author of the brutal street classic "Blood Money" returns to breath life into urban lit. with his new masterpiece "A Lovely Murder Down South".

This is a real heart wrenching bloody tale of three young ladies coming of age amongst the hustlers, strippers, lesbians, sexual predators and even a serial killer.

Atlanta has never looked so good or felt so bad as Lovely Sinclair and her friends Candace and Joy leave broken hearts and dead bodies in their path to the top.

Consequences of Oppression:Hell on Earth is n un cut, undiluted and un apologetic look at the plight of black America. The gloves have come off and Pen Black is our modern day crusader.

Consequences of Oppression is raw, it's real and it's a needed wake-up call to an endangered race. In this book he attacks the problems created, sustained and furthered by a system in place, a present oppressor and even blacks themselves.

After Pen Black forcefully remove the veil from your eyes, he lovingly replaces it with a wide- eye view and some necessary solutions. With controversial chapters like "Women let the Boys be Boys","Why they want a white girl", and "Who's a Dog?". This is a book that shouldn't be ignored.

Order Form

Purchaser Information

Name ______

Reg. #______

Address ______

City, State, Zip ______

Qty.		Cost
____	Blood Money: Crime Incorporated by Paul Johnson	$14.95
____	A Lovely Murder Down South by Paul Johnson	$14.95
____	Consequences of Oppression by Pen Black	$9.95

Shipping and Handling $2.50 first book $1.00 each additional book.

TOTAL------$___.___

Make check or money order payable to:
TruLife Publishing P.O. Box 21224 Brooklyn, NY 11201
www.TrulifePublishing.com

WWW.TRULIFEPUBLISHING.COM
Call Today 347- 409 - 0757

DESIGNED BY: OCJGRAPHIX.COM -1.800.964.6309

A NOTE TO MY READERS: I sincerely appreciate your support, and I promise to always deliver top quality work to the best of my ability, experiences, and creativity.

I would enjoy hearing your comments and suggestions.

You can write to me at:

Paul Johnson #07515-067
FCI Williamburg
P.O. Box 340
Salters, SC 29590

Or

TRU LIFE PUBLISHING
c/o Paul Johnson
P.O. Box 21224
Brooklyn, NY, 11201

Thank you, Paul Johnson

TRU LIFE PUBLISHING

P.O. BOX 21224 Brooklyn, NY 11208

Shabazz, Rafael and Pat are true friends for life who spend years building a criminal organization, an East coast drug empire to rival any business corporation on Wall street. Now they've decided to walk away; retire with their riches and go legit.

Can three friends just walk away from the drug game?

Can money stained with blood ever be washed clean?

Who will pay for the innocent blood? Before it's all over one will be killed.

One will be sentenced to life without parole, and one would have saved himself by putting his best friend in prison for life.

maybe the only way to really play this game and win is never to play this game at all.

Blood Money is Paul Johnson's debut novel. It is a thrilling tale of the lies and the deceits of the drug game. Its politics and its power to corrupt. A must read diary of the way the drug game is played- and the way it plays you.

Paul Johnson author of the brutal street classic "Blood Money" returns to breath life into urban lit. with his new masterpiece "A Lovely Murder Down South".

This is a real heart wrenching bloody tale of three young ladies coming of age amongst the hustlers, strippers, lesbians, sexual predators and even a serial killer.

Atlanta has never looked so good or felt so bad as Lovely Sinclair and her friends Candace and Joy leave broken hearts and dead bodies in their path to the top.

Consequences of Oppression:Hell on Earth is n un cut, undiluted and un apologetic look at the plight of black America. The gloves have come off and Pen Black is our modern day crusader.

Consequences of Oppression is raw, it's real and it's a needed wake-up call to an endangered race. In this book he attacks the problems created, sustained and furthered by a system in place, a present oppressor and even blacks themselves.

After Pen Black forcefully remove the veil from your eyes, he lovingly replaces it with a wide- eye view and some necessary solutions. With controversial chapters like "Women let the Boys be Boys","Why they want a white girl", and "Who's a Dog?". This is a book that shouldn't be ignored.

WWW.TRULIFEPUBLISHING.COM

Call Today 347- 409 - 0757

Order Form

Purchaser Information

Name ________________

Reg. # ________________

Address ________________

City, State, Zip ________________

Qty.		Cost
____	Blood Money: Crime Incorporated by Paul Johnson----------	$14.95
____	A Lovely Murder Down South by Paul Johnson----------	$14.95
____	Consequences of Oppression by Pen Black----------	$9.95

Shipping and Handling $2.50 first book $1.00 each additional book.

TOTAL------$___.___

Make check or money order payable to:
TruLife Publishing P.O. Box 21224 Brooklyn, NY 11201
www.TrulifePublishing.com

DESIGNED BY: OCJGRAPHIX.COM -1.800.964.6309